MY BOOK
—— OF ——
REVELATIONS

MY BOOK
—— OF ——
REVELATIONS

Stories that burst the bubble of believability

GERRY BURKE

iUniverse

MY BOOK OF REVELATIONS
STORIES THAT BURST THE BUBBLE OF BELIEVABILITY

Copyright © 2020 Gerry Burke.

All rights reserved. No part of this book may be used or reproduced by any means, graphic, electronic, or mechanical, including photocopying, recording, taping or by any information storage retrieval system without the written permission of the author except in the case of brief quotations embodied in critical articles and reviews.

This is a work of fiction. All of the characters, names, incidents, organizations, and dialogue in this novel are either the products of the author's imagination or are used fictitiously.

Editing: Kylie Moreland

iUniverse books may be ordered through booksellers or by contacting:

iUniverse
1663 Liberty Drive
Bloomington, IN 47403
www.iuniverse.com
844-349-9409

Because of the dynamic nature of the Internet, any web addresses or links contained in this book may have changed since publication and may no longer be valid. The views expressed in this work are solely those of the author and do not necessarily reflect the views of the publisher, and the publisher hereby disclaims any responsibility for them.

Any people depicted in stock imagery provided by Getty Images are models, and such images are being used for illustrative purposes only.
Certain stock imagery © Getty Images.

ISBN: 978-1-6632-1323-5 (sc)
ISBN: 978-1-6632-1322-8 (hc)
ISBN: 978-1-6632-1324-2 (e)

Library of Congress Control Number: 2020922504

Print information available on the last page.

iUniverse rev. date: 12/08/2020

Contents

Preface vii

HISTORY
The Central Pacific Railroad.. 1
God Botherers... 8
What I've Learned About America.. 18
Cigarettes, Whiskey, and Wild, Wild, Women 29
Horse Tales 45

HEROES
Servants of the Crown 59
Melanie Marple 73
The Banana Republic.. 87
War and Reese 97
Valour and Courage 106

HORROR
Albert Stein... 123
Donald Tuck and Mickey House 135
Kevin in A State Over Virginia 143
How Do You Wear Your Genes 159

HOLLYWOOD
The Investigation 181
Hands Across The Water 186
Sam Spade Down Under.. 198

About The Author... 207
Author's Previous Works 211

Preface

The stories you are about to read are, for the most part, unbelievable. That's what fantasy is all about. Even history can sometimes be blurred by multiple versions of the same event. In some instances, the scribes have neglected to report at all. I'm here to put that right.

It is true that I am prone to exaggeration, and often my imagination exceeds recommended tolerances. Nevertheless, I hope the following pages will entertain, as a refund on your investment is not an option. To supplement my historical revelations, I have included a menu of murder, mayhem, mystery, and marvellous moments. I know you like this kind of thing.

As my yarns have global appeal, I considered writing them in Esperanto, the international language. By choosing English, I am aware that some incongruous interpretations might arise to confuse readers who live beyond the boundaries of the colonies. One can only embarrass oneself by playing around with some inane aspects of these idiosyncratic interpretations. I blame it on my advertising background.

As a Christmas bonus, I have included a number of stories relating to discount detective Patrick Pesticide and his enigmatic girlfriend Stormy Waters. This is a marketing exercise brought about by the fact that my previous volumes about Paddy Pest have been discounted at retail level. He is outraged.

Her Majesty, Queen Elizabeth II, keeper of small dogs, and patron of the RSPCA, has urged all Britons to support their fundraiser at the London Palladium.

Corgi and Bess
starring
Shirley Basset and Snoop Dogg
Tickets through usual outlets

HISTORY

The Central Pacific Railroad

Some people think Henry Ford was the first marshal of Dodge City, but, in fact, it was Lawrence Deger, his assistant and successor being Wyatt Earp. Others believe that Herbert Hoover made vacuum cleaners, and that Jerry Lewis married his cousin. The initiator of this convenient romantic pact was actually Jerry Lee Lewis. God bless him.

So, as historians, we are rather lazy, which must diminish the memory of those pioneering men and women whose deeds should have been preserved and perpetuated in the pages of posterity. Many names slipped through the cracks, and I don't propose to pay homage to them all; just Ida Ho.

By the 1860s, construction of the Pacific Railroad was well under way, snaking across the Sierra Nevada Mountains, intent on meeting its counterpart, the Union Pacific, somewhere in Utah. The workforce attached to the aforementioned consortium was almost totally Chinese, while the beasts from the East employed Irish workers.

Once tracks had been laid in Utah, the Mormons appeared from nowhere, knocking on doors, even though everybody lived in tents.

"Hello, we're the Mormons. Does anybody here sing?"

Ida Ho, a courtesan from San Francisco, boasted many patrons, including the rich and famous. Although no-one found fault with her services, she was always vulnerable to the whim of the law, then regarded as the best police force money could buy. Many of her fellow immigrants had moved on, accepting employment with the new railway project that promised to open up the country like never before. She also relocated.

After just five weeks, the new arrival opened her own whorehouse, and, within six months, she operated brothels at numerous whistle-stops along the construction route. This was the best of times. Conscripted employees from the Far East, on lower wages, received discounted rates on slow days. New towns started to appear on the map as each portion of track was completed, and cheap land surrounding these communities attracted both ranchers and farmers. Of course, they didn't get on. In the words of Oscar Hammerstein II— "The farmer and the cowman should be friends."

One of these friends, potato grower "Spud" Murphy, preached peace and tranquillity in the district, and was more than a match for the likes of Butch and Hopalong Cassidy— gunslingers hired by ranchers, notably the Dalton brothers.

The region around Lovelock, Nevada didn't attract the same Indian insurgency as those involved in shaping the Union Pacific route. With no Sioux or Cheyenne interlopers to worry about, the cattlemen and the farmers turned on each other.

Jack Murphy cultivated a sizable spread, with a large family to help him. He had five children: Jessie, James, William, Bonny, and Cisco, the kid, born in the city of that name. When Cisco turned twelve years of age, James and William began to tutor him in the art of the gun. The girls, Jessie and Bonny, could ride and shoot like Annie Oakley, so the family presented as a potent force.

Ida and Jack may not have hooked-up if his wife had not been killed in an industrial accident while mashing potatoes for the annual "Salute the Sausage Day." The poor woman fell into a vat and was mashed to death.

The Paddywhacker liked this straight-talking woman, who trusted him to the extent that she became his silent partner in several ventures. The bordello queen had made her pile, but some townies considered it tainted money. Nevertheless, she invested in real estate, with the potato prince as her financial advisor. For example, P. King Poultry and Produce, the town's general store, was supposedly owned by Pete King, a successful Californian trader. There was no such person, and few people connected Mr. King with the capital of China, Ida's home town. The couple also financed a silver mine near Reno, and a beauty parlour. Young Bonny managed that money-spinner.

The madam danced dangerously with certain other chancers, including young Randy Hearst, the editor of the local rag. Ida's horizontal girls would extract tittle-tattle from their customers and pass the info on to her. She would relay same to her friend when he came to visit every Sunday. Eventually, the salacious gossip became too spicy and the townsfolk drummed Hearst out of town. He boarded one of the first trains to head west.

Even with all their property holdings, the Ho/Murphy conglomerate wasn't the biggest player around. With the opening of the railway, the Dalton brothers found new markets for their beef, and their sale yards and corrals emptied regularly. The brothers also controlled one of the two saloons, which sometimes featured touring dancers with exotic names like Fatima and Cleopatra. On one occasion, the owner booked a lady called Faith for the duration, and the pastor looked set for a coronary.

"I suppose you'll have Hope and Charity appearing next week. Have you no shame?"

"No shame, no charity, preacher man. Are you going to pay for that whiskey or what?"

Another investment opportunity arose in healthcare. In the Midwest, the ubiquitous sawbones and snake oil salesmen ruled. Lovelock's immigrant workers relied on Ida to import medicines and herbal remedies. These became available through her P. King Pharmaceutical outlet. Dental care was another matter, and people waited some time for the tooth fairy to arrive from Arizona, in the form of the unreliable Doc Holliday. The drifter usually turned-up, accompanied by his lovely wife, Big Nose Kate.

What can you say about crime in the Old West? Lawmen found it tough to keep the outlaws under control, not to mention the Indians; becoming a distraction in their own right. They attacked the Pony Express, plundered the rail network, and gave Colonel Custer a haircut. Some settlements were more dangerous than others, and one immediately thinks of Tombstone, Dodge City, Deadwood and Cripple Creek, Colorado.

The Chinese influence!

The communities which grew around the Sierra Nevada Railroad were often dominated by Chinese tongs—gangs spawned in San Francisco that followed the money.

Prostitution became the specialty of the tong, but Ida gave her countrymen solid competition. The mobsters, operating in the city by the bay, forced the smaller mobs eastwards, where their influence was conspicuous but constrained—especially if Doc Holliday was in town. Also, the Chee Kong and the Hong Tong hated each other as much as anyone else. If they amalgamated to become Hong Kong, that would be a different matter.

Celebrations and parades were common in Lovelock, be it the Year of the Dragon, the Easter Parade, St. Patrick's Day, or Thanksgiving. Abraham Lincoln set the date for Thanksgiving, and Fu Manchu may have had something to say about Zodiac signs. The Catholic Church controlled the rest.

"Due to the Teamster's strike, there will be no Easter buns this year. We'll be serving hot cross bagels instead."

Jack's female partner always received an invitation to attend the St. Patrick's Day celebration at the Murphy spread. Spud would let his hair down, serving green beer with his prairie praties. Jessie did train whistle impersonations; James sang "Danny Boy"; and William, Bonny, and the Cisco kid put on a shooting display. The terrific trio once shot an outline of their pa on the side of the barn.

The Dalton family also claimed to be Irish, but they were never invited, which upset them no end. At City Hall, racial overtones bubbled along, as blacks and Chinese were equally demonised. The royal Daltons considered themselves God's gift, and then the Mormons arrived, followed by the farmers. Murph and his gun-toting children gave as good as they got, and the Church of Jesus Christ of Latter-day Saints seemed intent on turning everybody into pillars of salt.

Until that time, the Episcopalians held the moral high ground, and that's where they built their house of worship. In comparison, Boot Hill was like a pimple on a porcupine. Fast-talking preachers, a dime a dozen in these lawless towns, brandished their bibles like Moses. Some of them, for their trouble, were gunned down, packed in wooden coffins, and delivered to the aforementioned pimple. The Mormons provided a different approach. They knocked on your door, offered you a pamphlet, and enquired whether you would like to purchase some sourdough bread.

Chee Ming, one of the tong leaders, was a churchgoer, and people accepted this because he had accumulated a lot of stuff that needed forgiving. As a senior member of the Chinese community, he demanded respect, as did Ida. Then there was the old man who dispensed parables and quotations for a small fee. Every week, Ho, Chee Ming, and old Benny Wong met to discuss their ancestors and the way forward, with Confucius always having the last word—never give a sword to a man who can't dance.

Moose Mountain!

By the time the female pioneer reached early middle age (her description, not mine), the historians had hardly sharpened their pencils, and they missed quite a bit. For example, the massacre at Moose Mountain did not rate many column inches in the dailies, and those who did report got it wrong. Fancy blaming the Native Americans!

The Shawnee inhabitants of the area were all passive people and avid traders, with most of their blankets, shawls and tablecloths being contracted to the P. King Five and Dime. Peace pipes and tobacco pouches usually sold a few hours after delivery. These tribes lived a long way from Moose Mountain, and way north of the Vegas Trading Post.

Chee Ming was the one who helped establish this community on high, dedicated to those free spirits who enjoyed drinking, gambling, prostitution, and the many saloons and opium dens which had opened up in the small town. The Hai Ho Massage and Moonshine Parlour also proved to be a winner, and Ida visited regularly to collect the takings. She was completing her monthly audit when the puritans rode through town, guns blazing.

Somebody recognised the outriders as Calvinists. These were mean outlaws, who gunned-down everyone in sight. Of course, you don't put together a team of blood-thirsty killers like this without employing freelance muscle, and this wild bunch recruited Vlad the Impaler as part of the posse. Having come from a particularly harsh winter in Transylvania, he had been taking the waters at Lake Tahoe when offered this one-off contract.

For the first twenty minutes, the tables remained open, but when the chips were down and the gamblers had their backs to the wall, they fought back. So did the ferocious femmes at the palace of serenity. Their mistress lined them up on the second-floor verandah, each cradling a carbine. The good-time girls picked-off the Christians as they careered down the main street with their flares and fire-bombs.

The terrifying tragedy lasted for less than an hour, but that proved enough to terminate the town as a tourist destination. Most of the croupiers had been killed, and Chee Ming, wounded critically, failed to make it through the night. Madam Ho became the heroine of the day, although not mentioned in despatches. The incident was hushed-up, and everyone got on with their lives.

The new territories!

A seminal moment for those folks concerned with the new territories was the Golden Spike Ceremony, which took place in Utah on 10 May 1869. The two companies now combined to be the Transcontinental Railway, providing an uninterrupted journey from Omaha to Sacramento, with return tickets available. Around this time, Ida moved from her house of joy in Lovelock to the Governor's mansion in Salt Lake City.

Cyrus Governor was a successful timber merchant, having secured his fortune by selling wooden sleepers to both rail companies. The chap enjoyed his frequent visits to Ida's establishment during his many marketing trips, and they became friends as well as lovers. After his wife died, he invited the mercurial madam to move in with him, which she did. The lady's great friend from the potato patch had passed, and she was happy to let her top girl, Big Hips Betty, run the business. Before she left Lovelock, the comely woman attended the farewell party for Spud's eldest, James, about to try his luck in the new territory, north of Utah. There was talk that this part of the country might be heading towards statehood, and he wanted to introduce his father's potato farming techniques.

Once settled, Ida felt comfortable. No-one was aware of her profession in these new surrounds, and she fitted-in easily with the ladies who lunch—wives and paramours of the movers and shakers around town. You could also get a good lemon chicken in Plum Alley. Cy'n'Ide were a lethal combination on the seniors tennis circuit, and dominated the many soirees that punctuated the social season in Salt Lake City.

HISTORY

The music was the only negative. Cyrus possessed a fine baritone voice, and he knew it. A valued member of the Tabernacle Choir, he chose to rehearse day and night. "The Battle Hymn of the Republic" with your grapefruit at 8 a.m. is pretty hard to take.

A further complication would be Cy's children, who were somewhat less than enthusiastic about the second wife (tell me if you've heard this before). The second son took things a little too far. The cold shoulder is fair enough but an Arizona bark scorpion in the sowing basket? Come on. Sadly, the maid who tried to intervene, was bitten, and her funeral was one of the biggest ever seen for a domestic. People still talk about the size of the wreath produced by her employer. Mr. Governor not only gave the eulogy, but also warbled a stirring rendition of "Amazing Grace." The girl's name was Grace, and it was rumoured that she had filled the gap between wives. People can be cruel, can't they?

Ida's twilight years proved to be both peaceful and fulfilling. She liked nothing more than to sit outside in the sun and read the morning newspaper. Often, she would catch up with the exploits of young Jamie— what a success story. Within one year of arriving in the thriving new territory, he had everyone growing potatoes. He even became an elected official, loved and respected by all. When the time came to ratify entry into the Union, the Boise bureaucracy needed to provide a name for that piece of dirt that was to become a new state. All eyes turned to James Murphy.

"Just remember, Jim," said his City Hall associate. "Look for a word that encapsulates everything we stand for. We're friendly, welcoming, attractive, and exciting. We have imagination and creativity, and will do almost anything to please you."

On 3 July 1890, Idaho became the 43rd state of the Union. The party rolled on to the next day and, sitting on her verandah in Salt Lake City, an old woman smiled.

God Botherers

Lucretia Borgia is a saint. This is not a matter of historical fact but an opinion voiced by her father, the pope—the Holy Father. The comment could only have been a comparative assessment, as her sibling, the notorious Cesare, supposedly killed his own brother, among others. In those days, family squabbles could get serious. Pope Alexander VI may not have been aware that his daughter had slept with Cesare, but didn't he remember that he, also, had been to bed with her? With so much Black Death about, they probably needed to share bedrooms. Whether these rumours were true or not, sainthood was a stretch.

Because Lucretia wed three times, she earned a reputation as a bit of a hussy, which was totally unfair. Lana Turner married eight times, and she still boasted thousands of fans. Liz Taylor also turned-up for eight nuptials and Zsa Zsa Gabor nine. Were they hussies? Don't answer that.

"Lucy, sweetheart," said the pope, one morning at breakfast. "Can I ask you a small favour?"

"Of course, daddy; have I ever denied you anything? Is it another one of your alliance problems? Who do you want me to screw?"

"Lucretia! Mind your language. Remember we are in Vatican chambers. Nevertheless, you are your usual perceptive self. I want you to marry Giovanni Sforza, Count of Catignola. We need his money and influence."

Marriage, thought the irreverent princess of piety. *Now, there's a papal decree from left field.*

"You do realise, father, that I am only thirteen years of age. Giovanni might want and expect a more mature companion."

This was a big decision for Miss Borgia, as it was no secret she had the hots for the Kiwi gladiator who played the Coliseum twice a week, with a matinee on Saturday. Of course, such a union would be impossible as he was a slave from the antipodes. In fact, they didn't let anyone from this part of the world into the Vatican until the 21st Century, and Cardinal George Pell was grateful to be there.

Was Alexander wrong in using his daughter as a pawn in his political games? Of course he was, but we do tend to be judgmental, don't we? Sure, some people deserve bad press, and I'm not trying to gild the lily. Hitler, Stalin, Simon Cowell, and Jack the Ripper all did things they might not repeat, if given another chance. Unfortunately, historians don't allow retrospective editing of bygone biographies. The Borgia tribe will live with their reputation, enhanced by the salacious reporting of the Vox media.

Local news outlets always employed a professional town crier (male), who was able to slant his story with the deft use of inflection and emphasis. Some of these scroll readers made good money, and we are talking about a time when the Roman scudo was strong against the Spanish ducat.

"Hear ye, hear ye! Far right pollies left-off invitation list.

A number of prominent conservative figures have not been invited to Rome's wedding of the year. A spokesperson for Pope Alexander cited budgetary constraints. His daughter denied these people were intimate friends.

This edition of fake news is sponsored by Caesar's Palace & Casino. Qui totum vult totum perdit." (He who wants everything loses everything.)

Because of the Borgia's Spanish roots, they were not trusted in Rome. However, from those roots grew a family tree of power and influence. You might say Alexander wrote the book on nepotism, giving property and position to kinfolk, principally his two sons. Never let it be said that he didn't possess a generous disposition, because his financial contributions to the arts and architecture are well documented. Leo Da Vinci and Lord Byron both benefitted from his interest, but he did attract detractors, notably the political scholar Machiavelli. I'm not sure whether this chap lived in Florence or with Florence, but he always had plenty to say.

As the years rolled by, and the gutters ran red with the blood of obstructive opponents, Lucy moved to Ferrara with her third husband. In 1505, this gentleman became Duke, and was required to step down from his role as chief executive officer of an organisation specialising in high performance chariots.

Many historians have analysed the lady's time in Ferrara and found little evidence to support her horrendous reputation. Has there been a plot to demonise women in general, initiated by male chauvinist pigs of the literary kind? The commentary has been controversial and the movies bloodthirsty. Through it all, I believe an opportunity was missed. Not since Pope Joan, in the year 855, has there been a woman ruling Vatican City. With her beautiful complexion, hazel eyes, and long blonde hair, Lucretia would have been a hit at any Papal Conclave—definitely a white smoke girl for mine.

Fun and games!

When Jesus asked Lazarus to come forth, he couldn't have been referring to the athletic competition held every four years in Olympia, unless he was on a commission from bookmakers. Someone talking-up the contest was Thaddeus Excititas, a smooth-talking public relations guru from Athens, reportedly being paid big drachmas to publicise the event and recruit athletes. Some of them were not enthusiastic.

"What, you want me to perform at the Naked Games without an appearance fee. You are delusional, my friend. Not that I couldn't beat most of those slackers, with or without my clothes on."

It has never been officially explained why the organisers of the inaugural Olympics asked the contestants to compete *au naturel*, but there is a theory. In one of the heats of the 200 metre footrace, one of the competitors lost his loincloth and slipped on it. Evidently, the punters in the stadium applauded the decision to go thereafter without clothes—Greeks with nothing to hide.

Let's ignore the comments of the aforementioned narcissist. Most participants embraced the opportunity to show-off their skills and manly physiques. This band of brothers also knew they would enjoy a gay old time during and after the closing ceremony. Some of them travelled enormous distances to take part, including Leonidas and Diagoras from Rhodes, Chionis from Sparta, and Astylos and Milon from Croton.

The latter gentleman, a pupil of philosopher Pythagoras, proved that you didn't have to be a Rhodes Scholar to receive all the accolades. Milon

HISTORY

was a multiple Olympic wrestling winner. Notwithstanding that, on one island all roads lead to the statue of celebrated champion Leonidas: twelve times on the victory dais to collect his laurel wreaths.

As we know, the ancient Greeks skipped the middle rung of glorification, not bothering with saints. If you cut the mustard, you immediately became a god, with substantial authority in the stratosphere, and they all displayed different personalities. Poseidon was a wet blanket, and Hermes, a handbag. For the record, Nike didn't just do it. Women are called sluts for that kind of thing.

Thaddeus Excititas, for all his trouble, never made it into the history books, although future biographers might redress such an omission. At the time, Athens was a hotbed of philosophical dispute, and guys like Plato, Aristotle, and Socrates dilly-dallied and demonstrated little urgency in their deliberations. The ad man cut through the crap and came up with spin that really worked. His agency *Hot as Hades* might have been the *Saatchi & Saatchi* of the BC age. They were way ahead of their time, being the first to utilise a new visual medium called Telly Savalas.

Prior to this optical phenomenon, wall and rock advertising was the way to go, perhaps combined with a papyrus campaign over a designated period. The media marvel would have loved to use his favourite Olympic champions as spruikers, but sport tended to be strictly amateur, a situation which would exist for a long time.

Thad did promote an arrangement with Odysseus to produce some travel documentaries, but the blighter went off to Troy and didn't return for years. During these times, the economic climate changed, the entrepreneur lost money, and he transformed from saint to sinner.

As his clients dropped off, the PR guru searched for new ones and, in so doing, exaggerated the abilities of his people. Alexander the Good became great, and his tennis manager, Nick, the stinker, became team thinker. Even Mary-Alice, the person who generated singing commercials, was promoted as Maria Callas.

Sport in general needed a shot in the arm and it was left to a local politician from Acropolis to provide it. Fabled correspondent Aesop had written several pieces promoting a new affirmative action group called He's Through, which supported women's liberation and, among other things, their right to participate in the Olympics. Con Volute knew this to be a complex issue, as many senators kept female slaves; so did Thaddeus Excititas, and two of his wives were also female. With Con's encouragement, the matter was debated in bath houses across the city, and when it came to parliamentary consideration, the member for Acropolis produced all the answers. Women would now go to the Naked Games.

The only person to openly fight this new wave thinking was you know who. Did that make Thad bad?

One of the few client accounts to survive the cleansing enema of change was the tourist office. They still liked the idea of his Hellas Hot Pants promotion. Of course, during an Olympic year, they didn't wear any pants at all, but word of mouth was enough to market that product. When Odysseus returned to town, Thad used his influence to try to obtain an interview with Helen of Troy. He wanted her to be one of his publicity girls, as long as Paris didn't object.

"Gee, old pal, I don't know. The last time I saw Paris, he fired an arrow at my friend Achilles. What a heel!"

Fortunately for the brash promoter, Melina Mercurial had become available, and the model and massage therapist gave the campaign the sex appeal it deserved. She possessed dark probing eyes, olive skin, unexplainable blonde hair, and a body like Venus de Milo. If this wasn't a call to arms to fight the prissy ladybirds, what was? Con Volute, appalled to see a government promotion hijacked in this way, made a long-winded speech in the Ecclesia, to no effect. Melina actually stood against him in the subsequent election and won. How about that?

There are a few elements to this story which you may find hard to believe, but I tried to be as Greek as possible, and generous in my interpretations. No doubt, those who didn't make the cut will be disappointed, and I salute the likes of Archimedes, Hippocrates, Euripides, Nana Mouskouri, Vangelis, and Yanni, plus the many fish and chip shop proprietors around the globe.

From Jerusalem to Jericho!

Buddy had been hanging around Bethlehem for some months, looking for work. The odd-jobs man boasted experience at everything from baby-sitting

HISTORY

to garment-beating. Joseph, the carpenter, taking pity on him, gave him some chores in his workshop: sweeping-up shavings and sharpening tools et cetera. He was a bit of a tool himself, but Joe didn't know that. The kind-hearted employer was not an ambitious man but a lucky one, having snared the best-looking gal in the village and then fathered the baby Jesus, now two years old and touted to be the next big thing.

This prediction didn't sit well with the current rulers, who protected their privileged status with determined ruthlessness, especially that nasty child-killer King Herod. Buddy, a simple person, soon earned the respect of his employer, who made him the official nanny of their son, a position requiring him to be forever alert for head-hunters like Herod.

"Now, Jesus, I don't want you wandering off by yourself. There's a nasty person in the neighbourhood, who likes to chop-off the heads of little children. He may entice you to his side with offers of treats."

"Don't worry, Buddy. I don't eat treats unless it's Halloween."

Mary may have suffered from post-natal depression after the birth, because she did confess to someone that she was glad it wasn't twins, which might have required some explaining. After all, one child from a virgin is strange enough, but two?

The Madonna considered her man to be a good catch, who was smart enough to see their future elsewhere, which is why they moved to Nazareth. Talented chippies were hard to come by, so the shekels rolled-in every week. The women of this town were simple folk who relied on their husbands and sons to provide for them, which they did. They fished and herded their animals to market, all the while being envious of those wankers (merchants, architects, goldsmiths, and sculptors) who lived on the top of the hill. The only people the villagers looked down on were bricklayers, who couldn't do anything right. No sooner had they finished a contract wall in Jerusalem when it started wailing. This happens when you get the cement mix wrong. What about Jericho? The whole bloody structure came tumbling down.

People thinking of biblical carpenters sometimes forget Noah. How smart was that move into shipbuilding for an ambitious man? Joseph seemed happy with his lot and, quite frankly, didn't mind the repetitive life he led. Without his son and his soapbox, Nazareth would indeed have been dull and boring.

Enter out-of-town author Moses, with his best-selling scroll *The Bible*. This page-turner, released to much acclaim, captivated and amused, with many scroll worms looking forward to more of the same. In fact, the fellow was prolific, writing five volumes in a frenzy, which is why they gave him tablets—a precursor to Valium, perhaps?

Jesus charmed his faithful with eloquent rhetoric in his sermons, and his parables were quite fantastic. Moses related the one about the loaves and fishes, but I am sceptical.

Rabbits might multiply in this fashion, but fish? Making bread would be no problem, just as it isn't today. Billy Graham used to start every prayer meeting with zilch and end up with a fortune. Of course, I am talking in colloquial terms. I hope you understand that.

Read *The Bible*, and you will notice there is nay a mention of poor Bud, who may not have seen eye to eye with Mo. Buddy, now the saviour's press agent, might have made access difficult for the pushy correspondent, and then suffered the consequences; iniquitous omission from the pages of history.

"Whaddyamean, there's no interview until I trim my beard. What is this, personal hygiene week?"

"Exactly," said Buddy. "You've been up that mountain for too long, and the good Lord is promoting social distancing. It's a sign of the times."

To me, one of the mysteries of biblical times is the lack of focus on the distraught parents after the Calvary cataclysm. What happened to them? Certainly, Joe didn't possess the drive of Noah, and was too thrifty to take chances. Did he have money salted away in the West Bank, waiting for a rainy day? In retrospect, this would have been an excellent investment because it did rain for forty days and forty nights, which, by the by, proved a boon for Noah's pleasure craft business.

Joseph went looking for an ark, and saw a frog sitting on a little rock near the pier.

"Bonjour, mon ami! Monsieur Noah's Ark de Triomphe; c'est gros, oui?"

"It certainly is big, but the smell? All those animal droppings! None of that was mentioned in the brochures."

If you wanted to put a bad week behind you, a two week cruise on the Dead Sea was a given, but it was expensive; not that there wasn't substantial prosperity around in those days. Wealth was a significant motivator, and recorded within the good book are over two thousand references to riches— most of us familiar with money being the root of all evil. I want to know who told the Jews that a great profit would come amongst them.

I'm a man of simple beliefs. There are two ways to achieve success. The first starts with hard work, followed by character building and luck. The other way is to sell your soul to the devil in exchange for immeasurable pleasure. Harvey Weinstein possibly chose this path.

One of Buddy's many tasks was to set up JC's speaking engagements—a difficult task while under scrutiny from those who would take him and his master down. The entrepreneur developed a formula of frequency: publicise the dates and then advertise the venue site by word of mouth, just like a floating crap game. Sometimes there were leaks, as there always are, and misconceptions. Spartacus, looking for love, arrived for the wrong reason, and got caught with the second collection. A bigger donation and he might have been blessed.

Buddy was also the go-to man when there were nuptials in the wind. He knew where to go to buy the best beverages and must have been devastated when the vino ran out at the wedding in Cana.

The guests were friends of Mary's, so you wouldn't think they're going to be booze bandits, would you? Wrong! The liquid refreshment had been consumed before the couple made it to the chuppah canopy, and the Madonna was distraught. So was the other virgin in the room—the bride. The son of God may not have realised he could perform miracles because he had never done it before. Nevertheless, you've got to mollify your mum, and he reached out and transformed 150 gallons of water into vin de table. With a lot left over, the shrewd organiser bottled same, and then sold the whole consignment to one of the invitees, St. Émilion, recently canonised for services to the wine industry.

"You're from Gaul, aren't you?" said one of the guests to the sainted sommelier, who was enjoying his canape in blissful silence. Inebriated wedding guests have been around since time immemorial, and this one was taking no prisoners.

"He brews a lovely cup of tea, but I prefer it when he changes water to wine (hiccup). Don't you?"

"Mais oui," replied the amused monk, as he tried to extricate himself from an awkward conversation. All the same, he was envious of JC's skills, and could only agree with the fellow's comment.

Wine is such an intrinsic part of religion, but I can't understand why they produced it for the last supper rather than the first. Some clerics are excellent after-dinner speakers, with their confidence and composure often invigorated by alcoholic exposure before, during, and after courses. It is true that too much vino can shrink the brain, cause behavioural change, sexual dysfunction and infertility, but members of the clergy don't worry about things like that.

Sadly, a name that never comes up in these frequent dissertations is Buddy, yet he did much to mould the apostolic delegation known as Team Jesus. For a start, he honed their communication skills. Peter, the fisherman, spent much of his life at sea, and his grasp of the vernacular hardly extended beyond bawdy tales and sailors' songs. In no time at all, he praised the Lord in a most erudite manner, but he still liked his sea shanties. One of the Israelites, Brother Cohen, had written a hymn to him called "Hallelujah," and Peter opened and closed each of his orations with the dirge. This was really the start of music and religion as we know it. When the main man gave his Sermon on the Mount, The Carpenters provided musical support. Some apostles went into the desert and preached amidst sand and hard rock, while the likes of Genesis and Black Sabbath performed. Up north, Paul and his road manager Ringo paid tribute to Mrs. Christ with their rendition of "Mother Mary." The congregation loved it. However, all things come to an end, don't they?

I don't think anybody saw the crucifixion coming. In those days, a hung jury had different connotations, but, nevertheless, the outrage deserved to be more widespread. Perhaps, folks were complacent because they didn't want to lose those extra holidays at Easter. Anyway, the music died, but I am happy to say it is now back bigger than ever.

Last year, I witnessed the choir from the Baptist Church in Dallas in action—200 choristers, all dressed in colourful smocks, and seven lead singers. Beautiful!

This is religious commitment in the Bible belt of America, but everywhere is different. You can see a young man sit on the knee of a priest and discuss the Ten Commandments, or observe Allah ride in on a rocket with his own version of retribution. Some other faiths have fallen by the wayside. These days, the Quakers make porridge, and the Latter-day Saints have less access because people now lock their front gates. Then there are the forgotten people like Buddy. The trusted companion was a big man in more ways than one, and, for mine, deserves this sympathetic attempt at historical accreditation.

For this insightful piece, I wanted to sign-off with the traditional Amen, but times have changed. A woman will now be the voice of reason, and who would argue with that? For the writing of this story, I was dressed by Yves St. Laurent.

What I've Learned About America

History has many versions and sometimes censorship and suppression can affect truth and candour. Those with the will and the want to defy convention and conservative viewpoints are often punished by ridicule, public scorn, and even imprisonment. This hasn't happened to me but it should be considered.

McDonalds and the Klu Klux Clan!

There's a place in Western Kentucky called Glasgow, home to the Highland Games, second only to the real thing in Scotland. Octogenarian Jack Laing put up the road sign many years ago, and built a bench seat under it for contemplation. You just can't rush into a town like this willy-nilly.

If you're wondering where all the Caledonians came from, go back to 1815, when Captain John Horton, choirmaster with Slaughter's Militia, reported on the proceedings of a well-remembered skirmish.

> "We fired our guns and the British kept a-comin'
> There wasn't nigh as many as there was a while ago
> We fired once more and they began to runnin'
> On down the Mississippi to the Gulf of Mexico." *

One can only assume the Scottish contingent within the British forces didn't fancy life south of the border, or the foot soldiers baulked at the long journey. So, the establishment of a hamlet in Barren County probably seemed like a good idea at the time. Of course, when one thinks Hamlet, one thinks of William Shakespeare, but don't brand the residents of this new village English. It turned out that the Scots and Irish hated their Pommy comrades more than they hated Americans.

Reliable intelligence is hard to come by regarding the early evolution of some new settlements, but extraordinary events, when they happened, managed to filter through the information impasse. The opening of a new restaurant always pulls in the punters, but food without eating utensils—wow!

"Who is this red-headed clown who thinks he knows how we like to eat?" screamed the conservative push from nearby Bowling Green, a town without pity. Only when their neighbours began travelling the thirty odd miles to try this new taste sensation did the fundamentalist foodies sit-up and take notice.

Roland McDonald didn't get it right at first. He started out with hot dogs, which he imported from the state capital Frankfort, but the animal lovers cried foul. People who owned sausage dogs were beside themselves, as dog-napping had become rife in the area, and Mr. Mac paid good money. Eventually, he hit the jackpot with his haggis-burger, which established his reputation, allowing him to open branches elsewhere, and even expand with ancillary dishes on request.

One of McDonald's suppliers was a potato farmer (there were a lot of them about), whose French wife fried spuds in her own peculiar way; and you could eat them with your fingers. What a revelation!

Some people in Kentucky claimed this fast food phenomenon to be offal, and it took the government many years to agree, later banning the importation of haggis from the U.K. Nevertheless, this cheeky upstart was up and running and had moved-on. However, let's not get ahead of ourselves. We have to discuss the competition.

We only need to consider one such person: a military man, who, in his own mind, served with Andrew Jackson when they sent the Brits a packing. He arrived in Glasgow with his herbs and spices, and immediately purchased all the ad space around town. The town-folk could only marvel at these colourful billboards displaying just one word—chicken.

The rest of the words came with the second advertising phase, and it soon became apparent that Roland McDonald had a rival. What could he do?

History tells us that this family descended from Conn of the Hundred Battles, one of the clans instrumental in colonising the Hebrides. So, they understood how to fight. Unfortunately, Roland's issue was all female, and, although one doesn't wish to denigrate their capabilities, real brawn was required here.

Enter the husbands of said issue, Angus Klu and Logan Klux, both exponents of paramilitary exercises long before such things became de rigueur. These guys thought nothing of stringing up a few coloured gentlemen before breakfast, and they could do it with complete anonymity, as their pal and soulmate Jed owned the general store, and provided their camouflage. Serious consumers in town questioned why this shop always came up short when they wanted bed linen, in particular white sheets.

The chicken man soon made inroads into his competitor's bottom line, putting him on the sharp end of McDonald's retaliatory offensive. The chap would not be easily intimidated. After all, they hadn't made him a colonel in the Confederate Army for nothing. Klu and Klux firebombed his premises, raped his serving wenches, and strung-up many of his chickens (which he intended doing anyway). The malicious misfits generally made a nuisance of themselves.

Although not a young man, the fellow with the white goatee gave as good as he got. On one occasion he chased the torch-bearing Klux down the street with his blunderbuss, and shot him in his rear end. Logan failed to out-sprint him due to his fallen arches.

Because the firebrand couldn't sit on his buns for three weeks, hostilities were put on hold, which gave the colonel time to refurbish his building and re-brand his product. The publicity which surrounded the feud proved to be beneficial for business and both outlets prospered in the aftermath of the conflict. The feuding food barons decided to declare a truce and co-exist, which is the situation as it is today.

The Clan, the only people not happy with this outcome, bristled, as they now had no-one to burn, rape, or rope. Angus and Logan eventually bought into a bakery in Glasgow. They hired local girls to sell the tasty pastry, and eventually made a lot of dough.

HISTORY

Every year for the Highland Games, the lads put their tarts in tartan, and called their shortbreads cookies. When it was all over, the two fellas always took a wee drop, and repaired to old Laing's sign, where they would spend the night watching the traffic go by.

*Composer: Jimmy Driftwood, 1936

Down among the cotton and the corn

Those of us colonials schooled under a British education curriculum are fortunate and should be eternally grateful, according to our parents. Some parental guidance was accepted without fear or favour, and one such assumption was that Americans had no culture. So, it proved a pleasant surprise to me when, prior to my first visit to the land of the free, I learned something of their opera house. I was excited when I stepped-down from the aeroplane in Nashville, Tennessee.

Billy Jo was to be my driver, and I had no idea whether this person would be male or female. After meeting her, I still had no idea, but I did like the large hat and cowboy boots she wore. Could Joan Sutherland have committed to a production of "Annie Get Your Gun?"

Initially, I perceived there to be a language problem, as I couldn't understand a word she said. I just went along for the ride, hoping I would find an English/American dictionary at the hotel. We would be lucky to find the hotel. The Cumberland River, having flooded its banks, surged into the streets and caught everybody by surprise. Billy Jo suggested a diversion, and we ended up in a honky tonk, drinking sour mash whiskey and listening to hillbilly music.

This detour didn't shock me as it could have. I remember singing cowboys from my youth, and those Saturday afternoons down at the Lyceum Theatre. I couldn't recall any of the songs, but the gunslingers who sang them came to mind freely—Gene Autry and Roy Rogers. Roy's horse Trigger didn't sing, but you half expected him to.

I'm afraid we stayed too long at the fair. My chauffeur certainly imbibed too much for someone supposed to drive me home. She also gave up more than I anticipated. Did I need to know she often came here looking for Willie? Then there was the embarrassment with my credit card in a cash only saloon. Even the entertainer on stage called himself Cash—Don or Donny or something similar.

I awoke with a hangover—Sunday Morning Comin' Down. You'd better believe it. There were any number of churches to attend, but even short sermons lasted two hours, and you had to sing a lot. I don't like to sing much, unlike the locals who walked around with their tonsils hanging out.

That morning I conversed with four people, three of them called Hank. I think this moniker is a derivation of Harry and, evidently, the trouble with Harry is that it can be confused with Barry, Larry, or Carrie, if you're a girl. The most famous person to carry this name, one Hank Williams, often dominated conversation in this town. I asked one of my new friends if he might have been an opera star.

"Oh yeah. He had the Lovesick Blues and a Cold, Cold Heart."

"Gee, I'm sorry to hear it," I said, not wanting to elaborate on what appeared to be conflicting emotional problems of a confused person. I subsequently found out that he also got into trouble for setting the woods on fire.

It took me some hours to recover from my breakfast burrito and grits, and I was no nearer to finding out the location of this damn opera house. Everyone kept saying "Why man?" but I really didn't think I needed to explain. Later that day, I walked past an ancient but distinguished building with its name engraved over the portico—Ryman Auditorium, Home of the Grand Ole Opry.

Hello Dolly, it's nice to have you back where you belong.

Being late in the afternoon, I had little time to put out a contract on my travel agent, but I made a note to do it the next day. In the meantime, I figured I should bone up on country music before I rocked up to the aforementioned auditorium to hear Waylon and other contemporary sounds of love and associated catastrophes. I wondered if Billy Jo still fancied Willie over at the Honky Tonk. By co-incidence, the lady in question honked me as she drove by in her Tennessee Ernie Ford. Why on earth do people give names to inanimate objects?

We caught up later at the refreshment palace, and my new best friend introduced me to some of her chums, who were on their way to the Ryman to perform. The girls parked their commercial vehicle outside, packed full of musical instruments. Loretta and Emmylou loaded it up with enough booze to tide them over—Tammy was standing by her van, and supervising. They were good kids with lots of hair, which made me glad they would be on stage. I'd hate to sit behind them in the cheap seats.

I managed to score a ticket for a forthcoming show, sourced by Billy Jo from her friend Billy Ray. Some people are not aware that every performance goes live to a radio audience, and that some of the sponsor's mouth-watering products could be desirable to a cow. Over the two-and-a-half hours of the show, many high-profile personalities performed, and the quality of the various acts was exceptional. To my mind, these supposedly uncultured rednecks in the audience really appreciated this exquisite talent, and enthusiastically applauded those who gave them joy.

Off-stage, life could be a bitch. Hank drank and Bobby McGee lost his me. Janis Joplin expired before her time, as did Patsy, the boy from Rocky Mountain High and others. Merle spent time at San Quentin, while Johnny Cash entertained the boys at Folsom Prison. These stories I learned in a few short days in Nashville. Did Pavarotti or Pavlova ever experience any of these deprivations? Devotees named a pizza after Pavarotti and a dessert after Pavlova. Surely, the Dixie Chicks are just as tasty.

Discovering all these treasures proved timely, as I was leaving on a jet plane just when the tide appeared to be turning. A wave of social comment epitomised a world of discontent and turbulence, and some of the new music sounded a bit Peter, Paul and Scary. One of the folksingers even had a lead belly. What about that?

I would like to learn more about these people and their ten-gallon hats, and in time I will. As soon as I find myself a new travel agent!

It's a shame about the name

Some people can be extremely patriotic, with their umbilical cord often attached to the town of their birth. It is rather quaint that some of those individuals perpetuate this relationship by deed poll; hence Dinah Washington, Tony Orlando, John Denver, Whitney Houston and Victoria De Los Angeles. On investigation, I discovered that none of these super stars were born where they should have been. However, Muddy Waters was native to Mississippi and the late River Phoenix was born in Oregon. Strangely, River arrived before Rain, the latter being the name of his younger sister.

What about Tex Ritter and Minnesota Fats? Yes, Texas for the former, but New York for the latter. And what a town that is. You can sit at a bar, drink Manhattans, and root for the Yankees or deliver them Bronx cheers. Do you remember that old codger Will Rogers who eulogised the Dodgers? Fortunately, the dude died before the team relocated to L.A. The shock might have killed him.

Sitting in a bar is one of the joys of New York, and the inhabitants are a particularly knowledgeable lot. I was told that John Wayne's mum christened him Marion, which was true. My informant had no knowledge regarding the parentage of that boy named Sue; nor James Bond's friend Pussy Galore.

You can't be in Gotham or the nation's capital without being aware of political shenanigans, and I was fortunate to be in a bar where one of the customers knew the whole story about the first settlers, most of them fruit-growers. They divided the nation into the Big Apple in the east and Orange County in the west. Everything in-between was pear-shaped.

Food, glorious food! Maryland and Kentucky are both supportive of chicken but there are other options down south. Local hero Muhammad Ali used to eat black-eyed peas after every fight. Crawfish, catfish, blue crab and other delights are always consumed prior to a man-size serve of pie, be it pumpkin, pecan or shoofly. I have to admit I preferred anything I wanted at Alice's Restaurant, washed down with a glass of woody Chardonnay.

The original restaurant was in Massachusetts, although I recall enjoying a Chef's Salad at a franchise in Westwood during the seventies. I saw Chevy Chase roll up in his flash vehicle, and I'm sure Kate Hudson was there in diapers. It was a time of recovery after the Vietnam War and few things were working as well as they might. However, folks still went to Viagra Falls for their honeymoon.

Have I told you about my side trip to New England?

I don't know what they talked about at that tea party in Boston, but the English didn't bring much imagination with them when they started branding their new settlements. I mean, really—Plymouth, Manchester,

HISTORY

Bristol, Canterbury and Dublin. For God's sake! Dublin is not even in Old England.

Take the smug look off your face, America. You performed no better. I visited friends in Woodstock, Connecticut, and then moved-on to Vermont, New Hampshire, and New York State, passing three other Woodstock communities in twenty-four hours. When I Googled these apparitions, I uncovered twenty-two towns with this name. Where's the creative flair that gave us Ding Dong, Texas and Scratch Ankle in Alabama?

Then there is Salem. Give me strength.

They used to burn witches in this city, which to me seems like reasonable conduct if they were trying to get into your britches. Do you realise Massachusetts can be a brutal place to live? Rumour is rife that Lizzie Borden from Fall River chopped-up her pa and then gave her step-mother forty whacks? It is history that the jury didn't think so, but suspicion lingers.

They also have cemetery tours in Salem and fun things like that. Would anyone be surprised if they had ghost riders in their pie?

If you're an Australian, you can't think about America without thinking about cowboys. We see them in the highest office in the land, and the dustiest towns. Names like William Bonney and silent screen star William Hart come to mind. William Boyd found fame as Hopalong Cassidy and, of course, Wild Bill and Buffalo Bill. All these saddle stars had a will and a way.

Tick the cowboys. Now, what about the Apache and the Comanche chiefs? Were they in Indiana? I managed to find my way to Boulder in Colorado and charted my path towards Little Rock via Dodge City, hoping Vin Diesel would be there; then on to Tulsa, Topeka and Texas by and by. An onset of travel sickness hit me in Waco, but, as this was the home of Dr Pepper, I recovered quickly.

The Indians turned out to be very friendly. They welcomed me to their casinos and I learned of their struggle for recognition, not unlike our own colonial experience. However, we would never accept both zero and double zero on our roulette wheels.

Before moving-on, I needed to ascertain whether I could effectively report on the American way of life, based on my experiences. My advisors included their ambassador to Indonesia Frank Sumatra, and Paris Hilton from the French Embassy. I remembered with affection Julie London in the U.K. and, of course, the Vatican consul Deli Pastrami. They all agreed, without exception, that America was brave, but they probably didn't need any more visitors from Australia.

My own thoughts—you can spend too much time in bars talking to philosophers and pundits.

Where little cable cars climb halfway to the stars!

Everybody is aware Tony Bennett left his heart in San Francisco. Bully for him. I left my wallet there, containing money, credit cards, and a picture of my dog Rex.

Perhaps I am being simplistic. My belongings were removed from my pocket during a ritual associated with the annual "Hug Somebody Day." This is an international observance, but I'm sure it was some loon on the West Coast who first floated the idea. Could it be the same loon who thought it would be smart to build the elevator on the outside of the St. Francis Hotel?

I like television as much as the next person and I understood that the streets of Frisco might be awash with crime, although I thought Dirty Harry had all that under control. The police found Rex's picture floating under the Golden Gate Bridge, and I was devastated. Rex couldn't swim.

This was not my first visit to this city by the bay. The last time, I wore flowers in my hair and Friday was on my mind. Or was it Tuesday? In those days we never knew because of the amount of weed we smoked. The main haze floated over Haight/Ashbury but extended from Little Italy to the Big Sur, where it could be Sonny but without Cher. Clint started his eatery in this neck of the woods, and you could listen to Joan Baez, fresh out of Palo Alto High School, with a voice that could cut through glass.

Some people describe these times as decadent and they may be right. The governor dated a young girl, and underage women everywhere were being generous with their affections. If you lost your money, free love helped ease the pain. For those on a tight budget, there was fish on the wharf, milk in the city, and wine in the valley. The Napa Valley proved an exciting destination for me because Australia supported a vibrant wine

HISTORY

industry and I wanted to compare vintages. However, when you start taste-testing before breakfast, it can be a long day. Mountain View (later to become Silicon Valley) was another interesting piece of real estate, but nerds only went there when looking for jobs. Perish the thought.

Once the hippie generation turned into Jesus freaks, you knew there would be retribution. Remember the earthquakes of 1906 and 1989? This turned-out to be worse than that. They elected Ronald Reagan as governor. Why do Republicans recruit their politicians in Hollywood; they've done it twice now. Come on, this guy ended up as president. At least Arnold was colourful. Not so Pat Brown, Jerry Brown and Gray Davis—not one among them a whiter shade of pale.

There were winners and losers during that summer of love in 1967; the biggest losers being bra manufacturers Playtex and Maidenform. Few women wore their products and the fall-out became obvious. Some of their designers jumped ship and embraced other architectural challenges such as bridge-building and dam construction. Marilyn Monroe and Jayne Mansfield saved the day. Jayne's D size cup meant the defeat of liberation because icons are role models, and all the girls now wanted to look like Dolly or Diana Dors.

I know I'm starting to ramble, but that's what I did on my first trip to the West Coast, rambling up to Vancouver via Eugene, Oregon. I also travelled the coastline to Carmel and Monterey and then trekked Yosemite National Park, where I came face to face with a grizzly bear with designs on my baloney sandwich. I called him Teddy, after one of the Kennedys. He seemed very pleased.

It is always the people who surprise you, and I must say that this city boasts an abundance of male flight attendants and hair stylists. When they congregate, they know how to put on a parade. A similar pageant in my home town is called "Moomba," which is an aboriginal word meaning "Let's get together and have fun."

Before I lost my wallet, I committed to investigate a much loved institution—The Buena Vista Café on Hyde Street. Long held views regarded it as the home of Irish coffee in this country and I could believe that, as they always mixed with traditional Tullamore Dew whiskey. The proprietors have sold over thirty million serves of the delightful potion.

GERRY BURKE

When I arrived, I met a lady seated on one of the bar stools. She introduced herself.

"My name's Eileen. I lean on the bar and you buy the drinks."

It was Eileen who told me about "Hug Somebody" day. Shortly after that, she retired to the Ladies Room and I never saw her again.

Some of San Francisco's favourite sons & daughters!

Isadora Duncan	Dashiell Hammett	Steve Jobs
Clint Eastwood	Jerry Garcia	Mark Zuckerberg
Francis Ford Coppola	Johnny Mathis	Levi Strauss
George Lucas	Carol Channing	Nancy Pelosi
Natalie Wood	Mark Twain	Monica Lewinsky
Sharon Stone	Tom Brady	Robert McNamara
Tom Hanks	Joe Montana	Harvey Milk
Robin Williams	O J Simpson	Ellen DeGeneres
Bruce Lee	Naomi Wolf	Dian Fossey

Cigarettes, Whiskey, and Wild, Wild, Women

When Solomon David and Mary O'Brien married, there was consternation in the synagogue as many of the guests arrived for the ceremony wearing pork pie hats. So much for the marriage. The divorce was even more embarrassing.

Sol, an upright member of the community, had donated millions of dollars to various Jewish organisations throughout the land. His three sons were well-liked and solid citizens, but his wife decided to pull the plug. The sons weren't hers, but the money was.

The lady realised that it wasn't her charm that had dragged him to the altar, but her inheritance, although few people would say she hadn't been unattractive; very few I would think. Looking back, she might agree that too much babka and knish helped enlarge her rotunda, and diminish her self-control.

So, there you have it: a divorced woman of forty-two years, with no skills, and little cash left from her legacy. She had enough money to hire a personal trainer, which she did with trepidation, knowing that any physical transformation would be hard work. On the job front, employment opportunities became available with a tobacco company. To erase memories of the past, she changed her name to Davidoff, and went to work for Roly Morris, a British expat operating out of Richmond, Virginia.

Walter Raleigh introduced Queen Bess to the delights of smoking, and for his trouble he expected customs and excise exemptions; but her decree only involved herself and personal usage. So, the habit became expensive and didn't sweep through the empire as it should have. Nonetheless, Mr. Meerschaum from Germany soon passed through town, and people started to utilise his pipes. The roll-your-own folks followed, which saw the emergence of Mr. Morris, who had previously been a dancer with a village touring group.

Mr. Meerschaum

Because Mary performed with distinction, the boss promoted her to marketing manager, with an insignificant wage increase. The only other employee in the department was Roly's son Philip.

No-one knows where the rolling machine came from, but Ms. Davidoff watched the installation from the Chesterfield sofa in her office. Having considered the benefits, she delighted in the fact that the unit would improve production seven-fold. Could they expand the market by this much?

Early tobacco advertising targeted gentlemen of the realm, positioning the product as a habit of the wealthy and refined. Mary thought this to be rubbish. Cigarettes (the new name) should be available to everyone, and she formulated a plan to take their own line of lung-busters down-market.

Through Roly's entertainment friends, the marketeer met a young girl named Rose Lee, a flower-seller in the same mould as the infamous Eliza Doolittle. This girl had been tutored in dance rather than language and soon became a sensation performing at the Roxy Paramount as Gypsy.

HISTORY

Mary's plan saw Philip drift into the theatre at interval and give out single cigarettes to those who wanted to try them. One of the red-headed showgirls would accompany him with a box of matches. Once the audience, who were mainly men, exited the stalls, they would find Philip's girl waiting for them with the ciggies in packets. The design team had constructed a portable tray to hold fifty cigarette packs, the tray supported by a strap around the girl's neck. The leather support didn't distract from an uninterrupted view of the lass's buxom melons.

With the sudden upsurge in sales came familiarity, and the darling of the Davidoff clan increased her profile, as well as her bank account. Often seen around town with important people, she failed to squash rumours that she descended from Russian nobility. When the lady travelled to Europe, this rumour went with her and she was feted in many countries, including Great Britain, where the mayor put on a cocktail party in her honour in Pall Mall.

This is where she met an ambitious young politician, Winston, who embraced the new craze in a big way. However, being a large man, he was not happy with the trim contours of the cigarette and demanded more. She gave it to him—well, her new ideas division did. They boosted the tobacco content, enlarged the wrap around configuration, and packaged the coronas in boxes. Winston emerged as the candidate most likely, when appointed to the highest position in the land. Along the way, he became a living advertisement for the cigar, akin to Sir Walter Raleigh's efforts all those years ago.

By the time the esteemed lady resumed her life stateside, there had been a change at board level, with the retirement of Roly and the rise to power of his son. Chief Executive Philip Morris would bring all his skills to the table and develop opportunities like never before.

They looked at the native population and tried to think outside the box. Those peace pipes had to go, and the introduction of ciggies with filter-tips and flip-top boxes helped with that. Unfortunately, this limited the opportunities for meaningful pow wows with the white man, and hostilities dragged on longer than they should have.

In alpine regions, folks smoked to keep warm, but producers found it difficult to maintain supplies in areas of rugged terrain. Nevertheless, the inhabitants of these parts refused to miss out. Smokey the Bear arrived at the trading post once a week to collect his carton of Silk Cut. Sales were strong on the East Coast in places like Raleigh, North Carolina and Beaufort, South Carolina, birthplace of Smokin' Joe Frazier. Cigarettes were promoted as the ideal aftermath to sex and dinner, not necessarily in that order, hence the award-winning slogan "Nothing could be finer than smokin' in a diner."

New York proved a different kettle of fish. Rough town, tough opposition! A Dutch lad, Peter Stuyvesant, came up the Hudson River with a lot of leaf and magnified his influence quickly. His ideas were revolutionary, and the Virginians were continually outflanked by his preposterous solutions to his logistic problems. For example, those dry barren areas in the centre of the country, not yet serviced by the railway, still received his tobacco cartons. They arrived by camel.

The immigrant even opened a branch office in a place called Stogie Springs, which remains under quarantine to this day because it is a health hazard. The Philip Morris people had problems of their own, as the Marlboro man kept falling off his horse, and Virginia Slim put on twenty pounds. The matriarch also failed to preserve her trim, taut figure of recent years and reverted to past pleasures, which was her right. She aged gracefully, and enjoyed the fruits of her success, the benefits of which included a European classic car and a substantial residence in New Kent County.

As the years went by, Mary pulled back from the day-to-day operations of the company, but remained on the board until her retirement. During the latter years of her life, she continued her two-pack-a-day habit, but finally succumbed to lung cancer, a few days short of her 109th birthday. The living legend departed this life with little fanfare, but her remains were repatriated to a gold ash-tray in the boardroom at headquarters. The memorial, encased in a glass trophy cabinet with some of her lifelong mementos, included her father's pork pie hat.

The first family of fermentation!

Adam and Eve purchased forty acres of prime land in Southern California, and planted their apple orchard. They borrowed heavily, with little leeway should there be a crop failure or any other disaster. They didn't plan on any disasters, of course.

HISTORY

The snake in the grass lived on the next farm, and he was intent on acquiring their acreage. Luke Ledowski (his birth name might have been Lucifer) was a nasty piece of work, with a reputation for taking advantage of mortgage foreclosures to increase his landholdings. The Eden Estate included a cider production facility, and the raider had done his due diligence. In twelve months, the orchard and ranch would be a hot property, so an early strike would be fortuitous.

A gentleman named Tom Lehrer discovered a way to poison pigeons in a park. Ledowski devised a similar strategy to decimate the Eden fruit yield. He had read a book where the villain tried to eradicate France's garlic harvest with liquid Vegemite; just the type of contagion he needed.

Vegemite is a beef extract, mainly consumed by kiddies Down Under. Few people outside Australia are fond of this breakfast treat, possibly because it is black. Luke understood the sticky spread to be part of a population reduction scheme like China's one-child policy. Once you add arsenic and liquefy it, the fluid becomes deadly.

Getting hold of the stuff was not difficult, as Quinlan's Ocker Shop in downtown Los Angeles peddled the brekky favourite in many forms. You could even buy it mixed with peanut butter.

The rogue would spray the trees himself, at night, but a problem presented—a dog. It wasn't a major setback. The woofer belonged to the eldest child and had never known any guard dog training. Butch loved everyone and everything, and he was especially keen on steak. The marinated T-bone which sailed over the fence was tainted, but he couldn't help himself. Adam made the grim discovery when he came down for breakfast.

"Oh my God! The dog is dead. Wayne will go ape shit."

Mr. Eden's contemporary catalogue of the colloquial had always been impressive, intuitive, and accurate. The kid went ballistic, and it was down to his two siblings, Mabel and Beth, to try to placate him.

"Don't worry, brother," said Mabel. "Pa will get you another dog."

Next time it might be a Rottweiler. Pa, having decided to take a walk along the boundary of his orchard, discovered, to his horror, that all his fruit had turned black. Two months later, he learned that his bank account had gone into the red, with no way back. The manager was a Republican.

When the bankrupt family and the Rottweiler slowly drove away from their former property in a U-Haul van, the gloating Luke Ledowski watched them go. It was a delightful day for the despicable opportunist, who had already planned his first planting in the fallow paddock behind the line of cedar pine trees.

Marijuana growers are responsible for the largest crops in California, today— boosted by relaxed laws relating to the production and use of cannabis. *Lucky Luke's Honeycrisp Cider* would be a neat support business.

Down the road a bit, the Eden family found temporary accommodation. Although everyone chipped-in as best they could, they were doing it tough. Wayne was only thirteen years of age, but working as a lumberjack. Beth touted for business on the street corner, with her home-made lemonade, and Eve flogged Tupperware. In circumstances like this, marriage break-ups are inevitable, and it wasn't long before cracks started to appear in the relationship. Then Mr. José Miguel Garcia appeared on the scene.

Senor Garcia owned a chain of restaurants from Mexicali to Mazatlán, and had recently divorced from his childhood sweetheart Rose. Eve was ripe for the picking and José pounced. The kids liked Mexican food but said goodbye to their pa with a heavy heart. The dejected father accepted the situation with regret but realised he would be better placed to bounce back if not burdened with family responsibilities. That's when he received the call from an old friend.

"Hey, remember me? Joe Pensacola—Honest Joe?"

"I do remember you. You sold me that Ford tray-truck, which blew-up two days after the warranty expired."

"Nooooo, I can't believe it. It was owned by a little old lady who only used it to go to church."

If he had been aware of that information at the time of purchase, the naive farmer would surely have smelled a rat. After all, little old ladies are so maligned in the second-hand car business. Nevertheless, he remembered the fellow as a friendly soul with a vibrant personality.

"I don't know how you tracked me down, but what can I do for you?"

"It's what I can do for you, compadre. I have opened a car yard in Louisville, and one of my clients is looking for a distiller. I told him about your fabulous set-up and he's prepared to fly you over for an interview. Even if it doesn't work out, we can catch up and go to the races together. I know you like the punt."

Adam did like the ponies, and there is no better place to see them than at Churchill Downs. So, he said yes and followed the instructions that would see him settled in seat 33C on the American Airlines shuttle to the home of Muhammad Ali. The honest car dealer waited for him at the other end.

"Hey man, how are they hangin'?"

"Hi, Joe. Nice to see you. What's the program?"

The program was rather loose. The interview would take place the next day at a farm, a few miles out of town. In the meantime, the visitor accepted the accommodation offered by the car salesman and his wife, a comely lass with bedroom eyes. Then he was spirited away to a bar, a rib place, and another bar. There were people with large hats at all these venues.

"Gee, this is my first honky tonk. You don't expect me to ride that mechanical bronco, do you?"

He did, and the guest from the west made a fair fist of it. Certainly, there was no lack of female company after his dismount. In quick time, he met Anna May, Ellie Mae, Jo Ellen, and Laura Leigh. Can you believe they all ordered the most expensive hooch in the joint?

People in this city live and breathe bourbon. In fact, if it's made from corn and aged in charred oak barrels, it probably comes from Kentucky. Those infidels in Tennessee have their own thing going, but they don't know Jack, according to one local expert.

Adam was glad of the afternoon meeting, as he awakened with quite a hangover, and discovered Mrs. Pensacola sitting on the edge of his bed with a cup of coffee. She must have experienced a rough night also, having neglected to button the top three holes on her nighty.

The house guest found himself in an invidious situation, and as she came closer it became more invidious. Her laboured breathing seemed to accentuate the output of her scent, which was working overtime. Who wears perfume before breakfast if they're not hot to trot? The sunlight streaming through the window highlighted cotton as an enemy of modesty. He could see right through the nightdress, with only a morning brew between her curves and his nerves. Was this the time to evaluate loyalty in the face of opportunity? Honest Joe had been most gracious in providing him with a roof over his head, and the prospect of a job also beckoned (with his pal on commission). On the other hand, the bloke sold him a lemon, and left him for dead on that honky tonk horse.

He was saved by the bell; or, to be more accurate, a telephone call from Car City.

"Hey, buddy, sorry to walk out on you this morning, but I need to escort a customer to the bank. What if I pick you up at noon, and we'll drive out to the farm?"

Timothy Beanpole was not as tall as his name might suggest, and he wasn't that sprightly either. Adam came face to face with a wiry old coot, weathered and lined like an old boot. His family had run the distillery since the turn of the century but hit hard times during prohibition, as had their competitors. Those bootleggers and speakeasy owners preferred to get their booze from Canada. Kentuckians made moonshine in the mountains, but elsewhere they were hardly drinking at all. Now, Tim's business just bubbled along, making minimal profits, possibly because of the limited talent among the most recent breed of distillers.

"I don't know why you need me," said the orchardist. "My specialty is cider."

The old man smiled and conceded the point, but a man knows when he is past his use-by date and needs to be replaced. The job offer included three months training from the prospective retiree, and then Adam would assume control. The position came with housing provided, and a car supplied by you know who. It was the accommodation which sealed the deal—a lovely little cabin on the outskirts of the property. The cottage had been deserted for some time, but with a little work it could be made comfortable. It was far enough away from the owner's house, but an easy walk to his workplace.

The offer, once made, was accepted, and the car trader, who was surely on some sort of commission, helped his friend celebrate. The distiller-in-waiting needed to return to California for final family goodbyes, and would drive back with his few belongings in two weeks. In the meantime, Churchill Downs beckoned, and the honest one invited Anna May and Ellie Mae to make up a foursome for mint juleps all around.

Eve and the youngsters were all packed and ready to make their move to San Antonio, and the farewell was short and sweet. It is difficult to kiss your children if they're all wearing sombreros, but there were hugs and tears and fond farewells.

"As soon as you kids are old enough to drink whiskey, I want to see you all in Louisville, right?"

"Yes sir," they cried in unison. Then they were gone.

It was a long drive to his new home, and the chap arrived in an apprehensive state. In cider production, it is all apples, but he now had to get involved in cereal grains such as wheat, rye, barley, and corn. The mash is important as is fermentation, so there was much to be learned. Timothy would be a patient teacher.

The man let Adam follow him around for a few weeks to absorb the process. He explained the difference between the pot and column stills, and the secret of ageing. The smoking of the oak barrels was an eye-opener to the former orchardist, and he didn't know what to think of the intense rivalry between Kentuckians and their southern neighbours.

The product produced in Lynchburg was whiskey, not bourbon—well, according to just about everybody. They filter the spirit through dirty charcoal and that's what it's all about. Give us a break. This was plain one-upmanship and pure marketing genius... which worked.

One night, the new distiller buttonholed Tim and explained that his problems were not with the quality of his spirit but the poor promotion. He suggested an advertising campaign that would make people sit up and take notice, but the owner would have to make sacrifices, including paying for a research team and focus groups.

The first sacrifice would be the loss of his name, diminished for the sake of brevity. The whole family were happy to accept this, as they had already anglicised their name on arrival from Poland. Then there was branding; in this case, a dog with its tongue hanging out. Honest Joe made available the services of his graphic artist, who produced an advertisement which turned the dish-licker into a household name.

Tim Bean Sour Mash...The best liquor in the country.

The southern competitors laughed at this amateur promotional attempt, but they hadn't counted on the fact that many consumers were also dog lovers. The canine was shaggy, and definitely loveable. Dixie licked his employer to the top of the sales chart, to become market leader. Down south, no-one was whistling Dixie.

The annual general meetings of both companies occurred within weeks of each other. One of them was a family affair, as Tim's four children were co-owners of the going concern, the eldest son being chairman. Tom Bean was an accountant in Lexington, his siblings being Tilly Bean, Billy Bean, and Marjorie Mung. Adam had been invited, ostensibly to report on current operations, but he became the centre of attention as Tom eulogised him on his performance.

"On behalf of the board, we would like to thank you for your efforts over the past twelve months, which have been most productive for the company. Because of your strategies, we now find ourselves more than competitive. You have maintained the quality of our products, in line with our father's directives, and we announce today that you are now our official master distiller. Congratulations!"

This called for drinks all around, and the meeting closed with a stirring rendition of "My Old Kentucky Home."

Down south in Lynchburg, proceedings would be more sombre. Bad news was never easy to talk about under the gaze of the founder, who looked down on them from his nine-foot portrait, the only feature in this gloomy charcoal-coloured chamber. To make matters more uncomfortable, pigeons dumped on the forefather's statue, which stands with pride at the entrance to the tasting room.

The treasurer, after providing his report, sat down and left it to the others to try to work out a financial comeback. There wasn't much harmony in the room, even though the director from Nashville offered to write a song.

"That won't be necessary, LeRoy," said Kurt Speechley, Chairman of the Board. We'll give our advertising people one last chance to tip the balance before I call in my brother-in-law. None of you need to know anything about that.

Felix the Firebug, Kurt's more than embarrassing relative, would be available for contract work after he was released from prison in three months' time—the timeline given to the marketing folks to make something happen. They tried everything.

First-up was a Hollywood spokesperson, followed by a minor celebrity with big knockers; but the cash registers refused to zing. In desperation, the creatives turned to LeRoy for his jingle.

HISTORY

> "You've made your Mark, you drink that Turkey
> We've got you licked, we're down and dirty
> Down in the great state of Tennessee."

Sadly, the refrain bolstered the fortunes of brand competitors Maker's Mark and Wild Turkey but did nothing for the Jack boys. Kentucky was winning the whiskey wars, with Tim Bean Sour Mash the market leader. Big things beckoned, but bet your bottom dollar that the night of the fire put a dent in those ambitions.

Felix had driven to the state boundary and hidden his vehicle. There was no way he was going to be caught driving with Tennessee number plates, so the rogue rolled into town in a rented pick-up and grabbed some chow at a local diner. He knew his route because of the map provided for him, so it was just a matter of whiling away a few hours until bedtime. He found a place with beds but no opportunity for sleep, and although Ruby proved to be accommodating, she did like to chatter. The firebug told her nothing—well, nothing that in any way resembled the truth.

Felix's slow patrol around the perimeter of the Bean property was cautious but necessary. He noted the cabin some way from the central buildings, but nothing would prevent him from executing his plan. As far as plans go, simplicity is often the mark of a simple man; otherwise, he would not have walked into the distillery carrying an open flame. One can only assume the pyromaniac wanted to replicate past glories, mostly in the service of the Klu Klux Klan.

Alcohol is almost as dangerous as gasoline as a fire and explosion hazard. Sure, the mash wasn't flammable, but the vapours from the distillates were, and Felix would have been well-advised to walk-in with a Zippo lighter rather than a flaming torch. The intruder came out faster than he went in, and in little pieces. The copper still was the first to ignite, and the eruptions that followed were reminiscent of the finale to a James Bond movie. The explosions awoke everybody in the vicinity. Those on night shift at the fire station noticed the sky light-up and were on their way before they were called. This quick response probably saved many of the oak casks, which were more charred than usual.

A recent inferno in a liquor warehouse destroyed 45,000 barrels, at a loss of fifty million dollars, so Felix the Firebug was lucky he didn't survive.

Southerners can get pretty nasty when you rub them the wrong way. The blaze constituted a huge setback for the family, but having a good bean-counter in Lexington meant that there would be adequate insurance. The property and plant would be re-built and incorporate the latest technology.

All this happened just in time for Wayne's first visit to see his father in his new environment, and he was hanging out for a little nip of Tim Bean Sour Mash. The lad would then transmit his verdict to his siblings, in anticipation of their coming of age. Could this mean a thaw in marital relations? His pa was optimistic, picking-up on the fact that the kids were all getting sick of Tex-Mex food.

Gee, thought the nurturing parent. *If they don't like beans, perhaps I should change the name of our bourbon.*

Wild Women of the West!

Born Maybelle Shirley, the outlaw didn't become a Starr until she married a Cherokee man called Sam, and joined the James-Younger gang as the Bandit Queen. She always carried two guns, and this pistol-packing mama sure could shoot for a dame who rode side-saddle.

Her partnership with Jesse James had been long in the making. Having grown-up together in Missouri, a criminal cabal was a perfect fit, and one way to make ends meet. They made a career of it, until Belle moved to the Indian Territory, later to be renamed Oklahoma. If you discount rustling and a bit of bootlegging, life for her proved downright boring. The female trailblazer then read the advertisement in the local gazette, calling for contestants in the inaugural Miss America Quest.

The promoter, Ronald Grump, a carpetbagger from the East, had lost all his carpets and been drummed out of many counties. Nevertheless, cardsharps, riverboat gamblers and connoisseurs of the female form thought he was on a winner with this one. The prize of 200 dollars, guaranteed by Wells Fargo, was also a tantalising incentive for the girls.

There were three disciplines:
1. Pistol and rifle shooting
2. Rough-riding/rodeo
3. The swimsuit competition

Belle Starr was one of the first to enter the contest, but she already knew where her competition would come from. That sharp-shooting bitch Annie Oakley would be a shoo-in for the rifle event, but she couldn't swim to save herself. Then there was Martha Jane Cannary from the Black Hills of Dakota, aka Calamity Jane. What a dip shit!

Other names came to mind—Rose Dunn from Cimarron; Lillian Smith, the trick shooter; Pearl Hart; and Laura Bullion, who rode with Butch Cassidy. They all had different abilities and would do anything for money. This innovative contest sounded like a lot of fun and would progress the role of women in a man's world.

Maybelle didn't think highly of her two most accomplished challengers. It always helps to be confident. She played piano like all the others in her family and presented well, being a snappy dresser. Her black velvet riding habit and plumed hat became her trademark, and many folks thought she possessed movie star looks. I would suggest they were thinking about Boris Karloff, rather than Jane Russell, who portrayed her in "Montana Belle."

One problem—the Montana miss regularly appeared on the "Most Wanted" list, currently placed third. She hoped to do better than that in the quest.

Ronald Grump, with contacts in the White House, hardly broke stride. He obtained an exemption, and the gal commenced her training. If she could knock over one stagecoach a week, that would sharpen her riding skills. Her trusty Winchester '73 also needed a workout. Who would miss a couple of Indian bucks from a hunting party?

As it happened, Chief Squatting Cow was one fella who did miss the deceased—his son. Chief Cow wanted revenge, but the shooter had already packed her things, and departed for the judging preliminaries. She would try to pick up one of those new bikini swimming costumes in Dodge City, imported from France and all the rage.

The first competitions were the riding disciplines, which were to be held in Carson City. Kit Carson, himself, would be the MC and, naturally, the activities would get under way with a parade. William Cody picked up the contract to supply the horses, and he brought along a few buffaloes for no other reasons than to promote his *Wild West* show. The man had more front than a rabbit with a gold tooth.

Most of the contestants booked-in to the Last Chance Saloon and Casino. The beautiful one was shocked to learn it was owned by Chief Squatting Cow and his tribe, who were on their way to take-up residence as part of the deal that saw native Americans moved from Indian Territory to make way for the new state of Oklahoma. At the time of the announcement, the injun chief had been interviewed by a journalist from New York, who listened intently to his grievance.

"White man make us move. Just when corn grows high to a buffalo's thigh."

"Is that right?" said the journo. "I've heard it sometimes gets as high as an elephant's eye."

With a pregnant pause and a certain amount of sarcasm, the wise old man put the fellow in his place.

"There are no elephants in Oklahoma."

There soon would be if Buffalo Bill Cody had his way. His show grew bigger by the day, and while in Carson City, he signed up Annie Oakley and Lillian Smith. It would be good for business if one of them could win the Miss America Quest, and, unknown to others, it was he who filed the complaint against the participation of Ms. Starr. How could she enter being a married woman? Easy! A clause in the rules allowed you to participate if your husband had been shot dead within the previous two years. This revelation really pissed the showman off. He didn't think anyone in town could read.

Once the tournament got under way, Calamity Jane immediately impressed with her equine skills. Shooting that coyote from under her horse's belly was the clincher that scored her a ten from the usually conservative judges. At the side of the arena sat a worried woman, and understandably so. She could only ride side-saddle.

It was not a well-known fact that Belle collected critters of all kinds. On this occasion, she brought with her some shiny spike bur-backed lizards. They are not poisonous but mighty uncomfortable if they get under your saddle, which is where these were going—under Jane's saddle.

The poor woman! Did she fall-off the horse with a scream, or did she jump? In either case, there were no points in the offing, and the other girls scraped through to be still in contention, with the shooting heats coming up. These would take place in Tombstone in two weeks' time.

HISTORY

Horse Riding Discipline

Tombstone, Arizona—the town too tough to die; you couldn't pick a better venue for a Miss America contest. With the Goodenough Silver Mine providing opportunity, the place was full of chancers ready to make their fortune and spend it soon after. The township boasted over a hundred saloons, plus dance and gambling halls and entertainment venues such as the Bird Cage Theatre and Brothel. Tell me this wasn't a fun city!

Everybody loves a gunfight, and the prospect of seeing Miss Annie Oakley in action excited the masses. Many of the tourists that rode in for the show were women, and they were offered free tethering of their horses at the O K Corral, considered a safe place away from any saloon shoot-ups that might turn rough.

The judging committee consisted of the town's lawmen—Wyatt, Morgan, and Virgil Earp; this appointment stymied the efforts of those bookmakers who always liked to retain an unfair advantage. There would be no leaks from this trio of titans, not that anyone could really envisage the gal with a gun being beaten.

Having said that, Belle gave her a run for her money. Annie was unbeatable with any kind of rifle, but the Bandit Queen was a crack shot with pistols. Lily Smith's trick shooting also impressed the judges. She managed to shoot the cigar out of Ike Clanton's mouth.

With little in it, the festivities wound down in Tombstone and the competitors moved on to El Paso. The Rio Grande had been re-stocked with alligators, just for the occasion, and all the premium seats by the river were snapped up. The Mexicans had never seen a swimsuit competition where the contestants actually swam, and seeing Belle Starr in her bikini provided them with a mouth-watering experience. Even Davy Crockett and Jim Bowie came down from the Alamo to provide moral support for the only representative from their neck of the woods.

She needed it because Calamity Jane had all the favours. Wild Bill set himself up on the riverbank with his trusty firearm, and picked-off each alligator as it gravitated towards his lady, making steady progress in the time trial. Local girl Lorelai Lopez went in next, with the band playing "The Eyes of Texas are Upon You:" but it was the 'gaters who descended upon her, and she didn't make the crossing.

It was ugly, but a good time for the bikini babe to make her splash, while the carnivores were otherwise engaged. The minimal material in her swimming costume reduced drag, and she literally skimmed across the water, leaving little Annie Oakley in her wake. The dog paddle is fine if you're trying to sneak up on someone, but it didn't cut it at this level. However, with Buffalo Bill riding shotgun in a canoe being paddled by Indian Joe, the sharpshooter's girl made it to the other side, and received a typical Juarez welcome—a plate of Burritos and a Rhubarb Margarita.

Yes, rhubarb is for losers. Belle Starr shot her eyes out and won the day. Calamity came in second, and was in a foul mood, last seen waiting for the Deadwood stage, with Mr. Hickok attempting to console her. It's a shame these wonderful women of the West couldn't be friends, but conflict and challenge brings out the best and worst in us, doesn't it?

There have been many stories to come out of the Old West, and this one has been as simple as ABC—Annie, Belle and Calamity. I would have liked to furnish you with a more accurate account of these times, but I checked with a friend in Hollywood, and he says you can't handle the truth. Where have I heard that before?

Horse Tales

The most envied gentleman in Coventry was one Clifton Cutting, personal hairdresser to the lovely Godiva, Countess of Mercia. These jobs didn't come around very often, and he was not taxed too much because she never wanted her hair cut. Sure, one produced a bit of crimping, tinting, and styling, but those long blonde locks usually cascaded over her shoulders and down to her knees. Sometimes, she would wrap her tresses around her waist or other parts, especially when not wearing clothes.

Those of you not familiar with history may raise your eyebrows and wonder why I continually find an excuse to include naked women in my stories. In this case, it was all about the excessive tax required by Godiva's greedy husband, the earl. However, the guy turned out to be a peach. He offered to reduce taxes if she rode naked through the main street, and you know the rest. Only one person breached protocol, and had a peek—poor Peeping Tom was struck blind.

Sometimes there is a fine line between history and fairy tales. I know the Coventry Tourist Board would not want me to elaborate, so I won't. The forgotten man in all this is the redoubtable hair stylist, with more to him that meets the eye.

In some parts of the Continent today, especially in small settlements, there are not enough people to make-up the workforce, so everyone toils over two jobs. This doesn't say much for competition but puts food on the table. This situation also existed in the eleventh century, but who would guess that Clifton Cutting was MI5?

Medieval Investigations, a covert government organisation, employed him as Agent 005, but you deleted the zeros if you operated out of London. You can understand why they recruited the chap; where else do you pick up scuttlebutt but in a salon? On more than one occasion, the snipper suggested to Godiva that he could braid her mane, but she always resisted. One who didn't resist was Ami Badu, a Ghan again Christian from a nearby village. This lady had the only dreadlocks in the county, and was welcomed everywhere, as long as she could explain why she looked different. Most villagers were suspicious of outsiders, so this made Ami a perfect Joe for the MI5 network. Admittedly, the network only included the two of them, but they did experience success.

No-one knows how a Muslim village in the sticks acquired gunpowder, which was not freely available in Europe until many years later. The Chinese invented the stuff during their Tang period and used it extensively through their Song Dynasty. Asians were singing "Bang Bang" long before Cher, Ariana Grande, and friends.

Ami often shared a kebab with her new friends, keen to explain the teachings of Allah. She had promised to plait the hair of one of their virgins, when she saw a disturbing scene in the background—a terrified youngster being strapped up with pouches of gunpowder. This could only mean one thing, but who or what was their target? The Ghanaian girl excused herself, and rushed back to tell her boss what might be coming their way.

"I wonder what the kid did wrong to be sent to Coventry. Are you sure he's not going to Birmingham? After all, they beat us at toeball, the bastards."

"No, I'm not sure," said Ami, somewhat bemused at his cavalier reaction. Surely, they needed to man the bulwarks? Even a woman with a good strongbow would be some defence.

"O.K., sweet lips; let's err on the side of caution. I'll warn the Lord via his wife. Our protector has the arms and manpower to repel any attack on our fair town."

In fact, one person with arms and manpower was the giant Lance Strong. Year after year he had proved to be invincible in battle, and at the jousting tournaments around the country. His real name was Laurence, but once he became a tour de force, the popular press renamed him. The Lord of Coventry, having secured the services of the fellow under contract, felt obliged to protect his peasants. If they were blown up, there would be no more taxes to collect.

HISTORY

The suicide bomber came into town in an early model family cart, with two passengers. The dray could carry three hay bales, with a top speed of one mile per hour. Later models would incorporate round wheels, but who could afford that luxury? Strong's men searched every wagon that entered the city limits, but they all looked the same, didn't they?

The marketplace was in the centre of town, and Cliff, Ami, and a female archer had positioned themselves on a first-floor terrace overlooking the open space. They could see each vehicle as they arrived, ostensibly to deliver produce. The alert secret agent became suspicious when he saw three people wearing hoodies. Who wears a hoodie on a hot summer day? Then, two of the passengers jumped from the cart and ran away—time for the archer to take her shot.

Michaela Green, a graduate of the Sherwood Forest Academy in Nottingham, was proficient in both longbow and crossbow disciplines, and could take an apple off your head at fifty paces. In a matter of seconds, the sharpshooter raised her bow and found an eye line, just as the young man stood up in the front of his cart. The arrow whistled through the air and struck the lad where his heart should be. General reflection after the drama concluded that the victim and associates were heartless, wicked individuals, who maintained a perverted relationship with Allah. The two accomplices were rounded-up, boiled in oil, and then decapitated. Their village was burned to the ground.

Nice one, Cliff. This kind of thing makes the style game seem a little boring, doesn't it? Of course, it would be without those frequent visits from the delightful, delectable Lady Godiva. Few people in town would admit she was a trophy bride, but they all thought it. Some believed she spent far too much time with the hairdresser, her husband being one of them.

"I'm interested, darling. How is it every time you come home from that salon your locks are no shorter?"

"Are you inferring something, my love? You always want me to look my best for your friends. A girl needs a makeover occasionally."

Historians will be reaching for their records to determine whether the lady God had an affair with her hair stylist. Quite frankly, where would she have found the time? The woman produced nine children, and opened many priories, convents, and bingo halls, as part of her civic duty.

Watermills also started to appear all over the country, and she enjoyed breaking a bottle of bubbly at these opening ceremonies.

If anyone had an insight into her salon visits, it would have been Tom the tailor, the one caught peeping at the naked countess during her famous ride. The voyeur rented premises across the street but was now blind. It has not been revealed whether this affliction was down to heavenly intervention or the village people. He couldn't see what everyone was talking about, but he didn't let his condition interfere with his trade. The sleaze just measured his clients by hand, and the macho man loved every minute of it.

Back at the castle, Leo the landlord did what he always did. He increased taxes to financially distress the crimper, but the sums didn't gel. The locals coughed up a consumption tax of 15% on their goats, oxen, sheep, and cattle. Cliff only paid 10% on his mousse.

With no long-term enmity between the style king and the Lord of the Manor, the aggrieved husband redirected his fury towards the tailor, accused of groping his wife during a fitting for her Easter wardrobe. There's always something happening in these small towns, isn't there?

Coventry, a small town? Maybe not. At any rate, Godiva was not given her due. Yes, her ride was memorable, and not eclipsed until Frankie Dettori urged Stradivarius forward to win his third Ascot Gold Cup. This part god and part diva did have a kind heart, with her generosity well documented. This family were important benefactors of several religious institutions in the area, and she donated her own landholdings to establish monasteries. Cliff Cutting eventually resided in one of them. Having become bald before his fortieth birthday, the stylist couldn't live with himself. A report circulated that the monastery was also a MI5 safe house.

Harry the Horse!

I first became aware of Harry the Horse when I was seven years of age. He was an oddball character in a musical entertainment that had come to town. My invitation was memorable because this was the only theatre event that my old man ever attended. It was a Saturday matinee and coincided with the cancellation of the day's events at the track, due to inclement weather.

Harry's confreres were a strange lot. Most wore unfashionable hats, and each of them carried a rolled-up newspaper in their hand. Mistakenly, I presumed that they had brought their own toilet accessories to the theatre. In those days, outside latrines were in vogue and the daily news was an appropriate accoutrement.

The oddball characters didn't stop with Harry. There was Nicely, Nicely Johnson, Dave the Dude, and Nathan Detroit: all regulars at the Saratoga racetrack and forever immortalized by Damon Runyon in his newspaper column, *Guys & Dolls*. I even shared their pain and disappointment when they were unable to conduct their illegal gambling at their regular spot behind the police station.

On that cold day, many years ago, I was to meet professional gamblers for the first time. Not that all of them were involved in a game of chance. Some of them were bookmakers. I had never been to a race meeting but I was familiar with the hovering presence at the bottom of our lane every Saturday. If Mother was aware that Dad had a gambling habit, she didn't let on. As an older person, she would have known about bladder disorders and the like, but not me. I couldn't understand why our beloved breadwinner kept making those visits to the can every thirty minutes. Longer, if there was a protest!

I attended my first race meeting a few years later. The frenetic invitations of the competing bookmakers cascaded over the milling throng, as punters scrambled over each other to try and acquire the best price. As I silently looked on, my hand automatically went to my breast pocket. Three recently ironed bills were about to discover what a rough world it is out there. These were the proceeds from my six months on the newspaper round, and I was amazed that I had the willpower to blow it all in less than two minutes of anticipation, angst, aggravation, and regret. The adrenalin associated with a photo finish result would come much later.

You might wonder how a small boy would be allowed onto a racecourse, unescorted. Over time, I acquired a few artificial uncles from amongst the regulars and would slipstream in on their coattails. In later years, my real uncle was to become a confidante. While my pretentious relatives droned on about Renoir, Monet, and the French masters, we discoursed on everything from the Breeder's Cup to the Melbourne Cup. Let's face it. Everyone knew that Greg Norman won the French Masters.

In times of doom and deprivation, we turn to our heroes, many of them having made their name on the green grass of Flemington on that first Tuesday in November. During the Depression we had little money but were prepared to invest what we had on our champions like Phar Lap and Peter Pan. Illegal bookmakers actually operated from the rear entrance to kindergartens.

Even the clergy were implicated, and, at the time, it was assumed their only vices were gambling and alcohol. The clerics filled their pockets when Galilee, Saintly, Evening Peal and Sister Olive all won the Melbourne Cup.

Losing Uncle Tom was a great shock. The man maintained a cabin up in the high country where he operated many betting accounts. His preferred bookie was Al Packer, who he called "The Goat." I recall the Gorilla ($1,000) going on the 6/4 favourite, in a field of five, and the magnificent beast saluted by eight lengths. Thankfully, I might add, because when he lost, there was Al to pay.

Tom was pretty excited until the jockey weighed in light and the horse was disqualified. To say that the mountain man was flabbergasted is an understatement. He had a heart attack and expired on the spot. Bookmakers came from everywhere to try and resuscitate him, and I think it was uncharitable of some people to suggest that they were only trying to protect a guaranteed income stream.

My late uncle always asserted that bookies were a very generous bunch of people. He always secured a spot over the odds, and if you were a pretty lass with a good bod, you could do even better than that. Not that there is ever any real chance of losing when taking wagers from women. They like to bet on omens, astrology numbers, birthdays, and the colour of the horse.

I was recently asked to write a tribute to bookmakers and you are now reading it. Can you believe that they no longer give me a spot over the odds? I still love them. At a time when monopolies and corporate decision-makers are taking all the fun out of our industry, we should appreciate their historical significance and cherish them for what they are. Bookmaking can be a very stressful occupation and so can punting. When my dad became a little recalcitrant with his debt repayment, our whole family had to leave the country, until things cooled down. We ended up with a Taco Bell franchise in Tennessee. I suppose you could say that things didn't really cool down.

As you might imagine, gambling became a rather touchy subject in our household. My sister, the nun, saw my repeated presence at the track as not only sinful but foolhardy. I could only agree but chose to take the Oscar Wilde perspective: it is better to repent a sin than regret the loss of a pleasure.

Do they bite if they're white?

Everybody loves a white galloper, even if they are invariably called grey. Snow White had one, although the dwarfs couldn't ride it. Their legs were too short. Someone put a white horse on a whisky bottle, and a popular operetta was called "The White Horse Inn."

"Goodbye, goodbye, I'll wish you all a last goodbye."

This is the best drinking song ever. People sing it from Broadway to Beerenberg, and in some Abyssinian French dominion, members of the Foreign Legion sit upright on their white chargers and salute the mother country. God, how I yearn for a croissant.

Muhammad Ali once said, "Why is everything white?" The world champ had a point. If you watched cowboy movies, Tex Ritter, Hopalong Cassidy, Zorro, the Lone Ranger, and the Durango Kid all rode white horses. So did Napoleon and Simon Bolivar. Pegasus didn't need a rider. He had wings.

My first horse of this colour responded to the name Urbane, not Mundane, as some folks suggested. The nag hailed from New Zealand, which is often a good sign, but the yearling was not well-bred. On the other hand, he raced much better than his breeding might suggest, coming third at Caulfield at his first start (at 100/1). Meet our trainer, the optimist. Our previous conveyance had come in at the rear of the field, and Geoff gave us his typical report.

"She came last, but it was a good last."

Urbane won six races, including a number of black-type events. Believe it or not, our next grey was called Aubaine, French in name only, meaning bonanza. Ha! She couldn't have beaten Hoss Cartwright, given a start.

The world changed when Subzero saluted in the race that stops a nation. How cool was that? His gleaming white coat dulled somewhat in the wet and windy conditions, but, as he defeated two Kiwi challengers, most punters felt pretty good about it. The gristly gelding displayed a personality of his own, and joined forces with the clerk of the course for many years, as a travelling ambassador.

What some people don't know is that the horse was trained by the FBI—Freedman Brothers Incorporated. The four lads had come down from New South Wales, and immediately taught the Victorians a thing or two about training. Under the management of big brother Lee, they collected five Melbourne Cups.

Last year, I won the meat tray at the local RSL, but it's not the same thing.

So, to the tale you are desperately waiting for—The Snow Ponies of Macedonia.

Those of you who have been to North Macedonia will know that the extremes of temperature are acute, ranging from forty degrees centigrade to twenty below. The terrain is extremely rugged and mountainous, affording few pleasures to the inhabitants who live there. It is not known when the equine flesh first moved in but I suspect on the back of the Bulgarian coup d'état of 1944. One supposes the ponies rejected soviet influence, and wanted to do their own thing. Were they Arabians, Camarillo, Pinto, or Palomino? Probably one or the other. However, they weren't communists.

Over the years, reports of white lightning coming out of the mountains filtered through to the authorities. The thunder being the sound of hooves galloping across the high plains, as the high country horses announced themselves as a force to be reckoned with. Who can forget the day they all came down from the highlands and headed for Doxato in Greece (East Macedonia)—at least 400 of them.

"Hey, Luka, all these horses? We can't cross the road."

"Don't worry, my friend. You're talking to the mayor. We'll put in traffic lights."

Why Doxato, you ask? It was a question that couldn't be answered until they got there, an incredible journey of some 300 kilometres. In Thessaloniki, they stopped for food at the local market. In fact, the steeds destroyed all the produce stalls, and then ate everyone's hats.

Their next stop was the racetrack carpark at their destination. The curator received quite a shock when he awoke to find them all there. The history of thoroughbred racing in this region goes back to the Ottoman Empire and today such activities are regarded as a cultural occasions. The ponies didn't want to miss out, and why should they? Their arrival sparked a resurgence of interest in the sport of kings. The stadium owner quickly auctioned off all the animals and prepared a program of events. Some of the buyers were amateur enthusiasts always ready to ask the silliest questions.

"Tell me, Stavros, do white horses run faster than black ones?"

If you don't want Secretariat's statue to be torn down, you don't answer that question. In this instance, a white nag let track performances define his credentials. Tyrone the Power won fifteen races, only experiencing defeat on one occasion. Maximus the Great lowered his colours, but you would expect that, wouldn't you? Of course, some didn't excel, and that is understandable. Herd animals always follow the leader, which is not desirable when there is money on the line.

The losers were shunted off to become equestrian stars. Snow ponies became show ponies in an Olympic event that had been around since the days of ancient Greece. Others went dancing with the Lipizzaner and the Andalusians from the Spanish Riding School. All good fun. Of the rest, one hoped for a vegetarian owner with a sense of humour.

Many Macedonians had lived their whole life without being aware of the hearts that beat in the mountains, and this was a shame. That mass exodus from Mt. Korab to Doxato was witnessed by many, and became instrumental in influencing a number of town planning decisions. For example, traffic lights started to appear in a number of rural locations, which previously had been under-developed. In some of these areas, your neighbour wasn't human, but probably white. In a token gesture, the aforementioned mayor installed lights that flashed red and white instead of red and green. The snow ponies were grateful.

The Charge!

When you reside a few streets away from Balaclava, you are never far from memories of the Crimean War. To arrive at my favourite supermarket, I always pass Inkerman Street and Alma Road. I used to live in Raglan

Street. Of course, people only remember two things about this war—Florence Nightingale and The Charge of the Light Brigade.

One doesn't like to think British people do stupid things, but the Earl of Cardigan had his work cut out when he led his offensive through that Ukraine valley, with Russian artillery on either side of him. The whole exercise appeared to be a misinterpretation of orders, and, like today, it didn't take long for the blame game to commence. Most of those in the know didn't survive the conflict, so argument continued unabated for years. One area where the result did bite involved recruitment. The regiment commanders found it awfully hard to get would-be soldiers on a steed of any kind.

"My name is Alistair McDuck, recruitment officer for the 13th Light Dragoons. Can I ask you, sir, why you want to join the cavalry?"

Many of the ne'er-do-wells around Soho were skint, poorly clothed, and not well-fed. They saw the army as a way out of their life of deprivation and destitution. In this instance, Nugget Gold was also on the run from Johnny Law—nothing too serious, but worth a few months in confinement.

"Well, it's the money ain't it? Two shillin's and sixpence is not to be sneezed at, governor."

"I'm not your governor," replied the urbane officer, who knew he wasn't going to enjoy this interview. "And we deduct one shilling for equine expenses, like grooming, saddle polishing et cetera."

"Course, I understand that. Does this mean I don't 'ave to supply me own horse?"

"You don't have to supply your own horse," confirmed the soldier, a touch of weariness already creeping into his vocabulary. "Is there anything further you would like to know about the mounted division of Queen Victoria's armed forces?"

"To tell you the truth, captain, I don't ride that well."

"Don't worry. We'll glue you to the saddle. Is there anything else?"

Was the potential rookie going cold on the whole idea? This is when Major General Cardigan appeared, trying to whip up some patriotism, even reminiscing with the fellow regarding his dash of destiny through the Valley of Death.

"D-d-did you say the Valley of Death?" stuttered the now reticent recruit.

HISTORY

"I did, indeed, my man. There were Russian guns on our left, more guns on our right, but we thundered on into the pages of posterity. Dragoons, Hussars, Lancers, we had them all."

Nugget Gold, when he departed the recruitment office, breathed a sigh of relief. He could face those monsters from Moscow but listening to another of Cardigan's stories, that was another matter. Naturally, he retired to his favourite watering hole, where the publican, a smarty-pants of the highest order, was known as Google. No-one understood why. The year was 1854.

"Ahhh, yes, the Charge! I refer you to the recent report from our poet laureate in *The Rhymes*, a periodical for creative people in London."

> "Someone had blundered. Theirs not to make reply.
> Theirs not to reason why, theirs but to do and die.
> Into the valley of death rode the six hundred."

It is not clear whether Alfred, Lord Tennyson, said poet laureate, actually socialised at the same pub as the Soho sophisticate. He probably preferred the King's Arms when he was in town, sharing a lager with Dickens or Gladstone, the politician who had such a bag of tricks that he remained prime minister for twelve years.

Explaining the intricacies of military strategy to someone like comrade Gold would never be a simple task, but it was admirable of the pub owner to want to try. It is never easy contemplating a career change.

"Now, I accept that you like horses, old chum, but can I tell you, the Queen's Cavalry is not like the two-thirty at Haydock."

If Nugget truly loved the neddies and their welfare, he would have steered away from the idea of being a horse soldier. The human death toll at Balaclava was one hundred and ten, but many horses also died. Of the two thousand that were shipped over to the combat zone, only two hundred survived. At the inquest, the interrogators quizzed Florence Nightingale about the casualties.

"Good morning, Miss Nightingale. Sorry to drag you away from your patients, but we will deliberate as quickly as possible, and let you get back to your important work."

The Lady with the Lamp had become a revered figure throughout the British Empire, mainly due to her pioneering efforts on the battlefield during the Crimean War. Of the allies, England and France did all the hard-lifting, but the others in the resistance were the ones under the pump. Tsar Nicholas in St. Petersburg was continually picking on Sardinia and Turkey because he had an appetite for change in the Balkans. The Ottoman hero Omar Pasha became renowned for his oft-repeated warning—"Turkey is stuffed if we can't beat these bloody Russkies." The exact description of his invective has been changed for obvious reasons.

Florence was an unlikely heroine, but her efforts in improving sanitation and hygiene in the field hospitals decreased mortality rates dramatically. Her nurses reduced the need for hearses, but never let it be said that she wasn't a tough leader, even forbidding the patients to tell dirty jokes. Today, in Istanbul, there are four hospitals named after the Order of Merit recipient, and the feeling out of Constantinople, at the time, said it all.

"Turkey owes a debt of gratitude to Florence Nightingale. Those Russian animals caused havoc with their guns, but the sweet lady and her nurses provided sustained care and treatment through thick and thin. She will be well remembered."

The only other witness to come out of the investigation smelling like roses was Ronald, Lord Cardigan's horse. Without him, the earl would not have made it home. The brave animal led the charge and also the retreat, by-passing Russian Cossacks on his return. Conflicting reports indicate that three or four hundred horses died in the battle,* but Ronald lived to see Old Blighty again. After having to listen to Cardigan's stories for the next few years, he must have been delighted to retire to Northamptonshire, only a few hours away from Haydock.

Nugget was never accepted into the Dragoons, possibly because of his Jewish heritage—certainly news to him. The well-liked rascal was named after the most popular beer of the time, Newcastle Gold.

*Two hundred horses died in the making of the movie. Was the ASPCA asleep at the wheel?

HEROES

Servants of the Crown!

Paddy Pest arrived a little late for his rendezvous with the man from MI6. James Bond was not in a good mood, in the aftermath of some venomous invective regarding the preparation of his cocktail.

"Everybody knows I like my martini shaken not stirred," grumbled the spy who had come in from the cold wearing just a lightweight tuxedo, pressed not ironed.

"I'll have a chocolate milkshake with double ice cream," chortled the Aussie gumshoe, as he buttonholed the waiter. At ten o'clock in the morning, there was no way he would be sloshing down any vodka martinis.

The indefatigable public servant got right down to business.

"I'm not happy with this joint investigation, but Her Majesty is adamant we should keep the colonies in the loop. I understand a representative from the Australian Security Intelligence Organisation (ASIO) will also be attached to my unit."

"This is correct, Commander. Her name is Stormy Weathers, and although she often demands seniority, she indicated to me that she would be delighted to work under you."

The world's most famous secret agent noticed a slight twitch emanating from near Pest's nose as this information was relayed to him—possibly a nervous complaint acquired by watching too many Humphrey Bogart movies as a child. The lady in question was Paddy's girlfriend and the prospect of such a close personal relationship didn't sit well with the discount detective. Then again, it may have been an itch rather than a twitch.

In terms of the investigation, one should clarify an earlier statement. The assignment, in all probability, did not come from the supreme ruler of Great Britain and Northern Ireland. Her Majesty was a pseudonym given to the head of the Foreign Office, the paternal entity of MI6. Sir Percival Plantagenet embarrassed many people with his effeminate disposition, and his recruitment from Cambridge University in the same manner as Messrs Philby, Burgess, McLean, and Anthony Blunt provided cause for concern. No wonder 007 had his knickers in a knot.

It is also pertinent to note that Patrick Pesticide boasted no government credentials and, as such, would be a peripheral player in any covert action. His services were used by any number of foreign agencies, but this kind of contract work gave these people the opportunity to disown him if things should go wrong, as they often did. In Canberra, the intelligence controllers farmed out odd jobs to the little man, on the basis of his relationship with their ferocious femme fatale. Her day job as manager of a gentlemen's club (of which Pest was a member) provided a clever cover, even though the social establishment only opened at night.

Licensed to thrill!

The detective from Down Under tried to downplay the significance of this joint action with the mother country, but Stormy remained excited about her forthcoming meeting with this heartthrob from the Hebrides. Her plaintive cry of despair was nothing he had not heard before.

"Oh Paddy, what will I do? I've nothing to wear."

Feeling like the straight man in a comedy routine, the gumshoe could only say what he thought.

"I don't think this will bother him much. Are you dining alone or in company?"

Bond chose the restaurant himself—an upmarket bistro in Mayfair. He would be picking up the tab, so the lady with no clothes parlayed her expense account funds into a little black playsuit she discovered in a chic boutique in Jermyn Street. She would slip into her thong without her partner's knowledge. What he didn't know wouldn't hurt him. If her consort spent more time with her on her shopping excursions, he would be aware of current fashion trends, but what can you do with a caveman who thinks thongs are rubber footwear, often seen on white-sand beaches?

The lady's first meeting with the erudite know-all came two days after her friend survived his get-together with the testy titan of testosterone.

"Good evening, Mr. Bond. My name is Weathers, Stormy Weathers."

It is true that this man of mystery often meets women for the first time in an aquatic environment: for example, coming out of the sea or a hot tub. In this instance, Stormy's first drink was aqua and he followed suit—a refreshing moment for a man with possible cirrhosis of the liver.

"Nice to meet you, lass. I've heard excellent reports about ASIO. Beauty and brains—a lethal combination."

"I hope so, James. You don't mind if I call you James?"

"Of course not. It is my name."

Having dispensed with introductions, the diners prepared to order the meal and discuss the operation. Naturally, they checked the condiments tray for listening devices—standard operating procedure.

The angel from ASIO had seen men dispose of a dozen oysters with verve and elegance before but never accompanied by a Romanée-Conti Montrachet, supposedly the most delicious wine in the world. Without a glimmer of humility, he rabbited on about the aromas of honey, vanilla, and smoky butterscotch which typified the selected beverage. What they said about him must be true. The man was a snob.

The couple would not discuss the case until the main course arrived, which annoyed the enthusiastic and impatient junior partner no end. When the distinguished dynamo from Vauxhall Cross finally revealed all, Stormy recoiled, gobsmacked and almost speechless.

"Somebody has stolen "The Ashes," and we have to get them back."

"The Ashes" are a much sought-after prize for a sporting competition between Australia and England. You throw a ball at each other for five days, and alleviate the boredom by taking lunch and tea at convenient intervals. The broken wicket is heaven's gate for bowlers, and those two wooden appendages which often fall off are called bails. In 1883, one such bail was burned and presented to the English captain in an urn the size of your index finger. Today, this coffin of conflict rarely leaves the MCC museum at Lord's, but, when transported between countries, it occupies premium seating on a British Airways international flight.

"You have to be kidding," spluttered the lady, having rediscovered her speech capabilities.

"There's been a terrorist attack in Manchester, an Ebola outbreak in Bristol, one of the royals has a social disease, and you bring us over here because some joker nicked some silly cinders. Where are your priorities, man?"

It is likely no-one had ever talked to Bond like this before, but he did like feisty women and harboured ambitions to get into Stormy's pants later that evening. That alluring black number she squeezed into didn't hide the fact that the hottie from heaven was wearing a thong.

The man tried to defend his position.

"Most Brits would rather catch the Ebola virus than lose to the Australians. Without cricket we have nothing. The relic is priceless. One recalls with affection my hat trick when playing for Eton. Didn't Paddy play our great game?"

"My partner is half Irish," said the simmering senorita, now a little less aggressive. Perhaps they could solve this robbery quickly and get on with their lives. She resumed her assessment.

"You wouldn't put it past the Micks. I seem to remember some lady called Angela."

"They are not her ashes," confirmed the super spy, "but it's good to know you're thinking outside the square."

"Could this be a personal issue?" continued the woman with more questions than answers. "Not all spies love you. What about Mr. Blowfly, the man who likes cats?"

"You are obviously talking about Blofeld—a nasty piece of work. Yes, I suspect he would stoop to such levels. Once you acquire the holy grail of colonial rivalry, world domination can't be far away."

Thankfully, the chow wasn't far away, providing a respite from the thrust and parry of their conversation. The *plat du jour* lived up to expectations and the dessert came amidst a flurry of after-dinner wines and after-dinner possibilities. When Stormy passed on the coffee and reached for her coat, he mentioned his flat, not five minutes away.

"Oh, what a shame, James. I would have loved to, but Paddy is picking me up. He'll be dying to hear details of the heist. Can you contact me when something breaks? With that, she gave him a peck on the cheek and sashayed out of the restaurant, the silence only broken when the Bombe Vesuvius on table nine exploded.

Over the next ten days, the amount of beneficial intelligence harvested from the constabulary amounted to zilch. Sergeant Plod and the forensic people did their best, but no-one had any idea who purloined the embers of enmity. Most folks thought the offender would turn out to be an Australian and this is where the HQ boffins stuffed up. Somebody fed the computer some lazy intel, and they arrested the world's number one tennis player, Ash Barty. She used to wield the willow before she conquered the world with her racquet.

Could the super-spy's reputation be on the line? He was currently negotiating a three-picture deal with Eon Productions, and a negative result from this widely publicised crime would damage his standing and earning capacity.

Somebody with less to lose was Patrick Pesticide, presently rated neck and neck with Maxwell Smart as the most inept secret agent on the planet. Of course, these figures would not be formalised until returns had been received by KAOS, SMERSH and the Korean People's Army. Traditionally, subversive organisations such as this were slow with their paperwork.

The man had a plan. Why not purchase a replacement from "Urns are Us," and sneak the compact container back into the display case at the museum? A contrite letter from the apologetic thief would explain the theft as a test for the security people.

"What a brilliant solution," enthused his most ardent fan. Stormy envisaged people concluding that the bandit was employed by a rival protection firm. James Bond couldn't, but this may have been down to the fact that it wasn't his idea.

"Don't drink red wine with fish, or fish without a hook, or replace the bloody urn without ashes. Do you understand my point, laddie?"

"Aye, Jock, I do," said Paddy, now starting to become a little exasperated with this Scottish twit from the Foreign Office. "Why not burn somebody's balls and put them in the pot?"

Because it might be his genitalia on the line, agent 007 managed a grim smile as a mark of respect for the Aussie's telling remark. The lady in the room blushed self-consciously, as the dilettante from Down Under threw up another possibility.

"I hope you haven't discounted those calypsos from the Caribbean, who take their cricket seriously. The West Indies is also very agreeable at this time of year."

"This is no time for a junket to a sun-drenched destination," suggested the team leader. "Jamaica can be a dangerous place. Last time I visited, a demented doctor tried to kill me. Can you believe that?"

"No," exclaimed his talking companion, emphatically exaggerating his degree of surprise.

"That's right, Dr. No. How they ever let him loose with a scalpel is beyond me. Having said as much, I must admit I would like to show Australia's best the sights in Kingston. Have you ever had a rum swizzle, Stormy?"

People who manage gentlemen's clubs are usually conversant with every cocktail under the sun, but the adorable hornbag was nothing if not polite and expressed enthusiasm for the fellow's hankering to be a tour guide. Her jealous confrere, not so enthused, reminded everybody about the problem on hand, so the trio of investigators chewed the fat for a further two hours before they reached out for help from head office.

To catch a thief!

These days, when you are trying to catch a thief, you call in the computer guy. At Vauxhall Cross, there are many such persons, all working for a department head called C, Q, P, L, or W. MI6 even have a female chief in the form of "M," who was Bond's boss. The Down Under dinosaur found these *noms de plume* mystifying, but his glamorous offsider explained their meaning.

"Really, it's quite obvious. M is for Mother. James is a mummy's boy."

This explanation appealed to the doyen of detection, fighting to remain relevant in a world being taken over by technology. In this instance, nearly every robber, burglar, and shoplifter on Earth appeared on the MI6 database, and his or her special skills were evaluated in an effort to arrive at a short list for the people who would pound the pavement. Not surprisingly, they weren't the only coverts working this case.

Agent 009, currently operating out of New York, had reported on a tennis commentator of some renown, who was presently detained at the overseas air terminal. A small vase had been discovered in his baggage, unloaded from a flight originating in London.

"You cannot be serious!" screamed M's man on a mission, already jealous of 009's fast ascent up the greasy pole. Only nine months earlier he was Licence to Kill 027. Of course, sometimes this kind of promotion is down to natural wastage instead of personal achievement. Too many of his predecessors had been kicked in the shin by Rosa Klebb.

Royalties are forever

America implicated! Surely not? Didn't JB become party to a conspiracy involving an urn full of South African diamonds being delivered to a casino in Las Vegas, egged on by Dame Shirley Bassey, who made it clear that it was not his sparkling eyes which turned her on?

Eventually, authorities advised that the item in the luggage at JFK airport was not the one they were all after but a trophy, released after thirty years of incarceration, brought about by the winner's shameless behaviour at Wimbledon. So, it was back to square one for the intrepid investigators, or to be more precise, back to Boodle's, the Pall Mall club where all the government tittle-tattle went down.

"M" ordered her decaf soy coffee, and Paddy stared at the giant muffin about to be consumed by his partner. His Dick Tracy watch let out a warning howl, as his eyes lingered longer than the allocated ten seconds. Not being an advocate of the morning meeting, Bond contributed little but became incensed when he heard the latest news. Agent 009 had been relocated to France to follow a local lead.

"He understands nothing about the French. The imbecile thinks a bidet is a breakfast pastry."

The head of MI6 smiled ruefully, not wanting to take pleasure in the fact that 009 was now 006. Wisely, she kept this information to herself.

GERRY BURKE

The Octopus Detective Agency!

This organisation, based in Rajasthan, boasted a more colourful history than Pinkerton's; its tentacles of influence reaching far and wide. How Octopus got into bed with British intelligence is anyone's guess, but most double-O agents enjoyed working with their ginger-haired CEO, Rebecca "Red" Herring. For this reason, "M" decided that 007 should have two chaperones on his next assignment.

Using her serviette to brush away the crumbs of her lo-cal chocolate fudge indulgence, Britain's premier spook looked directly at her favourite operative and imparted her instructions.

"You're going to India, and your two friends from Oz are going to make sure you stay on the Yellow Brick Road. No romantic diversions, understood?"

"Yes, ma'am, but what about…"

"What about nothing, James. We have credible data from Octopus that the Indian Cricket Board is responsible for the theft of our national treasure. Their chairman, Virat Besu has been on our radar for quite some time and is unstoppable."

"But I doubt he's a wicket person," interjected Paddy, mangling the English language in his usual misguided manner.

"He is a wicked person," came the reply; "out to prove the Curry Cup is hotter than any other sporting contest on the planet."

Receiving this much-coveted prize for competition between Pakistan and India is just compensation for performance, but temporary ownership also entitles the recipient to bragging rights for the next twelve months. Therein lies a risk and reward situation, and both teams like to scare the living daylights out of each other. The spiritual home of this clash used to be Madras but, since they changed the name to Chennai, the Cup has travelled and it now resides in Udaipur.

"Do I look OK in this?" asked one of the most sublime creatures who ever fronted a mirror.

Ms. Weathers surveyed herself in their suite at the Shiv Niwas Palace. Protocol didn't demand that she dress traditionally, nor subscribe to the clothing variation of the region. She made do with a conventional sari and looked fabulous in a colourful cotton ensemble. Her man tried on the dhoti provided for him, and correctly agreed that he resembled a banana in pyjamas.

On their first afternoon in this city of lakes, Stormy opted for a massage and spa, James hit the tables, and Paddy went for a walk. The traders in the marketplace may not have anticipated the cash cow coming their way. In the space of five minutes, the eager tourist purchased a copy watch, a flute, some incense sticks, and a basket from "The Surprise Shop." You pay your money and then choose any wicker wonder on show.

When he stopped for coffee, the music lover decided to practise on the reed instrument, which is sold with instructions. Only later would he investigate the contents of his surprise package.

No sooner had he started assaulting the senses of those around him when another music lover appeared on the scene. The lid of the basket seemed to lift of its own accord, until one realised a cobra was coming to the concert. The snake may well have preferred Paganini but settled for a little rock'n'roll, if this is what Paddy was playing. Dare he stop? No way. If the serpent didn't get him, he would drown in his own sweat.

You should leave this kind of thing to the locals. They are charming people, but if you interfere with their income stream, there will be hell to pay. Khan the Magnificent left Colin the cobra with a friend while he took lunch. All care but no responsibility! When the stall proprietor departed the premises for his vittles, his son took over retail responsibility. Can you trust anyone under forty? Poor Paddy played rock'n'roll on his flute right through the meal break, until the owner retrieved his scaly friend.

From a turret atop his formidable island home, Mr. Besu observed this episode through his binoculars and couldn't stop laughing. Virat was aware that the combined forces of Britain and Australia were in town to try and take him down, and made a mental note to transfer his recently acquired prized possession to a place of safety. One might be prepared to hint he possessed the prize, but Bond and his cohorts would never recover the urn. Never! His home was a fortress.

Coldfinger, the cool kleptomaniac!

Virat Besu, the golden boy of the subcontinent, was regaled like royalty and constantly showered with accolades and gifts, all in direct proportion to his batting average. This cricketing legend became the only chairman of the board to hold this position while still playing his chosen sport. And what about that palace on the lake?

Can you have all this and want more? Of course you can. The trophies in the dungeon were the fellow's pride and joy, even if he couldn't boast about them. Pinching that priceless memento from the Lord's museum had proved easy. Such bravado! The cheeky chap simply pocketed the fragile receptacle after a photo opportunity, and left the reception disguised as a taxi driver.

The two media magnets met at the Governor's Tea Party: a small fundraising affair to highlight the plight of the homeless and hungry. Stormy and Paddy tagged along, but the Aussie wag seemed sceptical.

"I can see why they call it fun-raising. These people are so emaciated; they could use a good laugh."

"Paddy," rebuked his fearless friend. "Don't be so rude. This is a poor country and we need to do everything we can to help. Oh look. James is about to talk to that famous cricketer, helping himself to the Peking duck. I didn't think cricketers liked ducks."

"My name is Bond, James Bond."

"Virat Besu. How do you do?"

"Congratulations, old chap. You're off to Bollywood I hear. Does this mean your cricketing career is over? Your fans would be devastated."

"Not at all, Mr Bond. We Indians are quite efficient at multitasking and I look forward to leading my team to victory in the forthcoming Curry Cup, in a few weeks. This challenge is as fierce as your series with the Aussies. By the way, any news on the missing urn? It's a hot topic of conversation around the dinner table in this country. Many of my people cook their meals on an open fire."

The sportsman proved to be a generous listener with impeccable manners, but was there an element of arrogance, if not smugness, in his reply? JB thought so, and, in fact, concluded that the willow wielder might indeed be the thief they were after. However, trying to find anything specific in a 100 room palace, situated in the middle of a lake, would be a challenging undertaking. Getting a wetsuit over your tux is a lot more difficult than it looks.

Live and get by!

Sharma Shan, the riverboat man, had an awkward decision to make. The naive Australian, with the gorgeous bit of crumpet in tow, offered him big bucks to take them to the Besu home on the water...with a return journey after a two-hour sojourn. The owner was not on the premises, and he doubted the veracity of the chap's story. However, the guy offered to pay in U.S. dollars, so he accepted the charter.

The world's most famous secret agent failed to join the inquisitive pair on their mission to recover the stolen relic. Bond always organised his own transport, with help from a fellow government employee, the quartermaster, who liked to whip up the latest and greatest with no expense spared.

QBall was a Rotarian's dream. It could reach Mach 1 speed in sixty seconds, and bounce over small waves or tall buildings at will. Features included contemporary weaponry, afterburners, a coffee-making machine and a BOSE Hi-Fidelity sound system. Digital photography aids were incorporated, with a "switch to invisible" button on the major console—an invaluable tool for fooling parking inspectors.

Bond chose to give the ballistic ball a turn around the lake to acquaint himself with the many features of the GT model. The playful pilot even bounced the unit over Paddy's hire boat, while wondering how his friends were going to bluff their way into the mansion. Many eyes guarded the entrances.

Unfortunately, the ASIO manual of operations is exempt from freedom of information requests, and the chapter on avoiding resistance remains on a need to know basis. Take it as read that the amazing couple managed to avoid detection and found themselves underground.

"Paddy, I can no longer see any windows. We're below water level."

"You're right, sugarlips, but I think we're on the right track. The furniture in this area is decidedly more upmarket, and I'm very interested in that padded door over there, the one with all those signs."

"Yes," murmured his companion. "*Keep Out* in five languages."

Pest's keys opened everything except for Margaret Scanlan's chastity belt, but that was another story.

"You've done it," cried Stormy. "What a man! Quick, get inside before someone hears us."

Reacting to Stormy's encouragement, the wily intruder slipped through the entrance and silently closed the large oak door behind them. They snapped on their torches.

For my eyes only

"Get out of here. What is this? Bats and balls? Paintings on the walls? Rubies and diamonds?"

"Are a girl's best friend," gushed Stormy, whose alert eyes honed in on a large glass showcase in the centre of the room. She saw a three-tiered wooden dais covered in a burgundy cloth. Sitting on top of a silk cushion was the biggest diamond necklace she had ever seen. A small engraved plaque indicated that the piece of jewellery purported to be "The Star of Dravid."

"Ahhh, yes," muttered the masterful maestro of the mundane, as he joined his lady to look at the showpiece trinket.

"Appropriated some two years ago, ripped from the shoulders of Mrs. Dravid at a beer and bagel night in Lahore. Who would have thought Virat to be the culprit?"

"What about this, sweetheart? It must be solid gold."

Mr. Pest appeared a little nonplussed about this one, but he shouldn't have been. The International Sport Authority awarded "The Singh Trophy" every year for the best pregame entertainment world-wide. This particular cup had been presented to Meatloaf.

One wonders if the new owner of these hidden treasures might own up to being the coolest kleptomaniac on the subcontinent, or would he just play a straight bat, if challenged?

The prying pair from Oz soon discovered the whereabouts of the prized urn, holding pride of place on a mantelpiece above an ornate fireplace.

"What a bastard," howled the little man, who attempted to survey the display unit from every angle. The object of their desire was encased in glass, but the owner provided an extra level of protection which had evoked Paddy's outburst. Two tarantulas seemed to be diligently patrolling the inside of the outer case, and our man didn't like creepy crawlies. Not at all.

"Where's Bond when you need him?" bellowed the would-be burglar.

The man in question was actually right behind them, having docked his QBall beside their craft and turned on the invisible switch. Avoiding the guards proved to be no problem. He then activated his tracking device to find his friends, Stormy being unaware their last embrace involved the planting of such a gadget. What a bounder!

A slight cough was sufficient distraction to attract attention, and the two busybodies spun around in surprise. Miss Weathers reacted first, followed by her irritable partner.

"James, how wonderful to see you."

"Not before time. We need someone to reach in and retrieve the prize."

The new arrival had seen hairy legs before and suspected this would not be the end of the protective measures. The others wanted to grab the container and scamper. They could worry about the spiders later.

"Be careful. There might be one of those hidden laser blankets surrounding the perimeter. Bugger! The bottom of the case is bolted to the mantelpiece. Maybe there's a verbal code needed to open the damn thing?"

Paddy was not good at this. Anyway, no-one knew Virat's mother's maiden name. The Englishman tried a few cricket terms, while Stormy exhausted her supply of Indian idioms. Finally, the man who mostly gets everything right got this one right, when he started whistling his country's national anthem: "God Save the Queen."

The lid of the glass coffin slowly opened and the imprisoned arthropods made a run for freedom. With eight legs to propel them away from the hotbox, they made the safety of the floor before the British buffoon came at them with his shoe. Pest quickly went for the urn and managed to salvage same, just as the bells and whistles went off. Bloody hell! There really was a laser blanket in play.

The intruders immediately retreated to their entrance point, only to discover that the whole outdoor area had been floodlit, revealing guards and household staff everywhere, many carrying Kalashnikov rifles. The terrific trio were trapped on the side of the palace known as the Eiger Wall, and they saw their escape vessel reversing away from its mooring. Paddy had a fear of heights and Stormy a tear in her tights. The script was not going to plan.

Only Bond could save them and, fortunately, he possessed the means. The quartermaster, a rather devious fellow, often borrowed technology from Apple Industries to enhance certain mobile phone features.

"Siri, I want you to demagnetise the docking mechanism on the QBall. Renew visibility and arm all weapons. Prepare rescue options and instigate battle action against enemy forces."

God only knows what the enemy forces thought when they spotted a big ball of oscillating light appear on the lake surface, some 200 metres from their fortress. The agitated minions saw the brutal bubble coming at them across the water, and they panicked.

The puffy projectile accelerated in speed until it reached the shoreline, at which time the pod managed to scale the battlements and scatter the defence party. Only when the terrifying turbocharged wonder-ball had settled comfortably in Virat's swimming pool did the man from MI6 complete his instructions.

"Siri, calculate coordinates and release sky-plank."

The end of a James Bond adventure is always a walk in the park. The fleeing opportunists skipped along the sky-plank to the mother ship and prepared to reconnoitre with "M" and her submariner friends, waiting off the coastline. As the QBall once again bounced over Shan's retreating vessel, they spied his two sons, Rogan and Josh, hard against the rigging. They waved.

I thank the late Ian Fleming for lending me his suave creation, James Bond—vibrant and fresh as ever. Or did I steal him? I am also grateful to Alphabet Soup Productions, who waived contracts to enable the participation of "M" and "Q."

Melanie Marple

The murder of a groupie in the toilet of the Hammersmith Apollo was not a big deal as far as the media were concerned. Not that the Snig Snogs, the headline act, weren't big with the young people. They were. However, Melanie Marple would have preferred to investigate a crime involving a high profile personality, which would have seen her fledgling unit perform under public scrutiny for the first time. This was not a selfish, ego-driven pipe-dream. She wanted to repay those who had placed their trust in her.

Ms. Marple's transfer within New Scotland Yard (from the Dog Squad) was due to the personal intervention of her uncle, Hercule Poirot, the well-respected private investigator. The commissioner was a huge Agatha Christie fan, and he was delighted to learn that he employed a relative of one of the best female sleuths of all time. Putting together an entertainment unit that specialised in show business crime was his initiative, and he had no hesitation in promoting the young lady to head the unit. Her two sidekicks in the task force were Simon Hitchcock and Nigel Niven.

Simon, the overweight ferret, boasted few people skills but was retained because of his impressive computer talents. Nigel, in the opinion of others, should have been a window dresser, and he dressed rather well, himself. Nowhere else in The Met would you see such natty suits, and he always wore a handkerchief in his jacket pocket. In terms of suitability for this particular posting, his pedigree could not be challenged. His grandfather, an actor, was the author's choice to play James Bond. The final two members of the team were a make-up lady and a hair stylist. One always has to look their best when fronting the media.

It was Nigel who was first at the scene of the crime, and he was ready with his report when Melanie arrived.

"The victim is Daisy Dolores Delfinata, a seventeen-year-old lass from Leicester. There were no witnesses, but she was part of an entourage which we would colloquially call "groupies." There are a dozen of her pals waiting to be interviewed."

Daisy had committed herself to rock 'n' roll and, for her trouble, she had been garrotted with a guitar string in one of the toilet cubicles after the show. Melanie reckoned a long time after because you just don't see empty restrooms at rock concerts. Where else are the kids going to snort their cocaine and other prohibited substances?

The ladies loo at the crime scene was overflowing when Melanie arrived. Now she was alone with the medical examiner. Nigel was interviewing the female fans in the foyer of the theatre.

"I'd say the time of death was around 1 a.m., give or take an hour. It was fast and clean; the deep neck wounds were inflicted from behind by a tall person, using a guitar string made of nylon, wound with wire—probably from a Gibson acoustic model."

"Gee, that sounds definitive," said Melanie in surprise. "Do you play this instrument yourself?"

"Only at bar mitzvahs and weddings," replied the down-to-earth doctor, ready to pack up and head back to the cutting room. "I'll be doing the PM this afternoon if you want to drop around. Bring your friends."

When the investigator joined her partner in the foyer, the degree of informality decreased. One of the young girls quietly slipped off Nigel's knee and started to rearrange her make-up. The fellow certainly had a way with women, and, if this helped to put them at ease, Inspector Marple was all for it.

"Well, Romeo. Is there any joy, here, or is it a "saw nothing, heard nothing" situation?"

"Pretty much that, boss," said the suave policeman, handing over his notebook to his superior. The chap was meticulous in his note-taking, and every entry included a comment which might activate his suspicions at a later date. He had even given each girl a nom-de-plume, which he had written beside their birth name. The redhead he called Blaze, the two chicks with rings through their nose were Cow 1 and Cow 2, and the chunky giant he labelled Big Bertha. None of them looked like killers. Then again, they didn't look like detectives.

The drive back to headquarters could have been time better spent, but London traffic is what it is. Melanie was able to ruminate on the present situation with her squad. Her current mentor, Superintendent Larry Gunderson, was supportive but results were everything. It is true that the terrible trio basted in the glory of one key result on their report card—the murder of Morse. Most television viewers thought Chief Inspector Morse died of natural causes, but nosy Niven found a vial of poison in John Thaw's freezer. The actor was detained and the script-writers disciplined.

Melanie had first come to the attention of her peers while working for the Dog Squad in Midsomer. Barnaby's pet had been kidnapped, and Mel solved the case. However, since Morse, there had been no attention-getting results, and the unit was struggling to be relevant. Yes, they had arrested Rik Mayall for overacting and investigated Joanna Lumley, before she fled to her home in the Champagne region of France. These were slim pickings and Simon had a theory.

"Television no longer has any need for Scotland Yard. The coroners solve all the crimes and leave nothing for the boys and girls in blue. In America, it started with Quincy and ended with the CSI franchise. Australia has Dr. Blake, and we Brits are proud of the Silent Witness team, even though they have now moved to Midsomer. That's where all the murders are."

The unit commander had little time to consider Simon's thought-provoking analysis, because she had a meeting with her boss. She hoped the Hammersmith crime might be a chance to earn her group some respect.

The commissioner had elected Larry Gunderson to protect his protégé, which he did through thick and thin. The veteran police officer valued his one-on-one approach for maintaining morale and always liked to provide a motivational speech before any high-profile assignment.

"I can't tell you how important this case is for your career. The Snig Snogs are Prince Harry's favourite band, and if any of the musicians are involved, he may need to leave the country to avoid publicity."

"Why?" asked the attentive policewoman. "Does he personally know members of the group?"

"I believe so, but you should find out for yourself. I'm not going to impede your investigation in any way. Let's hope for a quick result, with no surprises. People need to know that they can go to the john without being wasted."

With that, he indicated that the meeting was over, and the underling silently evacuated the spacious office and returned to her rat hole in the basement, where her two cohorts waited with bated breath. They were pleased to be part of an actual murder investigation.

"Wire in the blood," said Mel Marple, as she reported the results of her crime scene visit to her deskbound companion. "Or more accurately, blood in the wire. The girl was quite tall, so I'm thinking the perp is also. No leads yet on colour, race, or religion, but the Snig Snogs are confined to their hotel until we can interview them."

"What about the post-mortem?" asked Sergeant Hitchcock, anxious to get up to speed as quickly as possible.

"This afternoon, white man, and you're coming with me. It's time you got out of the house."

On their way to the mortuary, the dogged duo called in on the hottest Aussie rock artists on the planet. Their present domain proved to be a less than salubrious hotel in Shepherd's Bush, but they did score the honeymoon suite. There was some reluctance about interviewing an ocker rocker, but Simon thought they should wing it. Trevor Frith, the lead vocalist, doubled as spokesperson, and he recognised the teenager in the pic.

"Sure thing, sweet hips; I've seen her around, but we were not pals. She had the hots for drummers, including our own, Bonzo Bradman, the bad man. Whaddya say, Bonz? Did you murder the little scrubber?"

The person in question was in no way composed, alert, or, in fact, listening to the conversation. Drugs can do that to you, and he might have been recovering from a torrid night. Is it possible the drum person murdered the mademoiselle with no recollection of the vile act? Ms. Marple decided to proceed in a different direction.

"I don't see your guitars anywhere, and I understood them to be your prized possession. Am I wrong?"

"Oh yes, we love our instruments, but we don't see them until rehearsals. That's what roadies are for, and they treat our Gibsons like fine china. You know what a China plate is, right?"

"A mate?"

"Correct, darling. Now, is there anything else? We're ready to rack down."

Melanie could see that Bonzo had already gone to bed, and the others, who hadn't said a word to date, would probably be happy to see the back of them. She produced one final question.

"You have been very helpful, Trevor, and I'm sure my partner agrees, but just one more thing. Can you tell us who plays which guitar? As you may know, the young girl was strangled with a string from an acoustic model."

The chap's response to this enquiry surprised. He slowly rose from his purple velvet wing-backed chair and ambled over to the corner of the suite, where a lot of gear and baggage had been dumped. After rumbling around for a bit, he then returned with a poster containing information regarding their tour dates. Naturally, a promotional picture dominated the advertisement. Having unrolled the flyer on Mel's lap, Trevor Frith proceeded to point out the boys in the band.

"That's Billy with his six-string on the left and Sad Stewart on the right. I mainly do vocals but sometimes strum on my acoustic for slow songs. These are all Gibsons. See that spare guitar at the side of the stage. That's a back-up, a Fender. We use it when we want to smash people on the head. We then retrieve the broken strings to murder young girls."

Was it Simon who suggested that it might be time to leave? They did so in an elegant and graceful manner, accepting the poster as a gift from Trevor. What a guy.

The visit to the morgue was more circumspect. The autopsy on Daisy Delfinata had been completed, and the medical examiner relaxed with a cup of coffee in the visitors lounge. She invited the two crime fighters to help themselves to a brew, while providing chapter and verse on her findings.

"Apart from the ligature wound, I detected no other bruises on the young lady's body. Her stomach contents yielded nothing more than a cheeseburger with a double serve of chipotle sauce. No alcohol, drugs, or recent sexual activity. Given the angle of the gash, I would suggest her assailant to be at least one hundred and eighty-five centimetres tall—six foot one for the dinosaurs. I can't tell you the gender of the attacker, but you would think male. Men are such animals."

Until then, the lead detective had not figured on the ME being a misandrist. She fancied herself as a bit of a feminist, but this appeared to be deep-rooted, and she didn't want to go there. Perhaps a throwaway line and then out the door?

"What happened to sex, drugs, and rock'n'roll? What's going on here?"

The afternoon visit to the ME didn't clear the air and the forthcoming reproach from Nigel, on their return to the office, did little to appease the general frustration.

"You do know you've been concentrating on the headliners and forgotten about the warm-up act, Vascular Obstruction?"

"Get out of here!" screamed Melanie in complete surprise, before reaching for the poster that Trevor gave her. Sure enough, appearing in small type was the telling announcement that Snig Snog would be supported by the best band out of Liverpool since the Wombats.

Simon saw an opportunity for a computer search and made the comment that, according to the dates advertised, the tour was now over. What if they checked out previous performances? Perhaps Newcastle?

"Looking for another felony that coincided with the date of that rock concert. Good thinking, Sherlock," said the lady in the leather jumpsuit. "Do you think Vera Stanhope still rules the roost up there?"

Vera had been a formidable presence on British TV screens for over ten years and gave Northumberland folks the kind of gritty police drama they craved. She was tough but fair and not someone you would forget in a hurry; and yet, where was she now?

"According to the TV guide, she does," offered Nigel, but his pal immediately gazumped him with an update.

"Bloody hell! She's now the chief constable. There's hope for you yet, Mel."

The conversation with the new chief constable started with congratulations, became mired in superfluous girl talk, and ended with a request for assistance in the matter of dirty doings in the music business.

"Don't know, pet. You have me between a rock and a hard place, but I'll check with my people in the relevant stations and get back to you. Expect something tomorrow."

The reply arrived by fax with photographs and newspaper cuttings. A nineteen-year-old girl had been choked to death with a football scarf on the same day that Snig Snog performed at the arena venue. Also, on this day, Newcastle United lost an away game and the police blamed the offence on a disgusted Geordie soccer fan, presently being accommodated in Stoney Lonesome at Her Majesty's pleasure.

"You're not going to believe this," said Simon Hitchcock to anyone listening. He had just profiled Vascular Obstruction and the story didn't read well, although the *Liverpool Echo* thought otherwise.

"The most exciting Liverpudlian band since the Wombats boasts one of the most extraordinary back stories to come out of our city. The four lads, now all in their twenties, met while serving time at HMP Altcourse in Merseyside, which is a young offenders' institution. They honed their musical skills, using equipment donated by Sir Paul McCartney, and have become poster boys for rehabilitation and reintegration programs all over the north-west."

The article included a photo of the four offenders. They looked like any other adolescent group, pimples and all. Nigel quickly pointed out something of interest.

"These kids are tall for their age. Three of them must be over six feet."

Scramble, scramble, scramble—Simon back to his computer; Mel on the phone to Queen Vera; and Nigel tried to locate the road manager for Snig Snog. Could they find Vascular Obstruction before they left London? Alas, no! The rising stars had been booked to take part in a Shirley Bassey tribute in Cardiff, and they were on their way, not knowing they now enjoyed the social status of being prime suspects for two murders.

Melanie Marple

The prospect of another investigation in Wales didn't sit well with Ms. Marple, as the unit had been involved in an awkward public relations disaster a few months earlier, having arrested Hannibal Lecter for scaring school children during a promotional tour. It was all a storm in a teacup, but Anthony Hopkins would not be breaking bread with mothering Mel any time soon.

Having said all that, the team needed to be there if there was a possibility of catching the murderer in the act. So, the three amigos piled into Mel's car and headed west on a cold and miserable day, which became a wet and miserable day as they passed through Bath and Bristol. Protocol demanded that the visiting force pay their respects to the local constabulary, and they did that, at the same time getting approval for logistical support at the venue. With three dozen pavement-pounders at the concert, this kind of back-up might prove handy. In Britain, coppers don't carry, and Melanie and her officers didn't even possess a truncheon. It would be three six-footers against a slip of a girl, a fat slob, and a dandy dude.

Finding squalid accommodation in Cardiff proved easy, given the parameters of their expense account. The next day loomed large, with many music lovers descending on the city to help pay tribute to one of the best. The Principality Stadium caters for over 70,000 fans, and most of them attempted to enter The Dead Canary, a small bar where Mel thought they could discuss the case in peace. Pigs might fly.

The info that Simon extracted from Her Majesty's prison records was pivotal in elevating one of the group to priority perp. Two of the former inmates were juvenile delinquents, one a drug dealer, and Big Daddy had convictions for assault and battery, including sexual assault. He also spent many hours in anger management classes.

Big Daddy (his stage name) was the tallest member of the quartet. Little Daddy (the keyboard player) the smallest. The others were Tom and Jim. Having absorbed this information, the consensus was that they should focus on the best suspect, which would give the targeted victim a better chance of survival. All officers carried handcuffs, and Sergeant Hitchcock expected to sit on the scoundrel while these restraints were applied.

Vascular Obstruction commenced their set with the Roy Orbison classic "Crying." Simon could hardly supress his excitement, while Nigel wept.

"Oh God, the national anthem of Wales. Can't they save it for their rugby matches?"

The three detectives worked their way to the front of the stage, close to the performers. A bunch of female groupies had the same idea, and their squealing and shouting didn't put Sergeant Niven in a sunny mood. A soothing soliloquy from his superior officer settled him down.

"Is there a hedgehog in your pocket, Nigel? Girls will be girls, even if they're Taffies. Maybe "Men of Harlech" will be next up?"

There was little time for a considered reply because, suddenly, a new act appeared under the spotlights. To keep in touch, Melanie decided to follow the giggling girls, which proved a wise move, ending in the hospitality room underneath the entertainment. Up above, The Stones ramped up their version of "Diamonds are Forever."

"Gee, Mel," said Simon. "The security is not too good here. Anybody can get in and it's a free bar."

The smart thing to do was to leave someone outside to cover all exits. Lax security is sometimes part of the plan. Nobody wants to deprive all those young girls of the opportunity to enjoy social intercourse with their idols. Big Daddy was already surrounded by three such persons, drinking sparkling wine as if it were Champagne.

Then, in the blink of an eye, there were two persons and no Big Daddy. "Damn!" cried the team leader, who didn't wish to exacerbate her level of disgust in the presence of so many young people. "Where the hell have they gone?"

Outside, Nigel couldn't provide a solution. He had been covering two exits with most of the traffic going in rather than out. Nobody bothered to check out the catering entrance. The prime suspect was now on the loose with a prospective victim by his side.

Their first break came when one of the local Johnnies spied a tall gent leaving the stadium with a young thing in a mini dress and wearing not much else. The couple hailed a taxi and sped off to an unknown destination but not before the shrewd constable had taken down the cab's number plate. By the time Team Marple regrouped outside the venue, the fellow had provided them with a drop-off address, courtesy of the minicab company. They couldn't pronounce the chap's name but thanked him for his contribution.

Dafydd Leek's Red Dragon Hotel proudly advertised their clientele, with quoted endorsements from the likes of Tom Jones and *Little Britain's* Matt Lucas. Female underwear, often found in both their rooms after departure, only added to the mystique. On production of her police ID, Melanie had no trouble in obtaining the room number of the randy rocker from Liverpool. The concierge even described the vicinity of the third-floor room in relation to the side lane which abutted the hotel.

"It's simple Simon. Nigel shins up the drainpipe and attempts to photograph the brute trying to choke the poor girl, and, when he gives us the word via his mobile, we come through the door."

It is hard to know whether her ladyship expected any resistance to this plan from the proposed climber, but it came.

"Do you know how much this suit cost? Why can't you be the rat up a drain pipe? After all, gender equality is the thing, these days."

Bugger thought the frustrated feminist, previously unaware that her partner was beholden to any of the teachings of Gloria Steinem. Nevertheless, in her comfortable pants suit, she could hardly object. So, it was Mel who ended up hanging precariously outside the third-floor window as the violator had his way with his enthusiastic companion. With the foreplay over, he would surely move on to his strangulation ritual; then again, maybe not.

In the hallway of the hotel, Simon wondered whether they should order room service. After four hours of doing nothing, hunger pains started to bite. The lady on the ledge had a bigger gripe. She was suffering from frostbite, and knew that both occupants of the room were sound asleep. With no obvious crime being perpetrated, apart from underage issues, they all had egg on their face, which was more than appropriate at breakfast time. The crime-busters settled for an omelette at a greasy Joe's around the corner.

Back at their hotel, the shocks kept coming. The morning newspaper was complimentary, but the headline would set them back quite a bit:

GIRL STRANGLED AT ROCK CONCERT.

Before Ms. Marple reached the bottom of the front page, the phones started ringing, most of the calls originating from Scotland Yard. One word repeated ad nauseam was "incompetent," although "inept" and "bungling" were also bandied about. Outside of London, offers of assistance came from various districts, such as Cumbria, Cheshire, and Somerset. The major crime unit in Cornwell offered to bring Inspector Wycliffe out of retirement, if it would help. Of course, the matter of residuals would need to be discussed.

Larry Gunderson came to the rescue again and poured oil on troubled waters, assuring his assertive acolyte that she had his complete confidence. Nigel was still in a sarcastic frame of mind.

"That means we'll all be sacked by next week."

"O.K." said the one person who was really under the hammer. "Let's wrap it all up before next week. Who's ready for another visit to the home of harmony?"

Simon, being half asleep, found himself left behind, which was just as well because the crime scene looked rather gruesome. The dirty deed had, once again, taken place in a toilet cubicle, and the young groupie died with her mouth open in pain. The mongrel had rammed a drumstick in one ear and out the other. Nigel recognized Blaze, the redhead he had interviewed in Hammersmith.

Mel, in no mood to go easy on members of her least favourite band, demanded answers and grilled the youths incessantly. Was the killer Terrible Tom or Juiced-Up Jim, the junkie? Her partner had never seen her so worked up.

Tom played the tubs, and he recognised the stick as one of his. The musician admitted drinking with the girl but wished her no harm. The lad appeared to be stunned by this turn of events. For once, Jim was seemingly unaffected by drugs or alcohol, but he still couldn't provide any answers.

Melanie had no choice but to let the musicians continue on to their next gig in Oxford but indicated that they were still under surveillance. Pressure also loomed from the venue manager in Cardiff, wanting her to rescind the stadium lockdown, so he could get on with business. Charlotte Church was due to commence her "Crying in the Chapel" tour.

"She's very good," said Simon, who didn't get out much. "I saw her at Convent Garden."

"It's Covent Garden, you berk." Nigel was continually frustrated by his partner's perpetual existence in an artistic and academic wasteland, and now they were moving on to Oxford by the River Cherwell. Swiftly flow the dons.

Vascular Obstruction was one of a number of groups invited to perform during "Quiver and Quake Week," an annual campus event at Magdalen College. Inspector Marple was pleased enough to be there because she enjoyed a good working relationship with the Thames Valley Police.

Her timing could have been better. Their top homicide detective, James Hathaway, had just been found floating down Castle Mill Stream, tied to a wooden cross. Their number two man thought the murder might have religious connotations. Need I say everyone in town wasn't an Oxford scholar?

After the mosh pit at Principality Stadium, the smaller venue seemed like heaven, and the three investigators once again found themselves in front of stage left, looking at the groupies at stage right, with one difference. There were only two girls remaining. This is when Simon Hitchcock did a double take.

"Hey, boss lady. Take a look at the blonde and tell me what you see."

"Well, she's definitely not a natural blonde, and her dress sense leaves a lot to be desired. If she was wearing a bra, I would say she needed a 36D cup. She's a big girl. Oh, my God—she's a big girl."

"And quite tall," added Nigel, now recognising Big Bertha, who had attended both concerts in London and Cardiff. All of a sudden, she looked rather fearsome.

"Surely not?" queried Mel, now prepared to answer her own question. "She's solid enough to overpower all the victims and the right height to choke them. Can you believe it? Have we been looking in the wrong place?"

"What about a motive?" said Simon, extremely pleased that he had been the one to open the portals of possibility. The change in direction also dragged Nigel out of his negative mindset.

"She has the hots for the cute one, the drummer. He only had eyes for the other girls, so they had to go. It works for me."

If Melanie had not seen a number of crazies go down over the years, she would have dismissed this theory as fanciful. However, the premise had merit and could be checked. The previous victim socialised with pretty boy, and for all they knew so had the others.

The lady produced her sternest demeanour and addressed the troops.

"We can't put all our eggs in the one basket as we did with Big Daddy. Simon, you're the tough boy, so you should attach yourself to Big Bertha. Nigel and I will cover the band and, if we are correct, one of our paths will cross when disaster is about to strike."

Disaster struck on the hour of 5 p.m., halfway through VO's first number. A divinity student, Oxford Don Dunleavy, having consumed too many beverages over lunch, streaked across the stage, only to be brought down by a security person in the proximity of Tom's drum kit. In fact, the sweet thing was knocked over in the struggle and started bleeding profusely. The two girls, fearing for his well-being, rushed to his aid and began to mother-hen him, like only women can do. Then they turned on each other, but there would only be one scrub sister on this stage. To validate her position, Buxom Bertha, the peroxide blonde, pulled out a knife.

When Melanie asked Simon to attach himself to the big girl, she was speaking figuratively, but he did as best he could and it paid off. When the dagger appeared from nowhere, he came at the flaky femme like a flying bun, all 95 kilograms of him. They bounced on the snare drum and then disappeared through the thin skin of the bass unit. Nigel quickly pounced on the dropped blade, while magnificent Marple stepped forward and read the lady her rights. Then they all left, and the concert continued.

Crimes of passion never give you time to plan properly, which makes it difficult to cover your tracks. Desperate Daniela (her real name) was caught out, well and good. The investigators found Gibson guitar strings in her purse and her fingerprints on the drumstick used in the Cardiff murder. Roll the closing credits.

Although this exciting crime story played out under the auspices of Scotland Yard's entertainment division, they were never going to make a movie out of it. Miss Marple may have become Ms. Marple, but one generally accepts that the original is always best, whether you are talking about biscuits or bubble gum. Once the prosecution got a conviction in the "Case of the Grumpy Groupie," Melanie and the boys grabbed a pizza and a video and promptly retired to the squad room to watch *Die Hard 5*.

The Banana Republic

Meet Quincy Carpenter QC, the most infamous barrister at the Queensland Bar. Any number of prosecution silks might testify to his amazing record of successful defence motions, resulting in acquittal for so many of his nefarious clients. His associates called him "the fixer," being the go-to man for many of the crims in Brisbane and the Gold Coast. This legal eagle even serviced a whole family.

Lonny, Bronny, Sonny, and Ronnie Filou were career criminals, with a proclivity for getting caught. They stuffed up a heist on a payroll van in Coolangatta, and were lucky not to be apprehended by a policeman on a bicycle. This is when Ron, the smart one, decided to go solo.

The bloke was not a hard man, with never any thought of drugs or violence. You could nominate burglary as his specialty and, over a period, he did well. Because many houses are holiday homes on the Gold Coast, breaking and entering is a common offence and treated with little respect by the police, aware that owners are usually more than happy with the insurance payout.

Solo is such a misunderstood word. The housebreaker employed an accomplice. Matthew the monkey would climb on to the roof or an upper floor, looking for an entrance or open window. Once found, the agile creature would enter the house and scamper down to unlock the front door or other aperture. For this, he received food, and not just any food. The scamp, a grade one prima donna, would only eat premium Queensland bananas, and if you didn't come to the party, he wouldn't come to the robbery.

One day, Ronnie gave him a bad banana, and did he put on a show? When monkeys jump up and down, beat their chest and chatter on, regardless, you know they're not happy. In this instance, he refused to eat any more, and went on a hunger strike. The drama queen also declined to carry Ronnie's house-breaking tools, thus depriving him of his ability to earn a decent living. A solution was in the offing, courtesy of an animal psychiatrist, one of the regulars at Ron's local pub.

"What we have here, my friend, is the inability to disassociate one bad apple with a good banana, if you know what I mean. The primate likes the yellow fruit, so you should try to get him something that tastes like a banana but doesn't look like one."

Filou was glad he wasn't paying for this advice, as it all sounded rather hypothetical to him. What could the solution be?

In fact, the solution appeared right before his eyes—an ad in the *Farmers' Gazette*. A Tully grower, Barnaby Binch, had been the first planter in Australia to grow straight bananas, and they were available at the Carrara market. Binch tried to keep the secret to himself, but everyone knew how he did it. At a certain stage of the plant growth, he injected Viagra into the palm. Matthew loved his new diet and was soon back doing the hard yards, although sometimes when you're out of practice, things can go awry.

Ron targeted a house owned by a well-known politician, Paula Jantzen, who he knew to be in Canberra. The two-storey mansion at Paradise Point was designed like a fish, and Matt went in through the chimney, ostensibly the fish's mouth. Once inside, the light-fingered larrikin helped himself to Paula's jewellery in her bedroom, and then came downstairs to find that his animal friend had decimated the lady's office, having pulled out drawers, turned over lamps, and scattered books everywhere. What caught Ronnie's eye were the three voodoo dolls on her desk, with needles sticking out of them— one black, another Asian, and the third Indian. Sensing a blackmail opportunity, he whipped out his phone camera, just as the alarm went off.

The monkey reacted quickly, and fled out the front door, followed by his master. The car was at least 200 metres up the road and, when Ronnie passed his hairy partner, he observed him to be limping, with blood pouring from his leg. Leaving his wounded associate behind was a gut-wrenching decision, but that security siren sounded ominous, and he needed to get out of the area. One can only guess what the little fella thought, but he accepted reality and scrambled up the nearest tree.

HEROES

The officer who responded to the alarm, Eva Sullivan from the Runaway Bay precinct, also photographed the voodoo dolls. One of them looked like her husband. In the office, she spotted blood on the corner of a glass occasional table, and obtained a sample for a DNA check. One doesn't often see this kind of efficiency from a local Blue Heeler. Then again, you have to be on your toes when dealing with a high-profile victim.

The disappointment came the next day, when the result indicated animal blood, possibly a primate. This led the sergeant on a wild goose chase to a nearby wildlife park, where pygmy Marmosets reigned supreme. None of them looked capable of turning over a politician's mansion. Before leaving the station, she asked one of the young constables to perform a computer check on any monkeys in the vicinity, not expecting him to access the Centrelink website.

"I've discovered a Matthew Monkey, who has been getting unemployment benefits for the last two years. There's an address but no telephone number."

Ronnie Filou was not the type of guy to leave a pal in the lurch, so he returned to Paradise Point, and drove around until he felt the thump on the roof of his car. Matt was back. They reunited, albeit with a little reticence; the sheepish felon realising that he had done the wrong thing by his friend. Back home, the bungling burglar settled him in the kitchen, and produced two Tully treats as a reward. Then the doorbell rang.

"Good afternoon, sir. My name is Sergeant Sullivan. Am I addressing Mr. Matthew Monkey?"

Are gentlemen allowed to blush a bright shade of scarlet when they see a pretty face? Of course they are. At least, that's how Ron hoped the policewoman would interpret his surprised response. His verbal reaction was a little slow, at first, but this chap could think on his feet.

"Ahhh, er, I'm afraid Matty is interstate at the moment. Can I enquire what this is about?"

Eva Sullivan wasn't born yesterday, and she noted his flushed cheeks and laboured reply. She didn't ask to come in.

"We're investigating a robbery in Paradise Point, and we think your friend might be able to help us with our enquiries. When are you expecting him back from his travels, Mr...?"

Ronnie gave up his name and the information that the person they were looking for had been away for a week and not expected back any time soon. He accepted the copper's card and promised that his friend would contact her on his return. Even before she started her car, Ron was on the phone to Quincy Carpenter. The delinquent offender would drop off his felonious friend with his mother, on the way to Brisbane.

"You can't be serious. You've been claiming dole money for your monkey for two years?" QCQC was in a state of disbelief, but he needed to concentrate on the facts of the case.

"I don't want to know whether you did it or not, but did you mention DNA left at the scene?"

"I didn't do it. I swear it. But, yes, Matt gashed his leg in the woman's office. The pork have already knocked on my door, and they will soon put two and two together."

The barrister hated competing against DNA evidence, and contemplated invoicing his client in advance. With a certain amount of bravado, perhaps he could blame it all on the mythical Mr. M, assuming he would never return from his interstate trip. If Ronnie steam-cleaned his home and car to remove all traces of the monkey, they might find it difficult to implicate him. However, the paper trail regarding the unemployment payments and tax implications might bring him undone. That's more or less how they caught Al Capone. Not that Ronnie would put himself in that league.

Neither would Eva Sullivan consider him to be in that league. The perfumed policewoman had been dragged upstairs to the presidential suite, to report on progress or lack of same.

"Tell me, Sergeant. How many zoo habitat surnames did you find when you trolled through the telephone directory?"

Grumpy Monkey!

"Sir, we are aware that the prime suspect might be using a pseudonym. Naturally, we investigated all the usual suspects, including Floyd Cox."

"Floyd Cox—the communist?"

"Well, he's more pink than red, but he does have form. The last time he was apprehended, he pleaded a momentary lack of reason, and that bastard Quincy Carpenter got him off."

"O.K.; what about Mr. Monkey's housemate? Does he appear on our radar?"

"Indeed, he does," said the enthused investigator, now on a roll. "He is also Carpenter's client."

If there had been a fly on the wall of the chief's domain, said fly might come to the conclusion that Sergeant Sullivan would prefer to lock up the eminent barrister. Some people just don't understand that these denizens of disputation are obliged to do the best for their clients, and the social standing of their clientele is immaterial.

Thirty minutes after leaving the boss's office, enthusiastic Eva found herself back at the crime scene. Paula Jantzen had returned from Canberra and was coming to terms with the violation of her abode.

Surprisingly, she didn't seem too fussed about losing her jewels. Ron Filou would understand this when he tried to flog the trinkets. Insurance is a complicated investment, isn't it?

The office, having been thoroughly trashed, was now restored to its original condition, although the alert copper saw that the voodoo dolls had disappeared from Ms. Jantzen's desk. The politician was ready with a verbal report on her losses.

"To tell you the truth, they didn't take much. Apart from my jewellery, the greatest loss is my Davey Jones CD collection. Since he moved on to a better place, his songs are now collector's items."

Eva had heard of Davey Jones, but had no idea he fronted a band called "The Monkees." Such a revelation would have progressed the case.

The CD's in question now resided with the guest at Mrs. Filou's home in Nerang. Playing the simplistic melodies usually placated the beast when he threw one of his tantrums. This coupling was not a match made in heaven. The woman, not prepared to pamper the petulant pet in the same way her son did, soon tired of his antics and dietary demands. She stopped supplying straight bananas, which didn't go over well in the jungle domain out back of the house. Finally, there was the run to the hinterland.

Janice Filou decided she would liberate her unwanted guest into the wild, only a short drive from her premises. It would be crucial that she not warn her first-born of this strategy, as he would try to stymie her plans. When push came to shove, the operation proved harder than expected. The bugger refused to leave the vehicle, and whenever Jan opened the back door, he would jump into the front seat and vice versa. How embarrassing!

The confused woman couldn't understand why he wouldn't get out of her car. As it was getting dark, she thought he might be afraid of the bush that surrounded them. With no friendly noises or chatty birdsong, the place did look a bit confrontational. The female farrago remembered that he did like cavorting with the birds in the backyard of her Nerang home, so why not go with plan B?

Although not a golfer, Janice knew there were a lot of birdies at the Royal Pines Resort and Golf Course, and even talk of eagles. She arrived at the hotel entrance, unlocked the car doors, and saw her son's best friend jump out. The homeless one did not head for the fairway but to the pool area, where members and guests were stretched out on banana lounges, drinking cocktails.

What a day for the Filou clan, but it wasn't over yet. Only daughter Bronwyn, very much a night person, spent a large amount of the evening prepping and preening herself for her appearance at Sin City Nightclub, one of the first stops for Satan, when he is in town.

Bronny was at a delicate age, with the bloom of youth fast disappearing. Some of those facial lines needed careful camouflage. Nobody believed her to be a true blonde, and the lady would never be a size twelve again. All the same, she scrubbed-up well for a thirty-something cougar, who presented best in the half-light of a darkened bar. As the clientele of this club consisted mainly of tourists, her resume was known to few: twelve citations for prostitution, five for burglary, and three grievous bodily harm charges. A hard-boiled Hannah, for sure.

The shakedown usually happened around 1 a.m. The proposition from a boozed punter would be accepted, and they leave the premises by the back entrance. The hooker gets short-term rates at a local motel, and he gets done-over when the ladybird hits him with a cosh and scampers with his cash, credit cards and gold watch.

In this instance, the victim was David Osborne, Eva's superior officer at the Runaway Bay precinct. Fortunately for him, he wasn't carrying his warrant card. Unfortunately for her, he regained consciousness in time to see her skipping across the motel forecourt. The lewd lawman followed the unmistakable scent of her alluring perfume.

Bronwyn lived in the ground-floor apartment of a three-storey nightmare off the main drag. The lights went out less than fifteen minutes after she arrived home, and Dave used his down time to satisfy his urge for a gasper. In his early days, many a young lady remarked on his likeness to the Marlboro man. He almost believed it, himself.

If the law enforcement officer had not followed his chosen career path, he may well have been a role model for many of the people he arrested. The chap's breaking and entering skills were impressive, and he made it to the head of the girl's bed before she could react. He gagged and bound her, not to be deterred by the fire in her eyes, which were sending out messages that are definitely unprintable in a family publication. The contents of Bronny's bedside table made the break-in worthwhile. Captain Osborne found his Mastercard and his watch, plus another twenty odd cards and cash—a lot of cash.

Being careful not to leave any fingerprints, he helped himself to half the money, and then noted the name on one of the other cards—R. Morton. Mr. Morton then reported a theft, and directed the troops to the downstairs apartment, where they found the door conveniently open. The police would find the girl in bondage, writhing on her bed, which was the way Dave hoped the evening would go, anyway. There are always variations of a theme.

The next day, the thief appeared before Eva Sullivan, in what proved to be a two-hour interrogation. She failed to explain who had tied her up and why, but the owners of all those credit cards confirmed their loss. The unmarried ones agreed to take part in a line-up, which certainly sealed poor Bronwyn's fate. Before returning her to the cells, the detective wanted to get something off her chest.

"I notice a resemblance to one of our favourite customers, Ron Filou. Is it possible you two are related?"

"Of course, you slimy slut. He's my brother. He'd eat you for breakfast, bacon breath. You'd better believe it."

"I do believe it. If not him, his pal Matthew Monkey! Are you familiar with that gentleman, Bronny?"

"Wh...at? How stupid can you be? Matt is a monkey, you idiot. Wait 'til I tell Ronnie about this. He'll fall over laughing."

As they led the foul-mouth away, Eva smiled, knowingly. Now they had a conclusive explanation as to identity, which would define the direction of the prosecution. It would now start and finish with Ronald Filou.

This knowledge certainty sustained her as she drove into Southport to meet her friend for lunch. The sunny personality on the radio was sharing stories with the ring-ins who he had deputised as amateur reporters. She couldn't believe what she heard.

"Hey, Roberto; the new dining hot spot is the Arika Pool Bar at Royal Pines, where a meandering monkey accepts Banana Daiquiris from the patrons. He is drunk every day by 3 p.m."

The police sergeant nearly ran her car off the road and had a mind to cancel her luncheon and head for the resort. In the end, she decided to delegate, hoping her young constable was up to the mark.

HEROES

"Proceed in haste to Royal Pines and arrest Matt the monkey. Yes, our perp is indeed a monkey. I want him in lock up by early afternoon, and don't put up with any crap from the RSPCA. Got that?"

"Yes ma'am," said young Billy, as he grabbed his cap and raced out the door. When he arrived at the hotel, meal service was in full swing in various restaurants, and management was not happy to release the tourist attraction, already a legend in his own lunch hour. They relented after receiving advice from their public relations guy. Simon Feely reckoned Matty had done his job and they should let him go and move on. The food and beverage manager was thrilled with his new idea to replace the monkey with a gorilla.

Because the hairy one was quite inebriated, and relatively docile, taking paw prints was not a hassle. They were a match to those found at the crime scene, so he was arrested. Would Quincy Carpenter represent him? If Animal Rights Australia was footing the bill, this would be a possibility.

Of course, the focus was on the best burglar on the coast, but all the Crown evidence was circumstantial. The QC would surely make that point. The jewellery had yet to be fenced, with no trace anywhere. A bright young constable then stepped up to the plate and saved the day.

"What about the CDs? We've searched the Filou house and they're not there. So, he moved them somewhere else. The fellow would have been wearing gloves when he snitched them from Paradise Point but probably not when he carried them elsewhere."

"Well done, Billy," said Dave Osborne, hoping to step back from this case. Nevertheless, he was the one who would apply for the search warrants, and the targeted properties would be those belonging to the matriarch and two of her children, Lonnie and Sonny. A twenty-four hour tail on Ronnie would have been nice, but the district station didn't retain enough personnel for that kind of thing. However, their Brisbane cousins reported that the prime suspect spent a lot of time with Quincy Carpenter—building a deniable case, no doubt.

Ma Filou came at them with a frying pan, and no search warrant in the world would have saved them from that. Nevertheless, Eva and two uniforms prevailed. Getting spit out of your eye is always the hardest part, but one of the policemen, with bulk on his side, overpowered the feisty woman. One of the constables found the compact discs on the back verandah, together with a cheap music system and a poster of "The Monkees." The whole area was covered in scattered banana skins. "Hey, hey, we're the cops," muttered Eva, as she delicately placed each CD in her evidence bag.

    You might think there is a nail-biting finish to this story but there isn't. Ronnie's dabs were all over the music, and the great Carpenter of the courtroom could do nothing to dissuade the judge from sending him down. The beak did offer the prisoner a discount if he promised to never vote for Paula Jantzen again. Quincy didn't come out of it that well, either, having accepted Ms. Jantzen's stolen diamond tiara as payment for his services.

War and Reese

When Reese Withers joined the Women's Army Corp, she had no idea she would be going to war. In fact, all the Germans she met were very personable people, notwithstanding the fact that they didn't appear to have a sense of humour. The British army, on the other hand, were full of it. They sent her to Brighton to serve with the tea and cake brigade. According to her superior, catering was a very important part of hostilities, as an army could not fight on an empty stomach.

One seriously doubted the army could fight at all with the calibre of soldier on show at this popular seaside resort. The head honcho of the Home Guard, Captain Mainwaring, had been asked to cobble together a fighting force to repel the invaders. The word was out that if the Jerries managed to get a toehold in Britain, they would use Brighton as an R & R destination for their troops. Reese would be serving up sausage and sauerkraut instead of bangers and mash. Not long after her transfer, Ms. Withers received a visit from Captain Mainwaring.

"Good morning, Lieutenant. I've come to see you because I'm in a jam."

"Well, we've got plenty of that," said the cheeky caterer. "And Marmite! Unfortunately, with the rationing, there is no butter available."

The senior soldier tended to mumble a bit, and Reese accepted this as such, rather than a grumble. She listened to his request.

"I have the big brass coming down from headquarters tomorrow morning, and all the food we have is stale. There is no time to have an official requisition approved."

When the lady from London flashed her ivories, insurmountable problems disappeared in an instant, and the captain could see that he had come to the right place.

"This is not a problem. I can have two dozen scones ready for you tomorrow, with jam and cream. We'll put them in a Harrods bag for presentation purposes. How are you off for sugar and fresh milk? I suggest you send Private Walker over here thirty minutes before your guests arrive."

"Very kind of you, Lieutenant Withers. Perhaps I'll collect the rations myself. If Private Walker gets his hands on the scones, we'll be lucky to see half a dozen."

As it turned out, the big brass were impressed with the quality of their morning tea offerings. Once the shooting started, supplies in London dried up, and gophers like Reese were highly sought after. Two colonels and a major returned to their operations base with her name on their lips.

The woman, herself, was more worried about her hips. Spending too much time around food can be fattening, so she decided to embark on a fitness campaign, which involved running some distance in combat gear. It wasn't her combat gear, but it gave her some insight as to what the male recruits had to go through. Her mentor in this area, Sergeant Dick Delahunty, helped her with her program, and also supervised pistol and rifle lessons. For a catering officer, she certainly picked up a number of handy skills. Her karate prowess was the result of too many arguments with her Japanese chef, prior to his transfer to Pearl Harbour.

The 1941 date of his transfer was unfortunate, as was his desire to open a Japanese restaurant in Honolulu. Reese's transfer was more relaxed; her new job in a London motor pool would add extra skills to her already impressive resume. And she made a new friend. Elizabeth Windsor, the mechanic, doubled as a military truck driver. They spent a lot of their free time together, often attending concerts at the Gaumont Palace, later to be renamed the Hammersmith Odeon. Elizabeth's children probably saw Queen and Dire Straits there. The girls had to make do with Vera Lynn and George Formby.

Reese was unaware that her achievements were observed and noted by people who spent a lot of time in the shadows. In 1940, a clandestine offshoot of the intelligence community was established, which recruited female agents of the quality of Nancy Wake, Virginia Hall, and Odette Sansom. A few years on, the head of the Special Operations Executive, Colin Gubbins, reached out to the recently promoted Captain Withers.

"I like you, Withers. I like what you've been doing."

"Thank you, sir. I wasn't aware of your interest."

The small smile that appeared on the commander's face was more of a smirk. His people could follow someone without being spotted; what a relief.

"That's the way we like it, here in the intelligence community. We're going to ask you to join our happy band of infiltrators. Do you speak German? What about parachute training?"

"No, sir. Just a smattering of French. Did you say parachutes?"

The latter comment may have been anticipated. Recruiters report that most prospective female spies are happy to jump into bed with anyone, but jumping out of a plane is another matter.

"That's right, lassie. We want to give you three weeks training, some language refinement, and then drop you into frog territory to liaise with the local underground."

"I see," said the astonished woman, who couldn't believe all this had happened so quickly. "Most of my work has been overground. Do you think I'm suitable?"

"Very droll, Captain. Yes, I think you are an outstanding candidate, and I do hope you will say yes. Think about it overnight?"

This is how Reese Withers became a spy. Who would have thought it had all started with a tray of scones in Brighton? She could only think of Captain Mainwaring and his Dad's Army with great affection, and wondered whether she should send him a real Harrod's cake.

There is no point in being nervous about a parachute jump. They push you out of the plane, anyway. When the time came, the now lissom lady entered French airspace alone but confident. She had heard good things about her counterpart in the French resistance but hadn't expected her to be so curt and bossy.

"Listen very carefully. I shall say this only once."

Hello, hello, thought the new arrival. *What have we here?*

Michelle Dubois was the very model of a model resistance fighter. She wore her beret and trench coat with pride, and only donned sunglasses at night when there were Germans around. When Reese landed in her designated field, there were Germans in the vicinity, lots of them. In fact, it was fortunate the new spy didn't realise how inept the allied plan was—if there was a plan. Nevertheless, she found herself safely entrenched in the bosom of La Belle France. The rest of the welcome committee emerged from the bushes and surprised her ladyship. They were all women.

Their leader was ready with her once-only dissertation, and the newcomer listened intently.

"We 'ave arranged to hide you at a local café. The owner, René, is a patriot, who will employ you if your language is *très bon*. Your brief from headquarters will be waiting."

Ms. Withers may well have wondered why she didn't receive her mission instructions before she left London, but those on the ground can usually produce a more accurate assessment of the situation, and the response required. In general, all the agents that had been recently slipped into France were expected to report on troop and tank movements. Invasion plans were under way, and such information was critical.

When Reese met René, she couldn't believe what an attractive man he was. His wife was also quite a honey with a voice like melted chocolate. The café doubled as a cabaret and every night the small bandstand became the focal point for some musical extravaganza or another. Edith Artois was the resident songbird and, although she was not as good as Piaf, she did bring in the punters, which were mostly German soldiers.

The Englishwoman was able to pass herself off as a French waitress, and, as such, had to put up with René's sexual harassment, often perpetrated when his wife was singing at the bandstand. It was usually the patrons who put their hand up the waitress's dress, but people in this community were reserved, except for the parish priest. Given his commitment to chastity, the girls didn't mind, now and again.

The opening of her orders was a pivotal moment for Reese Withers. Michelle had explained that once the seal had been broken, the despatch would self-destruct in forty-five seconds. The resistance fighter looked worried.

"You don't stutter, do you?"

With a look of contempt, Reese slit the envelope open and absorbed the contents. Fortunately, there were no telephone numbers to remember, and she closed her eyes as the treated parchment frizzled into oblivion in the ashtray. Her compatriot looked on in anticipation, but there would be no sharing of information, at least not for now.

"Tell me, Michelle. Who is Herr Otto Flick? Does he represent the Gestapo in this region?"

Mon Dieu cried the hope of a nation. "Does Goebbels like turkey? Of course he iz the head of Gestapo. Do we 'ave to eliminate him? We will do it if the allies ask. Viva La France!"

Patriotic pledges like this are usually followed with a stirring rendition of "La Marseillaise," but the girls were alone in the back room of the café. While Reese appreciated her new friend's devotion to the cause, she would maintain secrecy until she could assess Herr Flick and determine his contribution to the German war effort.

In truth, his contribution was minimal, but, for comedy writers, past and present, he was a goldmine. The man had a gammy leg, and an irrepressible personality of predictability. He demonised his underlings and terrorised his enemies. The relationship he maintained with Colonel Von Strohm's secretary, Helga Geerhart, was unprofessional and unbecoming. For Pete's sake, the man was the godson of Heinrich Himmler.

Otto would be lucky to survive the war, especially if he continued to employ Englebert Von Smallhausen as his deputy. The fellow was an idiot. The concept of the SS man up against the popular princess from Pimlico was a mouth-watering prospect, and one which had everyone salivating.

It didn't happen because priorities change, depending on circumstance. The aerial dogfight above them all was one such circumstance, and it was an event which you could compare to the bell in a fire station. Every resistance fighter in the village scrambled.

Two Spitfires had crash-landed in nearby fields, and it was up to Michelle and her crew to get there before the German patrol. This is something they did quite often, and there was a standard operating procedure in place. Dylan Snowdon and Ben Nevis, the rescued flyboys, would be hidden in Rene's cellar until they could be transported to a safe house on the coast at Calais.

The safe house was actually a tennis academy, run by prominent hero Nick Noah. The coach employed live-in ball boys, who were always available for clients. Dylan and Ben were both over thirty but didn't look their age, so they dossed in with the lads, even officiating in a match between Herman Goering and Benito Mussolini. At any one time, Chez Noah could be home to half a dozen allied pilots en route back to England,

and they were well looked after. On the second Tuesday of every month, Yannick would ask his wife Joan to escort the airmen to their small boat, and then she would manoeuvre the vessel out of the harbour under cover of darkness. Out in the English Channel, the men would be picked up by sailors from the Ark Royal, His Majesty's flagship carrier.

Because she made these night-time liberations so often, the good woman acquired the appellation "Joan of the Dark," and for her trouble received the Croix de Guerre from Charles de Gaulle, himself. Yannick had already been awarded the Legion of Honour for tennis.

The life of an underground resistance fighter is not easy. You never have time to stop and smell the roses. At the very moment Michelle, Reese, René, and others were about to celebrate the success of their latest repatriation, the whole café started shaking.

Sacré Bleu! cried René, as he crossed himself while heading for his crockery cabinet, to save it before it fell down. It was left to Michelle to provide an explanation.

"German tanks, and a lot of them. *Allez vite,* Reese. We 'ave work to do."

The first of the big brutes was some twenty minutes away from the village, and although they were all camouflaged, you could tell they were straight off the assembly line.

"My God," exclaimed Reese. "Our Tommy tanks are about half the size of these monsters. I wonder where they're going."

"Well, they cannot swim, so my guess iz Belgium. It iz in that direction, yes?"

They both knew what they had to do—follow the Panzers and report their coordinates to the air wing. However, bombing would not be easy with current weather conditions, and the area near the border was heavily wooded. Michelle decided that a group of five would be best and headed off to obtain a portable radio. Reese, the caterer, raided the Artois larder to provision up for the trek. Who knew how far they would have to go, and for how long?

Dylan Snowdon and Ben Nevis, when they were debriefed in London, waxed lyrical about the two girls who had saved them from the Hun in France. Naturally, the spy chief, Colin Gubbins, would get to hear of this, and was pleased his new girl was doing so well. There had been few communications since her departure, and he suspected she might be having a hard time of it. Then the call came in from the Ardennes region, which was not where he expected her to be.

"White Dove to Blackbird. White Dove to Blackbird. Come in Blackbird."

"Hear you loud and clear White Dove. Where are you? What are your coordinates?"

Reese Withers was thirty feet up a tree, binoculars in one hand and a radio transmitter in another. A little way off were battalions of tanks, spread out as far as you could see. There must have been a thousand of them. It wasn't what HQ wanted to hear, but she was glad to be the one that warned them.

"Weather permitting, we'll send over some reconnaissance, and then a little more. Keep warm, White Dove."

"Roger that. Give my regards to Tubby Gubby."

Reese knew that the Major General wouldn't actually listen to the radio transmission; otherwise she would not have been so cheeky.

When Blackbird reported the conversation to his superior, Gubbins was very pleased.

"I knew Withers would come through. She's a beauty."

"She is that," said the underling, "but aren't you getting a bit carried away? This is the first we've heard from her, and she has been over there for some time, now."

"No, no, no, this information is gold. We had no idea the enemy were heading for Belgium. The U.S. 9th division are trying like hell to protect the last bridge over the Rhine River, so they can get into Germany. Now we've got this tank onslaught, as well as the Luftwaffe. Get some planes over there now and inform Withers about the bridge at Remagen."

The fridge at René's café was full of explosives: C4, nitro glycerine, and any number of penny bungers. It hardly seemed enough to even slow down the bully tanks of the Panzer division, but Reese had a plan, which she slowly explained to Michelle.

"Now, if you can't understand my plan, don't worry. I am more than happy to repeat it."

When you are speaking to a person from another country, sarcasm is not always recognised, but the freedom fighter absorbed what the English woman had to say and agreed that it was a good strategy. Reese would swim across the river with the explosives on her back, and then set charges at key points around the large petrol dump on the other side of the waterway. The only way to stop the tanks was to deprive them of their life force—fuel.

This time it was patriot Yvette up a tree, providing intel to Michelle at ground level. The incursion had started and everybody had their fingers crossed.

"Withers on ze Rhine," reported Yvette, as she scanned the area with her binoculars. "Madam Artois and Mimi on ze river bank with weapons. German tanks à deux heures."

"Forget the time, Yvette. Where are the tanks?"

As it was two o'clock in the morning, the Panzers were all asleep, but in the morning they would be looking for their gasoline breakfast—not if the under ten swimming champion of Pimlico primary school had anything to do with it.

Reese made the crossing in good time and checked that there was no water damage to her precious cargo. She then slipped into furtive gear and found the wire fence that surrounded the facility. Snip, snip and the intruder was in. There were plenty of lights illuminating the depot but no guards. In twenty minutes, all five charges had been set and Reese was out of there. The swim back across the river was easy, as she was carrying nothing and charged by adrenalin. The fanatical five regrouped and headed home. They would hear the big bang as they slipped through the back door of René's Café.

Everybody heard the big bang. Lights went on all across the countryside, and some folks thought it was New Year. The commander of the Panzer division didn't enjoy the fireworks and cursed the allies in no uncertain terms. But he was beaten and knew it. With no gasoline, there was nothing to do but leave the tanks where they were and walk back to base. Hitler was not going to be pleased, but so what? He was the last to admit that his race had been run.

With the invasion imminent, the war would be won, and the Brits discovered that Churchill's victory sign was reversible. They used it most effectively on the Italians and the Vichy French, who had collaborated with the Germans.

Reese Withers came back to England as a decorated woman and was retained in government service after the war. Colin Gubbins was knighted, and his organisation was merged with SIS in 1946, thereafter to be known as MI6. Reese would initially be deskbound, but she was grateful to have such a good supervisor. His name was Kim Philby.

Valour and Courage

Patrick Pesticide had been ready for almost forty minutes, but it has to be stated that his sartorial demands were few. In contrast, his beautiful companion, the enigmatic Stormy Weathers, was relentlessly committed to perfection, and this meant deft control in areas relating to eyeliner, lip gloss, and the most time-demanding of all, nail polish.

The discount detective would never admit to being a patient man, but, in this instance, he was lucky to be straddling that Georgian armchair in their suite at the Dorchester Hotel. The garden party with royalty was to be Stormy's day, and it was only because of her insistence that ASIO pushed the Palace for a second invitation, so that her boyfriend could see Her Madge pin the Valour and Courage medal on her chest. Knowing the extent of Paddy's jealousy, agency insiders hoped the Queen wouldn't delegate the job to Prince Andrew.

"Tell me, sugarlips," enquired the little man, studiously surveying his lady, as she hung her fingers out to dry over the covered balcony above Park Lane.

"Could you ever love a man who wears glasses? Like that nerd, Harry Potter."

The Harry Potter novels didn't figure in this girl's idealistic childhood. Notwithstanding that, she well remembered having the hots for Clark Kent, long before the realisation that he was Superman. Knowing that Paddy had recently been to see an optometrist, she thought it best to 'fess up to some latter-day interest.

"Gee, what a question. Who knows? I don't fancy Woody Allen much, but I might get excited about Bill Gates."

This didn't help the shambolic shamus much. What woman wouldn't be interested in Mr. Gates or his money? Fortunately, the conversation

HEROES

foundered there, as the telephone trilled impatiently and the voice at the other end announced the arrival of their car. Full speed ahead to Buck Palace!

The garden party exceeded expectations, and even the caterers must have been warned of Paddy Pest's participation. They served Champagne and beef jerky. A representative from MI5 introduced Stormy to the Queen, who was obviously impressed with the amount of girl power emanating from the colonies. The week before, she rewarded the Aussie women's cricket team for winning their ninth World Cup.

Back in their hotel room, the secret service chap announced to the couple that the director general wished them both to stay in town and help out with an undercover assignment: the infiltration of London's club scene.

The spy lady possessed the credentials to gain access without any questions being asked. Sure, there would be a superficial check but her qualifications would stand up. In Melbourne, her cover as manager of a gentleman's club (owned by ASIO) defied scrutiny. The MI5 man, Jack Adams, was well recognised around Soho and the West End to the extent that he was easily identified as Patch Adams, the King of Clubs aka "The One-Eyed Jack."

Evidently, as a young man, he played fast and loose with a cocktail waitress, while she mixed drinks. She let him have it with her ice pick. Ouch!

The terrorist threat in Great Britain continued to be an ongoing challenge with security agencies continually stretched and often accused of being unimaginative. Bringing Paddy Pest into the fold would certainly debunk that theory. Pest could claim to be the most perplexing figure in the international intelligence community and probably the least intelligent, if you can ignore Maxwell Smart, whose very name was a contradiction in terms.

Nevertheless, one must acknowledge this insignificant small-town gumshoe, who has managed to elevate his status on the back of an incredible success rate, matched only by the likes of James Bond and Inspector Clouseau. He has ingratiated himself with world leaders, movie stars, buxom beauties, and little old ladies—a man of the people, now being asked to flush out home-grown terrorists who would challenge our very existence. With his capable companion by his side, there would be no lack of confidence, as long as he did things his way. The inveterate gambler couldn't wait to visit his first Soho casino.

"O.K., I understand this is a bit of a fishing exercise, but I'll need chips to maintain my disguise, and we'll want to continue with our upmarket accommodation to preserve my high-roller reputation."

"Negative, Paddy. You'll get your gambling money and you can still stay here, but we're splitting you and Stormy up. Work together but apart. We want to move your partner to one of our safe houses."

"Is there one near Harrods?" questioned the compliant lady, currently enhancing the fading paint on the nail of her little toe.

In answer to the obvious question, no, there was no imminent terrorist threat inside any of London's two dozen casino clubs, but someone in Whitehall wanted to investigate laundered money and its distribution to various clandestine organisations. The presence of lowlife cockney millionaires at these establishments was grist to the mill but, in recent times, arms dealers were more abundant than used car dealers. Many of the blackjack dealers also boasted criminal records.

Legs eleven and the perfect ten!

Mohammad Abbas Yousef Abboud was addicted to the roulette wheel, which became a cause for concern among certain intolerant Muslim clerics in the London borough. Although the man continued to be hounded by the drug squad, the imams were prepared to look the other way in such matters. However, they couldn't accept his penchant for gambling clubs and fast women. The man with five wives at home always attended Annie's Nightclub with a floosy on each arm. It had been mentioned to him on numerous occasions that this kind of behaviour precluded him from enjoying the fruits of the next life. "No virgins for him," says Allah's representative in Islington.

The alleged businessman achieved a great deal in his short but interesting life. He would never see forty again but wouldn't want to, remembering those early years as rather disgusting and best forgotten. Now, he enjoyed his days as a successful minicab driver and arms dealer, who could well afford to entertain his lady friends in style. The chancer always smoked a cigar and mostly sat at table seven, which wasn't his lucky number. That was eleven; legs eleven. This was the number of minicabs he owned.

Like many shady characters, Abboud used the casino to launder money and loved to watch it spin dry at table seven. Since incarceration is often a reward for tax evasion, criminal elements all around the world have now become devious and creative in the management of their tax-free funds. In this instance, the manipulative mauler from Maida Vale sold weapons of mass destruction to the owner of the club, one Duncan McTavish: industrialist and man about town, also an avid protagonist for Scottish independence.

Having agreed on a purchase price, the arms dealer would place the appropriate chips on number eleven on table seven and then reel in the rewards at 33/1. On this occasion, there was one other winner, the man sitting beside him, memorable because of his distinctive Australian accent.

"Bloody beauty!" shouted the lucky gambler, as he groped for the ever-burgeoning pile of chips before him. A lesser man might have gawked enviously at his neighbour's stack, given that each token was a larger denomination but not this visitor from Down Under. The two winners grinned profusely, shook hands and introduced themselves.

"Mohammad Abboud. Mo to my friends."

"Patrick Pesticide. Does this call for a drink or what?"

So they retired to the bar and the Champagne began to flow. Mo even sent over some readies to his lady friends, playing blackjack at a nearby table.

New pals always tell one and other their life story and, in this case, both stories were embroidered with exaggeration and embellishment. How often do hedonistic ladies' men with few scruples find each other? The more inebriated they became, the more socially embarrassing their utterances. Mohammed Abboud first spotted Stormy Weathers as she climbed the plaid-covered stairway to the rest rooms on the first floor.

"Get a load of that. If she's not a ten, I know nothing about women. How would you like to screw that one, Patrick?"

The sight of his girl in her figure-hugging Givenchy gown, slit to the waist, sobered-up the gumshoe, and he wondered where she was going. There were closer facilities on their floor and, should the truth be known, the lady had excellent bladder control. Something was definitely up, and Paddy knew he must drop his drinking pal and provide some support for the inquisitive snoop—his inquisitive snoop.

The arrival of Sandy and Candy with their friend Mandy gave him that opportunity. Mo had not met Mandy before, and was not to know she worked for the same organisation as "The One-Eyed Jack." The gentleman in question innocently hovered near the entrance to the gaming room, and noticed his friend slip away and ascend the stairs.

Annie's Nightclub was named after village poppet Annie Laurie, famous as one of the key figures in a Scottish version of Romeo and Juliet. Management classified the upper levels of this friendly facility as "Highlands," and declared same to be the owner's living and working quarters, naturally out of bounds to the punters. However, should a disorientated soul with an ample bosom find her way into these areas, where's the harm?

"Hello bonnie lass. Would ye be lost or is there somethin' I can do for yer?"

The bonnie lass, although chock-full of valour and courage, didn't anticipate being exposed so soon into her journey of discovery. She had been stopped in her tracks, and urgently racked her brain to come up with an excuse for being in the owner's office—obviously the nerve centre of his operation. TV cameras were aimed at every croupier as well as the entrance and all cashier points, and the monitors in front of her revealed all. If you ignored the technology hardware, the decor was half-decent, although a little confrontational. The art on the walls depicted various Caledonian heroes and heroines in all their glory. None of them looked like Mel Gibson.

"Well, er, ah...I'm looking for Jack Adams, who mentioned that if I should ever visit, I should come up and see him. "You're not Mr. Adams are you?"

"Nay child, and we dinnae let the intelligence services into our inner sanctum. Patch is a valued customer and we are always happy to take MI5's money, but..."

"Intelligence service? MI5? I don't understand."

"Och aye, you do, young lady. Yer bum's oot da windai fer sure. Even little Annie is unimpressed wit yer performance."

HEROES

Lightly grasping Stormy's elbow, the confident Scot escorted the intruder around the room, explaining the significance of each of the paintings. The girl from Australia had heard of Annie Laurie but thought she was married to a clarinet player in Putney.

"What about photographs, McTavish? Can you explain this one?"

The club owner spun around at the sound of a third voice in the room but Stormy didn't need to. She recognised the unforgettable nasal twang of her partner, as irresistible and irrepressible as ever.

"Who the hell be you?" spluttered the surprised highlander, while mentally cursing his security staff for their failure to stem the tide of visitors to his office. This latest arrival looked as if he had taken the high road instead of the low road. The bingo hall was in the basement.

Then he noticed the framed photograph in the stranger's hand. Normally, it would be hanging above the bidet in his bathroom.

"No-one will worry about who I am," said the self-assured trespasser, "but I'm sure MI5 will be fascinated by the company you keep."

Stormy grabbed the pic of the three amigos out of his grasp and stared at it with concern. There was Duncan the dastardly with his arm around European Union supremo Hercule Van Damme, whose own limb embraced weapons dealer Mohammad Abboud. Each rested one leg on an open case of armaments, while the Scot cradled a M20 3.5 inch smoothbore bazooka, capable of inflicting intense damage on the non-porridge-eating population, should this be his intention.

Eventually, a member of the security staff stormed into the room in response to the boss's surreptitious dab on the scramble button. The balance of power then changed again with the arrival of agent Adams and Mandy, both brandishing guns. At the end of the day, it was a great big hoo-ha about nothing. However, Mr. McTavish was now warned about MI5's interest.

Looking back, the whole scenario might have been scripted by those responsible for the Keystone Cops. The outcome also proved disappointing. Consorting with members of the European community was not a criminal offence (for now) and the gung-ho photograph might well have been doctored. So, the Scottish sleazebag walked, with renewed confidence that he could continue his efforts to attain independence for his people, by fair means or foul. This meant Paddy Pest would see his visa extended, but his controller moved him out of the Dorchester and into a bedsit in Earl's Court.

Home is where the hearth is

Balmoral Castle is the queen's much-loved residence and every summer she looks forward to her holiday in the highlands. The join-me invitations go out to most members of the family, including children and grandchildren, and woe beholds those who would choose not to participate.

Every year, Charles tries to dampen his mother's enthusiasm for the Highland Games, which are an integral part of the northern summer.

"Mummy, you really shouldn't be entering for the caber toss. Some of the other competitors will feel obliged to let you win, and this will leave the door open for more criticism from the independence lobby."

The table had been set for the first formal dinner of the season, and most kinfolk hovered with pre-dinner drinks. Subjects always up for discussion included Scottish independence, other intrigues, and family gossip. There always seemed something to talk about.

"This fellow McTavish is becoming quite a pain," said Elizabeth the monarch, prior to surveying the hors d'oeuvres tray for her favourite Bombay toasty. "Are you sure we don't have license to kill agents at MI5 and MI6?"

"You've been watching too many James Bond movies, Gran," piped up young William, so ready to contribute to the conversation. "But we do have reason to worry. I've heard that since the rebels can't win at the ballot box, they're starting to mobilise on the borders, and they're getting arms from someone. I don't know who."

His grandmother would not be put off so easily, as she explored other avenues of support. "What about our 7th Battalion? Shouldn't they be primed and ready for action at any given moment?"

It was not often that William knew more about troop movements than his gran, but in this case, he was up to the mark.

"I'm afraid Harry's taken them all over to Canada for the Invictus Games, but help is at hand. The security services are sending that Australian chap up here to sort things out."

"Is he bringing his curvaceous friend with him?" chirped in Prince Charles, always anxious to get the whole story.

As the dinner gong boomed and the echo resonated throughout the ivy-covered palace, all thoughts turned to the slow-cooked haggis, which would be served up with mash, turnips, and a whisky sauce. Slowly freezing to death in a café at King's Cross Station, Paddy Pest and his best girl possibly dreamed of anything hot or edible. Unfortunately, with the train to Edinburgh delayed, the cook took to the drink and the "toad in the hole" arrived the worst for wear. Stormy was not impressed.

Neither was her partner impressed with her decision to bring along three pieces of luggage, jam-packed with designer clothes. The fellow couldn't believe MI5 would run a safe house near Harrods.

"Darling, you can't expect me to meet the Queen in the same old outfit. You do know Priscilla will also be there?"

"Really?" replied Paddy with contrived surprise. "Should I wear shorts and my hat with the corks on it?"

This last comment might have been desert humour, but further conversation was curtailed with the arrival of the fast train. The changeover being relatively painless, they soon rolled on to Edinburgh, which gave the crime-busters time to evaluate the northern offensive. Having survived the "toad in the hole," Paddy had tidings to share.

"I have credible information that the first assault from the north will target the City of Manchester. The Minister of Defence is a Chelsea supporter and is not prepared to intervene—a totally irresponsible position to take."

"Gee, lover, as you know, I'm not a great football fan, but surely Crystal Palace would be an easier target. Even a high C could bring that place down."

An eavesdropper, listening to this kind of analysis, might well surmise that the whole country would be wearing kilts before the year was out. With the border crossing and the desperate weather came the realisation that Edinburgh was nigh, and, sure enough, the dynamic duo were met and whisked away to Deeside. As Duncan the diabolical employed spies at all transport hubs, he soon became aware that his fearless foe had set foot on his turf. How sweet would be his revenge?

The Queen was delighted to put on a barbecue for her two new Aussie friends, with Prince Philip in charge of the tongs. Priscilla fussed over the female visitor, while Charles and his son argued over the possibility of sanctions being placed on all Scottish products.

"Let's ban all imports of their liquor," said William. "Starve them of money to purchase weapons. We've got to stand-up to these traitors, Father."

As much as Father was impressed with his son's assertive opinion, he didn't think much of the idea.

"What are we going to drink, pray tell? We've got no fallback. We banned Irish whiskey, last year, when they beat us at cricket."

The small voice that came from behind the plate of burnt sausages belonged to Paddy, who, in the twinkling of an eye, discovered a solution to the problem. At least, he thought so.

"Why don't you put in an order for some Tasmanian whisky? It's extremely good and has won awards all over the world, even beating some of the highland producers at the last international show."

One doesn't like to denigrate a representative from the colonies, so, although Prince Charles' response was patronising in the extreme, he found the good grace to skittle the guest's suggestion with a measured reaction, somewhat short of humiliation.

"That sounds exciting, old chap. However, I doubt they can produce large quantities. After all, Tasmania is such a small place. How much Scotch per head do they drink?"

"Twice as much as you would think. Did you know that last century, in the eighties, many of the residents of Hobart possessed two heads?"

This comment managed to bring others into the conversation— William in shocked disbelief and the princess of the storm with a broad grin on her face. The future king was about to be diddlywhacked.

"You can't be serious. Are you telling me that in 1880, some people had two heads?"

"Not 1880," said Stormy. "1980." Some of them were arrested for voting twice."

At this stage, the young man realised the Aussies were taking the mickey and retaliated by pouring a glass of vino over Paddy's head. Who would have thought the Royal Family to be just as fun-loving as the rest of us?

That night the laughter died. Somebody crept into the castle grounds and poisoned the Corgis. This proved to be a strategic miscalculation by the tartan terrorists.

Dog day after-gloom!

The first lady of Great Britain and Northern Ireland was really pissed off; she had every right. Also, many of the independence people were aghast at this gruesome act. The separatists failed to anticipate that public support for their movement would evaporate on the back of his horrific attack on a couple of innocent canines.

Down south, community rage boiled over, with Annie's Nightclub trashed. Pubs refused to sell Scottish whisky and the Murray brothers quietly withdrew from their doubles final at Wimbledon. The Australians would have won anyway.

Duncan McTavish, now a wanted man, headed north with the dynamic duo in hot pursuit. Harry, former Duke of Sussex, offered to send the 7th Battalion back from Canada, but the two superstars thought they could handle any challenge. By now, the media had got hold of the story and revealed some aspects of the colonial help, making Paddy Pest the most famous male Australian since Don Bradman, cricket hero.

Before the couple left Balmoral Castle, Stormy was forced to put her foot down.

"Sweetie, we've no time for diversions. Please leave your clubs behind. This is not a golfing holiday."

"Well, maybe I'll just bring the drivers in case we lose our weapons."

Yes, the pair, now authorised to carry firearms, were fully armed with orders to shoot to kill. In the event that apprehension might be a possibility, handcuffs had been provided, together with an access-all-areas pass, signed by Sir Percival Plantagenet, head of the Foreign Office. Before he left, Her Madge pulled the gumshoe aside and whispered in his ear.

"Get this bastard who murdered my dogs and a knighthood might be on the cards. In the meantime, here are some shortbread biscuits for the trip. It's awfully cold and inhospitable in the far north of Scotland."

Some thirty minutes into the journey, the misfit from Melbourne told his girl about the possible change to his title but assured her that she could still call him by his Christian name. Her response was a concerted sigh. As manager of a gentleman's club, she dealt with night hoods every day. This experience would be worse than most, should it happen.

In an effort to avoid traffic delays and police interference, the canny driver placed two flags on the front of their vehicle, one being the flying kangaroo and the other the ubiquitous unicorn. Most of the Caledonians were now aware of the Aussie white knights, and they encouraged them as they cautiously drove through their village. Pointing excitedly, the rustics would shout loudly.

"Hoot Mon, he went that way."

Appreciating all this local help, the relentless Aussies arrived at land's end before sunset and herein lay the challenge. So many islands made up the Orkney and Shetland groups and they guessed the renegade had taken refuge on one of them. But for how long? Later that night, the coast guard intercepted radio traffic, indicating an undersea craft was heading towards the Orkneys. The captain had been speaking Flemish.

"What are you thinking?" said the girl spy, as she un-wrapped their evening meal. The shortbreads had long gone but this northern town of Thurso took pride in its chippies and the haddock looked edible. Paddy taste-tested one of the chips before he replied.

"I don't think Dirty Duncan is heading to the islands for sympathy because I recently read that local folk in these parts are not keen on independence. The presence of a sub has got me thinking, all the same.

A little bit before your time, honeybunch, but, during both wars, the Brits used a place called Scapa Flow as a naval base. It is a body of water that passes a number of Orkney islands, one of them being Mainland, which is where we're going."

In point of fact, Scapa Flow was only a dozen miles from Kirkwall, the largest town on Mainland. Surely somebody would see a vessel of any description if one turned up? At least, that's what Stormy thought.

"Not if they arrive at night, sweetheart. Remember, the Irish reckoned they could go on their voyage to the sun at night and beat the heat. Up here, no-one goes out in the evening because it's too bloody cold."

The couple decided to book into the Stromness Hotel, overlooking the harbour and just thirty minutes from Kirkwall Airport. This traditional four-storied Victorian monstrosity is always popular with tourists and constantly receives good reviews. Their porridge breakfast is outstanding, and the Whisky Room is always admired. The Aussie pair arrived by ferry, and the proprietor saw them coming. He immediately doubled the price, which he often did for non-Scottish visitors.

The first order of the day for the newcomers was to stock up for their night-time excursions. Comfort items like scarves, beanies, and thermal underwear sold only in tartan, but provided much-needed warmth. The shopping list included thermos flasks and hot nourishing soup, because it would be a long night or nights. Who knew how long the stake-out would last?

The night riders got lucky. At around 1 a.m. on their first evening out, as Paddy panned the coastline with his night glasses, he spied a flashing light, emanating from a farmhouse on a grassy knoll, some five miles away. Even though he couldn't read same, he recognised it as Morse code, with the reply coming out of the eerie darkness, well out to sea. The decision to be made was whether to intercept the renegade at the house or near the water's edge. The other question regarded logistical support. After all, everyone knows their limitations.

The main man decided that an assault on the residence was required and his offsider reported their intentions to Jack Adams at MI5 headquarters. Authorisation was granted and a squad of SAS paratroopers mobilised. The Vanguard class submarine "Vengeance" received a redirection order to the North Sea, with an instruction to scare off the European interloper.

The trek to the farmhouse was no walk in the park. There was gorse, of course, plus all kinds of bracken, sharp-edged blackberry bushes, and slippery wet grass. Nevertheless, the courageous couple made good time and scaled the top of the penultimate hill as the moon conveniently appeared from behind a cloud. What they saw before them came as a complete surprise.

The dwelling on the apex of the rise seemed larger than first thought but the surprise was the number of buildings at the bottom of the slope, all part of the same landholding. The large structure in front of them probably started out as a bluestone dairy, but the extension was purely DIY. The weatherboard exterior had been painted with a dark green matte finish, giving the place an eerie feeling of foreboding. The lack of decorative flair suggested camouflage might have been the intention.

"What a large construction for such a remote location," mused Paddy. "I wonder what's inside."

The garrulous gumshoe often talked himself out of difficult situations, but he was prepared to talk himself into this one. The building needed investigation, even with time on the wing. He heard the gathering in the farmhouse and the many voices combining for a heart-rending version of "Auld Lang Syne." If McTavish intended to depart in the next few minutes, that submarine must be close by.

"This is a big padlock but nothing we haven't seen before," said Stormy, as she rummaged in her purse for the laser lock-buster that Patch Adams had given her. His agency always competed with MI6 for the best gadgets and this unit always performed. The intruders were in.

"Oh my God," cried out the only Christian in the room. "Look at all those armaments."

The girl wasn't seeing things. Laid out all along one side of the building was enough firepower to decimate Dagenham: rifles, grenades, handguns and shoulder-fired rocket launchers, all with ample supplies of ammunition, stacked in wooden boxes. The other side of the warehouse contained many bags of soft cargo, piled to the roof. Each of the freight containers parked outside the building advertised their origin: AB Sea, Shanghai.

"Whatever is in these bales must be important," said Paddy, as he produced his Swiss Army Knife and began to cut along the seam of one of the bulging bundles. Ms. Weathers used her fingernail to do likewise.

"Bloody hell, I don't believe it. Kilts! Thousands of them. The man is stark raving mad. Does he really think the Sassenachs will go for this, even if they're defeated?"

"Welcome to the new order, my friend. Oh look, here's one in your size, and only forty pounds."

A gambler would take short odds about any Aussie male wearing a skirt of any description, although Dame Edna Everage may consider it. Further discussion on the subject was curtailed by the increased noise coming from the farmhouse. The singing group, having spilled outside, were moving towards the cliff edge, some 200 metres away. In their shaded area below the house, the couple could just distinguish the dog bolter, with friends helping him into some kind of contraption, not instantly recognizable. Beyond the precipice, an outline of anguish was the conning tower of a submarine. Only when the singers finished their farewell refrain did they hear the steady drone of an aircraft, but would the SAS be too late?

All of a sudden, the Scotsman's intent became apparent. He was going to jump off the rock face under a hang-glider. Paddy thrust his night glasses into Stormy's hands and raced back to the warehouse, returning shortly after with a rocket launcher and a couple of stingers, just as the misguided miscreant ran towards the moon and launched himself into the wild black yonder. The glider dipped alarmingly before rising again and turning like a gazelle, before flattening out on its direct trajectory to the waiting craft, which was bobbin' along on the surface of the flow.

Life on the edge was nothing new for Patrick Pesticide, now precariously perched on the verge of a rocky crag, with his partner endeavouring to anchor him to ground zero, while trying to avoid the fierce blowback of the weapon. Paddy would probably only get away one shot, and any help from the cavalry looked a forlorn hope.

What the two heroes didn't know was that there would be support at water level, should the villain ditch in the briny and try and swim for the submarine. Elizabeth, as patron of the RSPCA, had ordered their elite SEAL team to the hotspot, providing the services of two dolphins, a shark, a crocodile, a turtle, and a small whale.

Duncan McTavish was negotiating what he thought would be a three-point landing on the deck of his rescue vessel when the licentious leprechaun pulled the trigger. The rocket surged forward with determined accuracy, all internal projections predicting a direct hit on the retreating reprobate or his sky-taxi. The projectile actually shot through the space between the body and the canopy and exploded on the submarine, blowing it to bits.

McTavish landed in the water slightly before the paratroopers descended en masse from their Chinook helicopter. A number of brave lads also found the water, only to be taken by the shark and the crocodile. The fugitive managed to scramble aboard the turtle, which returned him to the shoreline, where he was quickly arrested and charged with treason.

The other conspirators were soon rounded up and all armaments confiscated, later to be purchased at auction by the IRA. The surfeit of kilts initially became a problem, but the Palace acquired them in a job lot, and the royal tailor redesigned them as curtains for Balmoral Castle.

Paddy and his lady returned to Australia bearing the gratitude of a nation. The little man never did become a Knight of the Garter, as promised, but he wasn't too disappointed. Stormy gave him one of hers.

HORROR

Albert Stein

Al Stein owned one of those mom and pop type gas stations just past the off-ramp at Northridge. He sold everything from hot dogs to home therapies and manned his two gas pumps himself. The chap could have installed a self-service facility, but he figured that drivers would be more likely to buy something else if they had time on their hands.

A clever plan but not a very successful one! Most folks avoided this servo in favour of a contemporary one up the road. Because of that, he tolerated certain customers who, normally, he would be happy to avoid, one example being the Bandido bikie group, who were crass, crude, and generally obnoxious. They were also racist, which got Albert's goat, and he was not averse to criticising their tattoos, even the quality of the artwork on their leather jackets. For their part, they thought he was a philistine, but maintained their custom because they enjoyed the confrontation.

One day, Stein decided he could cope with it no more, and, while the easyriders terrorised his assistant in the shop, he added a little something into the tanks of their motorbikes. *Hotfire* accelerant is not something you will find at many retail outlets, but it is extremely effective if you have murder in mind. The smooth flowing liquid blends beautifully with gasoline and slowly increases in temperature as the engine warms up—then kaboom.

Only five riders arrived that day, all riding superbikes, and Al watched intently as the throbbing monsters roared into life and rolled out of his drive, heading for who knows where. In point of fact, they were going downtown and ready to connect with the Santiago Freeway. They didn't make it.

The explosions started and finished on Nordoff Street, occurring within seconds of each other. Observers said the motorcycles just exploded and the riders had no chance. Body parts were recovered from various properties over a wide radius. Paramedics climbed trees to retrieve some limbs.

The highway patrol closed this portion of the street and commenced interviewing eyewitnesses. Naturally, no answers would be forthcoming until a lab analysis had been completed. The filling station owner heard the news report from a car radio while attending to a little old lady at the pumps. A small smile lightened his otherwise stern countenance.

"Will that be all, ma'am? We're promoting our special on speed radar detectors this week."

The cheeky chap still radiated goodwill even though he didn't get the extra sale, but this state of mind didn't last long. The absence of the Bandido business started to affect his bottom line, and he realised that he needed an incentive of some sort to stimulate trade. Who would have thought he would strike gold so soon?

The offer of a free butterscotch bagel with every purchase proved to be a winner, and his customer base improved markedly. Unfortunately, one of the new customers was also a racist pig.

Flight Lieutenant Virgil Brampton (Ret.) operated a pilot training school at Van Nuys Airport, and he always filled his tank prior to his first morning lesson. The bakery treat constituted breakfast, and he always consumed same as his student grappled with the throttle. It is pertinent to note that when Brampton purchased the going concern, two years earlier, he boasted a full head of hair—from bounteous to bald in two years.

As previously mentioned, the former navy pilot was a nasty racist, and always addressed the Northridge proprietor as Yid, Shylock, Hymie, or Heeb. Most distasteful!

Al's analyst had taken leave, presently enjoying a cruise with his wife. Otherwise, he would surely talk his patient out of the type of affirmative action being considered. Even if the shrink returned before the delivery of the flavoured strychnine from Amazon, he might not have been able to change the course of events.

The young assistant David rarely got to work the pumps, but he had been given this honour when the flight lieutenant descended on them early one Friday. The boss would attend to the cash collection and the issue of the free strychnine-laced bagel.

HORROR

"Thanks Jew boy. Have a nice day," said the flyboy.

The former air-ace tried to be more cordial towards his twenty-year-old student, who appeared to be very nervous, which was not surprising, this being his first practical lesson. The teacher would take off and land the Cessna, on this occasion, but give him the controls when they were airborne. This is when Brampton would bite into his breakfast with relish.

"Relax, Tommy. Just watch what I do, and also keep your eyes on the instrument panel, especially the altimeter and air-speed indicator."

With that, the flier revved up the engine and taxied onto the tarmac, gradually increasing momentum until the light plane lifted its nose and reached for the clouds. Tommy reached for his stomach and wondered if young people ever suffered ulcers.

There was some trepidation in the cockpit when the lad took-over the controls, so his co-pilot remained alert until he felt comfortable with the situation. Only then did the xenophobic aviator open his brown paper bag and reach for his breakfast. The whiff of butterscotch permeated the air and the young man seemed interested.

"I can let you try a small bit off the end," said the instructor, not expecting the boy to accept; but he did.

For a brief moment, both faces exuded joy and contentment, and then everything changed. Virgil grabbed for his throat as the poison took hold. He tried to get out of his safety harness but became disorientated, as all his muscles stiffened. First, he experienced lockjaw. Then he started frothing at the mouth. Finally, he slumped in his seat, dead as a door mouse.

Beside him, Tommy couldn't believe what had happened. Even his small portion had been infected, and he felt severe muscle tightness. The student pilot found it difficult to manage any of the instruments. The aircraft started to dip in a downwards direction, and the terrified youngster didn't like the sound of an overworked engine. He fought with the controls as best he could, but the Cessna was now in a spiral, heading for Beverly Hills.

The plane ploughed into the Wellness Spa and Beauty Retreat and caused havoc on Rodeo Drive. The fireball lit up the smog-laden morning sky all the way to Venice and Santa Monica and, thinking it might be a terrorist attack, the inhabitants stopped shopping. For the clean-up team, it proved a nightmare. They didn't know which body part belonged to which torso, and it didn't help that there might have been a transgender person in the facility.

Also, the assorted scents and fragrances associated with the anti-ageing process confused those who may have found the aroma of butterscotch a telling clue. At this early stage, there was no reason to associate the incident with a small filling station in the San Fernando Valley. Neither would the air-crash investigators liaise with the highway patrol. Why would they?

The following few months were uneventful at that particular filling station as everyone got on with their lives. It was a time of significant achievement for the Jewish people, and nobody felt inclined to denigrate Al Stein in any way. Mark Spitz had just won seven gold medals at the Olympics, and Neal Shipiro had tamed the tough equestrian fences. Sol Solomon, the astronaut, came up as an early favourite for the "Time Man of the Year," and Neil Simon had everyone laughing.

A few years went by and both of Stein's crimes ended up in the cold case files. Only when Silicon Valley came into its own could information be cross-checked and victim traced. The property in Northridge then became a pivotal point of interest, as all the fatalities except the student passed that way. Detective Lily Laguna from the homicide squad, now in charge of all cold cases, recognised these two unsolved mysteries as a tremendous challenge. Being a smart cookie, she had her eye on Stein, and poked around the perimeter of the property; even purchasing fuel there. Can you believe the servo still offered free bakery items as an incentive?

Albert had progressed, both physically and mentally, now being wealthy, well-dressed and at peace with himself. He even recorded quite a few German customers on his books, and not a Nazi among them.

In truth, many of the residents of this country are refugees from Westphalia or the Wehrmacht. Look around you—Helga, Olga, Gunter, Kurt, and at least fifty-seven varieties of Heinz. None of these people would ever abuse Stein, but there was one woman who did, and she needed to be expurgated.

Rose Carr possessed the biggest mouth and the smallest vehicle. She was a frightening spectacle at Parent and Teacher nights, and continually insulted shopkeepers and service suppliers. The Waiter's Guild once put out a contract on her. Not just because of her insensitive temperament—she also refused to tip.

HORROR

Al knew her as Wanda in the Honda, and dreaded her every visit. The aggressive virago always complained about the price of fuel, and continually cast doubt on the circumstances of his birth and the legitimacy of his forebears. When he changed his giveaways from bagels to a sauerkraut sandwiches, she didn't like that, either.

For someone who has been in therapy, it just takes small episodes like this to send them on the road to regression, and so the man regressed. Because he had been involved in unpleasant actions in the past, he proceeded with no degree of guilt or remorse. Determinedly, the schemer searched the Web for the address of the company he needed—Creatures Inc.

The rattlesnake was delivered by drone, with its own carrying case, and he hoped Wanda wouldn't be a stranger, as he didn't fancy having to feed a hungry predator, although there were quite a few rats about. He regarded the woman as a snake in the grass, so what could be more appropriate than a snake in the ass. She presented the next day, rudely commanding him to top up the tank, and headed for the ladies room. Perhaps that is where he should have liberated the serpent?

After fulfilling her order, he slipped the rattler into a comfortable spot behind the driver's seat, and hoped she would clear the immediate vicinity before the viper struck. One wouldn't want anyone to ask questions that might be embarrassing.

It may have been the sun coming through the back window that deterred the slimy creature from wanting to explore the confines of the Honda. Sunbaking is not a pastime restricted to humans. Because of this, Rose Carr travelled a lot further than one expected. She almost reached Granada Hills, before hearing that rattling noise in the back of the car. Luckily, the observant driver noticed another garage in the vicinity and decided to seek help. A polite young man greeted her, ready to provide service.

"There's a rattle coming from the back seat somewhere. Can you check it out?"

"Sure thing, lady," said the obliging auto-technician, as he opened the rear door.

"Arrrrrrrrgggghhhhh!"

The snake struck, and then made a dash for freedom, along the concrete forecourt and onto the grass verge beside the road. There, danger waited, in the form of a big black Doberman, out for a walk with his master. It was all over in seconds. The dog broke its leash and scampered after the retreating reptile. What a feast!

Back at the garage, the mechanic was in shock and sweating profusely. Mrs. Carr had fainted. The ambulance arrived in minutes and the paramedics attended to his bite, before racing him off to the nearest medical facility. The driver of a passing police car saw what looked like a medical emergency and drove up to render assistance. Having heard the story from the recovering Rose, they decided to submit a report, which would eventually find its way to investigator Laguna.

Some people think cops in cold case departments are just biding time before their pension kicks in. This is not true. Older officers are retained because they are more likely to remember crimes that happened in a past era. Lily, only thirty-eight years of age, deserved her seniority because she was a talent. The ferocious female was also competent in front of a computer, whereas her associates owned-up to being technology dinosaurs.

Three cases from the departmental database were isolated and linked, with one name standing out—Al's Gas 'n' Carry. This information proved enough to renew the senior detective's curiosity, and she explored the archives to see whether her person of interest had form.

The person of interest was not a felon, but his nephew was, being a pyromaniac who had been arrested on numerous occasions. Francis Nicholas Stein had spent much of his youth consorting with his cousins, the Burnsteins, who all worked for the fire brigade (except for Leonard, the musician), which is why he became a fanner of flames.

"I can see how most of these victims link to the same fill-up station," said Sam Secateur, Lily's number two, "but they are Valley people. Why shouldn't they get their gasoline at Al's?"

"O.K., fine. But all of them within an hour of their so-called accident?"

"I understand your point, but what's the motive? Could it be drugs? A plane for importation? Bikies for distribution? If so, what do we do? Put the guy under surveillance?"

Having said that, Sam knew this was not an option, as their department operated with restricted resources. He agreed with his boss that it was time to interview the proprietor of said business, so they both piled into one of the available pursuit cars and headed off to Northridge.

HORROR

"Good afternoon. My name is Detective Laguna. This is Sergeant Secateur. We'd like to talk to you about former clients of yours, some of whom met with nasty accidents after leaving your premises. Do you know who I am referring to?"

Albert Stein narrowed his eyes and seemed to spend an inordinate amount of time formulating his reply. Realising these were not paying customers, he closed the cash register and walked around the counter, offering his guests the use of two hard-backed chairs, pushed up against the window. The third chair offered him a view of arriving motorists.

"I am not aware of any of my regulars suffering nasty accidents, unless you are referring to the motorcycle group, but that happened years ago."

"That's right, Mr. Stein. We're from the cold case squad. What can you tell us about the Bandido motorcycle group?"

Once again, the man became a reluctant conversationalist, delaying his response, which irked the two crime fighters. Finally, he emerged from his reverie with an astonishing reminisce that was far from the truth.

"I remember them as fun-loving kids, quite misjudged and misunderstood to my mind. One of them even had "Mom" tattooed on his arm. And they always donated toys to my Children's Christmas Appeal."

"Very nice," said the mother of three. "Do you have children of you own, Mr. Stein?"

"Sadly not. Only my nephew. That's him out there by the pumps. He's been a great help to me over the years."

Frank Stein was, in fact, not near the petrol bowsers. He was hovering around the patrol car in the parking bay, with a durian fruit under his arm. In recent years, the proprietor of this growing business had reached out to immigrant families and now stocked a vast array of produce not available to the average American. The rapacious retailer even packaged his own line of Al Hal food. Durian is a delicious tropical delicacy with a horrendous reputation because it smells like skunk. In many countries it is banned on all public transport, as the aroma tends to hang around for a week or two.

Both coppers sat with their back to the forecourt, so Frank was able to open the back door of the sedan without detection, and squeeze the fruit under the driver's seat. For good measure, he slashed the side of the ripe durian in order to release its pungent odour.

It appeared that the two homicide heroes would not be leaving anytime soon. Lily moved the conversation on to the flight lieutenant and his butterscotch bagel, but Albert had trouble remembering that particular gentleman.

"We service quite a few customers from Van Nuys, most of them flyboys. That particular giveaway was one of our successful promotions, but we've moved on to Kardashian Toons."

The unsophisticated male policeman couldn't restrain himself. "What the hell is a Kardashian Toon?" Relishing the opportunity to move into promotional mode, the mercurial marketer reached down below the counter and came up with a box full of small rubbery figurines.

"You just stick fashion icons Kim or Khloe to your car dashboard, and she wiggles all the way to your destination. Is that great or what?"

The two officers exchanged glances, and the female interrogator wondered whether there was any point in continuing the interview. The man lived in a world of his own. Nevertheless, she brought up the name Roseanne Carr and immediately sparked a reaction.

"Oh yes, Rose Carr—Wanda in the Honda. Thankfully, she has moved on to another provider. She didn't like my sauerkraut sandwiches. Can you believe that?"

"Somebody put a rattlesnake in her vehicle," said the policewoman. "We think it might have been you."

"Alright, already, enough is enough," claimed the besieged merchant, as he arose from his chair, an indication that the discussion was over. Without losing his temper, the silver-tongued devil shepherded the two investigators through the door, while inquiring as to the condition of Mrs. Carr. All in all, he figured he had weathered the storm and come out of it smelling like roses, which was not the fragrance about to be unleashed on his departing visitors.

Lily and Sam had persisted for three blocks, initially thinking the oppressive odour might have been each other, or an outside source like the abattoir they passed. Finally, Sergeant Secateur pulled over to the kerb, and both exited the cabin in haste, almost gagging as they histrionically searched for clean air. The squad car would not be roadworthy for three weeks. All the seats were removed and steam cleaned. No-one would go near the carpets. The union demanded double time for those in the precinct garage. If the cold case supremo was not already fixated on Stein as a suspect, she was now. The lady was livid.

Back at the gas station, a mutual admiration society existed. Frank thought the smelly fruit lark to be hilarious but hardened his viewpoint when he heard that his uncle was in the police crosshairs for the rattlesnake prank, plus the murder of seven people. This man had looked after him all his life, and there was nothing he wouldn't do for him. When a pyromaniac gets hot under the collar, send him to the nearest water cooler.

Should the truth be known, the man under the microscope wasn't worried in the least, as Wanda still walked among them, and the other crimes were too old and only supported by circumstantial evidence. However, had he been aware of the vindictive thoughts racing around in his nephew's mind, he might have intervened on his own behalf. In the interests of brevity and precision, it may be sensible to now refer to the pyromaniac as simply a maniac. Young Mr. Stein's proclivity to offend certainly breached the borders of descriptive focus. The nauseating Neanderthal was ready to ramp up the level of his transgressions.

Burning Lily Laguna's house to the ground with her and her three children in it was quite a plan, but eminently achievable. Of course, he needed to find out where she lived, and this would have proven difficult if her name had been Smith. The online street directory gave him options, and that strap line for law enforcement engraved above her front door sealed the deal. Once he confirmed the detective as the principle inhabitant, he started to formulate his strategy.

Most people, when they imagine a firebug, see a man (it is usually a man) with matches or a cigarette lighter, and, yes, this is how they start out. Francis graduated to a blowtorch with safety precautions, the precautions being a fireproof jacket, a ski mask and an LA Dodgers baseball cap—all purchased from his Uncle Albert at a family discount. No questions asked!

The detective's house in Tarzana was as cute as a button. Sitting on 2000 square foot of affordable real estate, the single-storey hacienda came across as a Mexican mix-up with a two-car garage and well-kept gardens, boasting an array of drought-resistant plants and shrubs. If there was one element of untidiness, it occurred on the roof. A large water tank dominated one side of the house, while an air conditioning unit and solar panels occupied the other side. One could say that this equilibrium appeared to be a measure of the woman's economic prudence.

A really committed villain would wait until the early hours of the morning, but Frank wanted to get home to watch *The Late Show*. He emerged from the bushes just before 11 p.m., and was gratified to see the house lighting in the immediate vicinity of Chez Laguna dim. Lily's bedroom lights lit up her second floor, with the rest of the house in darkness.

Fearless Francis left the two jerry cans of fuel on the front drive, and slowly moved to the back of the property, hoping this would be a dog-free zone. The intruder was in luck. The only movement came from a rabbit hutch and who's afraid of a cottontail? Nevertheless, he roasted the innocent little bunny with his blowtorch.

By the time the cad drenched the base of the house with petrol, the only light source in the area was the moon, and Frank hoped his target was not a romantic, or an insomniac. He quickly ran around the house igniting the fuel, and then high-tailed it to his pickup. It wouldn't matter if he missed the opening routine of *The Late Show*.

Lily, in fact, wasn't an insomniac, but no sooner had she turned off the bedroom lights, when she realised that she had asked her partner to deliver, whatever the hour, the forensic report on fingerprints found on the remains of the rattlesnake. If she couldn't get Stein on a first-degree homicide charge, she would settle for attempted murder. As she slipped into her dressing gown, she became aware of a strong smell of smoke, followed by the sinister sound of a crackling catastrophe.

"Oh my God," she cried, as she rushed to rouse her children, who awoke sleepy and disorientated. By the time the family gathered at the front of the house, the exits were not an option. The fire had taken control. The basement beckoned and the protective mother almost hurled her kids down the stairs. Her fourteen-year-old fashion conscious daughter had other ideas.

"Mom, I've got to get my designer jeans, and I can't face the cameras later without a bra or make-up." Her protests soon withered on the whine, as her mother produced one of her most contemptuous scowls. The trapdoor closed.

HORROR

Dolly Parton once said, "I burned my bra and it took the fire brigade four days to put it out." It looked like this fire would be over and out before help arrived. Then the help appeared, in the form of Sam Secateur, who couldn't believe the extent of the inferno in front of him. Pulling his gun from its holster, he fired six shots into the water tank on the roof and then repeated the action. The flow was more a spray or a spurt, rather than a cascading drenching, but it slowed the blaze down until the big red trucks turned up.

The TV cameras were there when the Laguna family emerged unscathed, but nobody wanted to interview young Lucille. That is, until the arson investigators arrived. They wanted to interrogate everybody. They liked the ex-husband for the crime, but he produced an alibi, having been in a gay bar in West Hollywood at the time of the fire. The break in the case came courtesy of the forensics folks. The firebrand had left his two jerry cans behind and, although burnt and scarred, a trademark was discernible, if you looked closely. Once magnified, the marking became easily readable—Al Hal Premium Gasoline: Not approved for terrorist activities.

Lily lost her house, but she was now confident that she would get her man or men. The investigation really opened up, with the arson squad joining the Cold Case team in trying to secure an indictment against Al Stein and his nephew. This meant a bigger task force and access to more facilities. Because of the demise of the snake and rabbit, the Animal Cruelty Task Force also joined the alliance. The jerry can revelation would give the investigators the opportunity to apply for a search warrant of the Gas 'n' Carry premises. Having acquired this court order and the one giving them authority to remove his business files, the scrutineers pounced. Detective Laguna bounced through the door with a big smile on her face.

"Good morning, Mr. Stein. This court order will explain why my officers are going to turn your place over and impound all your records. I should also warn you that you and your co-workers will be under surveillance until these files have been analysed. Do you wish to say anything?"

Al, all out of words and visibly shocked, didn't know where this was coming from, as Frank neglected to take him into his confidence. He saw the news report on the fire in Tarzana but gave it little thought. He now recalled that a law enforcement officer had been the victim, and the picture became less blurred. But, what did they expect to find in his accounts?

They didn't know themselves until they found it—invoices relating to the sale of two cans of premium fuel to Francis Nicholas Stein, plus a fireproof jacket, a ski mask and a Dodgers baseball cap. The cap was a giveaway as a substitute for Kardashian Toons. He already had enough of those.

The second discovery was a bonus. In the back room, the records were hard copies, as they related to pre-computer times. There amidst the dusty files in a filing box, the searchers found a label for *Hotfire* accelerant, a product manufactured by I M Lucifer LLC. The label must have slipped off the exterior of the container, and remained at the bottom of the box for all those years.

Let's hear it for Lucifer and the forensic accountant. Dom Pellicano, no relation to the mafia capo with the same name, traced the sale of the accelerant to Al's Gas 'n' Carry and the package was signed for by A. Stein, a few days before the bikie explosions.

"Game, set, and match," said the proud detective. "Ninety-nine years," said the judge. The only hiccup was the disappearance of young Stein just prior to the endorsement of his arrest warrant.

Some months after Al's conviction, Lily received a drone-delivered package with a replacement white rabbit in it. The sender's name was Frank N. Stein.

Donald Tuck and Mickey House

Donald came from a family steeped in religious tradition, one of his early forebears being a friar in northern England, not far from Sherwood Forest. Not that he claimed to be spiritual. His career path was quite pedestrian, him being a parking inspector and all that. The "all that" relates to his relative unpopularity, both at home and at work. Handing out fines all day didn't endear him to the general public, thus giving him the incentive to seek solace in the pub on the completion of his duties. His ever-suffering wife later bore the brunt of his inebriated rants and violent acts.

Mickey House, his drinking buddy, also shared the ignominy of being a parking inspector, not to mention his shame as the black sheep in his family. His brother was a well-known doctor, his sister an architect, and another sibling sold cheap wine to the hotel trade—quite successfully I might add.

So, it was Donnie and Mickey against the world. They already had the wealthy toffs in their sight, and woe betide if you owned a Mercedes in a no-parking zone. How they moved from stop and go to Geronimo is beyond me, but Don Tuck's plan became more feasible with each glass of beer.

"Hey Mick, whaddya think? If a couple of Arabs could bring down the twin towers, surely we could dynamite the Sydney Opera House."

Initially, Mr. House wasn't that keen on demolishing a building that might have been named after him, but, on the other hand, he was a Victorian, and inter-city jealousies were rife in Australia.

If the harbour city advertised the best football match, Melbourne would claim the top horse race. If one state operated with a Labor premier, the other would have a Liberal incumbent. Residents continually argued about respective weather conditions, culture, coffee, and the quality of life. Boasting one of the most iconic structures in the world, on one of the most beautiful harbours in the world, Sydneysiders always lord it over the southerners. Did this smarminess irk those intoxicated grey ghosts from the streets of Melbourne? Yep. It sure did.

"O.K., Donald, I'm in. How much TNT will we need?"

"Well, let's not rule out other possibilities, my friend. We could dive-bomb a plane into the building. El Qaeda must retain pilots in Oz. With the lay-offs in the airline industry, they probably don't have much to do. Or we could ram the Ruby Princess into Bennelong Point. Nobody would be disappointed to see the end of that nightmare."

The Ruby Princess was the cruise ship that brought many cases of Covid-19 into Australia, and what would be more appropriate than its swansong at this concert hall?

This kind of hopeful speculation over a brew is often forgotten in the cold light of the next day's sobriety. Not this time. That morning, every car with an interstate number-plate received a ninety-dollar fine. Late afternoon, the two plotters ignored the pull of the pub and met at the public library, in that section devoted to historical disasters. They started with Guy Fawkes and the gunpowder plot and moved forward.

If one is conspiring to inflict an unlawful act on anyone or anyplace, you don't want to do the research on your own computer, for fear of discovery. Most subversives use an internet café, but in Melbourne the public library is more comfortable and elegant. You can conspire and connive to your heart's content as long as you don't speak too loudly.

The reference books didn't throw up much good news for the would-be terrorists. Although there have been recent success stories, there have also been some shoddy attempts to destroy our most cherished treasures. The Sphinx just lost its nose, the Leaning Tower of Pisa failed to fall, and Buckingham Palace survived The Blitz. Mr. Tuck, having investigated the acoustics of the Opera House, came up with a novel plan.

"We blow the bloody place from the inside, which is designed for sopranos, tenors, baritone, and bass voices. Let's bring in some country singers who can yodel. This will shake the foundations, and the walls will cave in. Maybe the sails will escape across the harbour but the pride of Bennelong will be all but gone."

"What a terrific plan," said Mickey, who wished he had thought of it. "Perhaps we'll get the yodellers from Queensland, so they won't suspect us."

That night, Donnie came home with a smug look on his face and didn't beat his wife. She knew something was up.

"I'm heading up north, darling—to a civil enforcement convention. Even the Green Onions are coming from Montreal."

The Green Onions, so named because of their colourful uniform, provided authentication, but there was no convention. The despicable duo had drawn on their accrued leave and dipped into their savings to finance the Hillbilly Hootenanny, the first concert of its kind to be held at the Opera House. If they could also dispose of a couple of thousand boot-scooters during the course of their destructive act, who would blame them?

Country music in Australia usually starts in Victoria with a whimper and gradually increases in volume the further north you get. The lady with the loudest whine came from Mt. Isa, the Queensland hometown of Greg Norman and Pat Rafter. Lois Griffin performed as a star attraction every year at the music festival in Tamworth. However, her agent Jerry Daniels operated from downtown Sydney, and the opportunity to put on a show at the Opera House would be a coup for him.

It is true that the fellow had never heard of these promoters from Victoria, but Tuck & House had managed to cobble together enough funds to book a date at this renowned performing arts centre. Daniels would source the acts and put on the show. Naturally, his brother-in-law Benjamin Hennig would win the marketing contract.

"Lois is not big in this town," said Ben, as he weighed up the challenges associated with his appointment. The consortium didn't possess the funds to implement a saturation TV campaign and the woman rarely performed within a ninety-kilometre radius of the city, thus denying some of her fans that fraternal feeling of familiarity. Where were the excitement vibes going to come from?

"Lois is not big anywhere, but she is popular with the die-hards. I think you'll find they'll jump out of trees to support this show."

And jump they did. The 2000 odd seats of the Concert Hall booked out in four days and the free list was to die for (I hope I am not getting ahead of myself).

Nearly every theatrical craft sails with a bunch of free-loaders. These are the society and media personalities who give the occasion that sense of approval that is so necessary to the promoters. In this instance, Ben and Jerry were delighted to see the prime minister's name on the guest list, together with Kylie and Dame Edna—absolute Australian royalty.

Donald and his fellow conspirator were not so pleased. After the devastation, nobody would miss the PM, but Kylie Minogue and the possum person originated from southern parts. The plotters hadn't counted on this. As usual, Mickey was the one with questions.

"We can't obliterate Victorians. It's unpatriotic. How can we stop these people from attending the clambake?"

"Easy," said his friend, renowned for thinking on his feet. "Let's kill someone they both know. Neither personality would dare attend a concert while they are in mourning."

"Preferably a local," added his partner, now warming to the suggestion. "What about Russell Crowe or Cate Blanchett?"

"I was thinking talk show host Alan Jones, but they'll do."

The day before disaster!

Russell Crowe in his *Gladiator* outfit is an imposing sight and would not to be taken lightly by potential aggressors. Tuck was a 170 centimetre pear-shaped butterball, with poor eyesight and misplaced confidence. Underneath that absurd blond combover wig, he would fail to intimidate anyone.

Crowe, in the preliminary stages of auctioning off many of his mementos and movie memorabilia, was being photographed in his harbour-side apartment, when the parking inspector from Melbourne chugged by on the 3.15 p.m. ferry to Woolloomooloo. The enthusiastic assassin's binoculars worked overtime, and that bulge in his pants was a Raven Arms MP-25 Saturday Night Special. Through the front window, the boat passengers could see that the actor had moved on from his toga publicity shot, and now brandished his snub-nosed revolver from the movie *L.A. Confidential*. Terminator Tuck was thinking midnight. Would this be their *High Noon* moment?

In truth, Donnie wasn't thinking straight at all, having failed to consider Russell's state-of-the-art security measures. The multi-level apartment, situated at the end of Finger Pier, boasted multiple cameras and locked gates were in place to deter uninvited guests. Neither should the would-be intruder have assumed that Mr. Crowe's lifestyle would, in any way, replicate his own. Whereas Donald Tuck's most adventurous midnight adventure would entail falling asleep in front of his TV set, the movie star would be out and about until 4 a.m.—as he had been since his divorce.

The upshot of all this was that the fearsome killer arrived at a quarter to midnight to find the gate locked and no-one answering the doorbell. When Russell appeared a few hours later, he discovered the Victorian asleep in an alcove near the front door, with a crowbar in one hand and a gun in the other. The actor's rage may have been activated by too much alcohol, but what the heck. He grabbed the 170 centimetre weakling by his coat lapels and threw him over the railing of the pier. Pear-shaped people tend to make a large splash, but at three o'clock in the morning, who's listening?

Finding himself airborne in the early morn, Don realised something had gone wrong. With little distance to the water, he had no time to initiate a swan dive or anything approaching a face-saving drop. The poor slob hit the waves hard and suffered some form of concussion, as nothing slowed his descent into the murky depths below the wharf.

I don't know whether this is an appropriate time to talk about luck, but it is fact that there are two types of luck—good luck and bad luck. I also don't know how many sharks there are in this stretch of water, so beautiful when viewed from above. Those coastline areas below piers are a constant source of food morsels for the marine population, and no-one is hungrier than a 5 metre white pointer. Maybe the inept assassin saw it coming, and you can imagine what his last words were, "I hope you enjoy the yodelling, Russell."

Over the same period, Mickey House stalked Cate Blanchett, who, that day, had entered discussions to play Kylie Minogue's mother in a forthcoming production. The lady, regarded as a chameleon because of her ability to instantly transform herself into a person of any age, was actually one year younger than the singing budgie.

Of course, the potential intruder didn't know what this was, and thought she had bred a camel with a lion. For that reason, he gave her known residence a miss. Guard dogs were one thing but a chameleon? What he also didn't know was that the lady had moved to England, her current time in Australia being temporary. However, he did locate her favourite café and obtained details of her daily pilgrimage to said café at around 10 a.m. every morning. Having not heard from his partner, who promised to report on the Russell Crowe offensive, he could only proceed as they planned.

Mr. House didn't like firearms, so he looked elsewhere to find an equally effective killing agent. Although blowguns are illegal in Australia, antique reproductions are not and he managed to source a working model. Where he acquired the lethal curare poison to tip the darts is anybody's guess.

When Mickey arrived at the café, Cate Blanchett was already there with two friends. The place served *al fresco* customers, so he sat outside with an eye-line to his target. He would need to be careful of anyone walking by. The clandestine Victorian ordered coffee and loaded the dart into the blowpipe, while surreptitiously looking around for prying eyes.

Unbeknown to him, he was being watched from across the road.

Roger Gyles, regarded as one of the most successful barristers in the nation, had acquired a reputation for having a photographic memory. Noticing the face across the street, he tried to put a name to it. Then it came to him—Mickey House, five times a client for house-breaking, before he moved to Victoria some years earlier. Given that he proved to be an entertaining villain and a constant income source, Roger decided to say hello and crossed the street. In retrospect, he shouldn't have slapped him on the back, but how was he to know the fellow had a blowgun in his mouth and was about to send his projectile in the direction of his target, the fabulous Cate Blanchett.

Yes, you guessed it. The villain breathed in instead of out and swallowed the poisoned dart. He immediately fell to the ground and started writhing around on the pavement, obviously in great pain. Unfortunately for the café owner, his customers concluded that there might be something wrong with the coffee and most of them departed, including Ms. Blanchett and her guests, one of whom was her agent, who slipped a business card into the pocket of the poor fellow on the ground. Actors who can perform a good dying scene are hard to find.

Roger Gyles acted responsibly and called an ambulance, but Mickey House died on the way to hospital. No-one else in New South Wales remembered him, so Jerry Daniels didn't get to hear the sad news. The Hillbilly Hootenanny would proceed as planned.

The night of noise!

What a day and night it would be. Willie Nelson arrived mid-afternoon for rehearsals, complete with his customary bandanna around his head. He couldn't fail to see bales of hay on both sides of the steps leading up to the front entrance of the concert hall. Cardboard cut-outs of cowboys hung from the roof, and all the ushers were dressed as cowgirls. For one wonderful night, the Sydney Opera House would be the Grand Ole Opry.

Because she was the headline act and the last performer on call, Lois Griffin took liberties. She did her rehearsing on her tour bus en route from Tamworth and, need I mention it, two buildings with suspect foundations collapsed as the bus passed through Singleton. Because of traffic problems, the singer and her entourage would not arrive at Bennelong Point before the show started.

Cherokee Charley and the Tom Toms opened the hootenanny to rapturous applause. They were an American native group of five that included four guys on drums and one vocalist with a banjo. On their way off-stage they encountered Dame Edna Everage, trying to find her seat with as much publicity as possible. She handed out gladioli to the thunder-struck musicians and received the plaudits of the audience.

Forty minutes into the show and not one artist projected a high voice or any desire to yodel. More noise came from outside the hall, rather than in it.

The demonstration came from nowhere, and hundreds of young people with placards milled around all the entrances to the venue. In fact, they came from Macquarie Place Park, having walked down Pitt St, and then past Circular Quay to the Opera House. Their grievance was not unfamiliar to Sydneysiders, most people being aware of the Noise Abatement Society Tertiary Youth, or NASTY if you would prefer their acronym.

The movement started in the U.K. but opened up at the University of Sydney campus on the back of a few exchange programs. Their present leader, a seventeen-year-old Swedish student named Bea Kwite, didn't like country music and chose to focus on its flag bearers. It is my own personal view that if she had taken the time to listen to Cherokee Charley and the Tom Toms, she would have been impressed.

Sadly, that kind of thinking was water under the bridge. Right then, right there, were hundreds of youngsters in the shadow of this iconic structure, and they surrounding the concert hall. Lois and her band couldn't get in and the fans couldn't get out. Not that they wanted to. Willie Nelson had taken to the stage and was singing up a storm: "All the girls I've ever loved," with the artist not naming one of them. What a spoiler that must have been.

In the end, nobody missed Lois, or yodelled, and the walls didn't come tumbling down. Jerry Daniels didn't make money because he was obliged to pay damages caused by the NASTY people and repatriation costs for Donald and Mickey's remains. In Donnie's case, this was only one leg, a torso and his blond wig. The only winners proved to be the people of Melbourne. Over the following six months, parking fines decreased by 20%.

Kevin in A State Over Virginia

Looking at Kevin, you would say that he appeared to be a healthy individual. The fellow stood tall at 180 centimetres, straight and erect, and carried no excess weight. His top end was years away from the baldness bandit, as his abundant blond locks radiated responsible hair hygiene, with no sign of dandruff. His dark penetrating brown eyes were clear and bright, his blood pressure was normal, and his diet was not dependent on junk food. He played squash twice a week, consumed alcohol sparingly, and was voted the guy most likely in a secret ballot undertaken by the ladies in the typing pool.

Kevin was just twenty-five years of age when they rushed him into Dumore General Hospital with suspected appendicitis. The patient came out four days later minus his prostate, which must have been quite a shock, as there was nothing wrong with it.

Everybody blamed the nurse who dropped his chart and put it back on another patient's bed, thus causing great consternation in two operating suites, when the scans didn't make sense. But time was on the wing, and the urologist had a luncheon date with his accountant. Questions could always be asked later.

After a hushed-up investigation, a hospital supervisor apologised profusely and offered the distraught patient discounted sanitary products for twenty-five years. Being a good-natured fellow, and initially unaware of the effects such an operation can have on your sexual performance, he accepted the offer and tried to move on with his life. Sometime later he met the lovely Virginia, who became the first person to notice his recently discovered inadequacy. Being quite competent in the kitchen, she understood the analogy of trying to bake a sponge cake without self-raising flour.

Did it surprise anybody that the poor chap would lose his good-natured outlook on life and seek revenge?

The nurse!

Felicity presented as a fun-loving flibbertigibbet who frequented fun places with her friends, mostly pals from nursing school. Thursday after work at the bowling rink rated as her favourite night of the week because there were always a couple of handsome interns on hand, ready to challenge her and the almost unbeatable team from Ward 2C.

The twenty-two-year-old bowled a good ball, and the young doctors must have been impressed with her form. She boasted the shortest skirts on the second floor, and legs that longed to be looked at. The rest of her wasn't too bad, either. Who wouldn't be mesmerised by those baby blue bedroom eyes, and enticed by ruby red lips that promised so much? Nevertheless, it goes without saying that this potent L'Oréal weapon should only be produced after dark. On the ward, a more muted lippy colour blended with her conservative uniform. With her union-approved stopwatch hanging from above her left breast, she projected confidence and capability and continued to be a constant source of comfort to the patients under her care.

The girl did have a problem, however—a severe case of dropsy.

Nurse Felicity

If there were two places where such an affliction would be awkward, I nominate a hospice and a ten pin bowling alley. In her short career with the *Bedpan Belles*, the young woman broke two of her own toes and damaged the ankle of Dr. Adrian. Admittedly, Dr. Adrian was the resident sleaze, and she didn't ask him to show her the Heimlich manoeuvre while she was clutching a 7 kilogram Brunswick Rhino ball.

By now you may have guessed that Felicity was the ward nurse who misplaced Kevin's chart. Nurses are not supposed to look at two charts simultaneously. Certainly, for this story they're not. So, she dropped them both, returned them to the wrong beds, and then clocked off at the end of her shift. This didn't rate as the worst cock-up of the week at Dumore General. That goes to the cleaning lady in the ICU, who pulled the power plug on the life-support machine, to accommodate her vacuum cleaner.

The situation with the latter case is a point of difference, there not being a survivor to seek vengeance. Kevin was very much alive and committed to finding every person who contributed to his botched procedure, including the asshole who told him that now he needn't worry about prostate cancer later in life.

The former patient remembered the hours of Felicity's shift and hovered outside the staff carpark, before following her home to her unit, where he checked her surname, printed on the door of her mailbox. He understood she didn't always go straight home and often met her girlfriends at a nearby hotel. Her boyfriend sometimes picked her up at the pub, and they often retired to his or her place to do what he could no longer do.

There would be retribution, but the fun would be in the fear that the stalker might instil prior to his final act. To get things going, he slipped a note into the nurse's letterbox.

> "Good day Felicity in apartment seven.
> Remember me when you get to heaven."

You wouldn't expect anybody to be terrified by this innocuous message, but the confused carer called her boyfriend, who suggested she run it by the police. They laughed and concluded it to be a prank, only giving the girl their time because she was so pretty.

The doctor!

Dr. Lou Gutman had moved on since the day of the unfortunate prostatectomy. In fact, he was on his way back from a medical convention in the Canary Islands, where he swapped experiences with his peers from around the world. He also lazed around the pool with models involved in shooting the *Sports Illustrated* swimsuit edition. Could you ever experience a better tax-deductible junket?

Kevin was waiting for the traveller when his plane touched down on home soil, and patiently passed the time of day as officials processed him through customs and immigration. He observed the kiss for the wife, who had driven to the airport to meet her man, oblivious to the fact that there were swimsuit models at the conference. Perhaps he would tell her when they got home?

The absence of children in their car pleased the vengeful predator, who had manipulated his wheels into a traffic stream just two vehicles behind his mark. The twenty-five-year-old was not an animal, and he had no desire to involve kiddies as collateral damage in whatever pain he would unleash. His heart sank when the Land Cruiser turned into the guy's drive and pulled up. It only took one beep of the horn, and three youngsters bounded out of the front door and embraced their father. From his position across the street in his beat-up sedan, the stalker absorbed this affectionate reunion and sighed. It would have been much easier if the diabolical doctor had sired juvenile delinquents with rings in their nose and Justin Bieber tee shirts.

For the Volvo driver, the next few days involved surveillance and more surveillance. The surgeon operated out of three private hospitals and two consulting rooms, and his day was so humdrum—advice and slice, advice and slice. He always arrived home for dinner at 7 p.m., in time to carve the chicken, roast the rabbit, or fillet the fish.

The rest of the family were just as predictable. Two of the kids caught the 8.15 a.m. fast train to a destination near their school, while mum drove the young one to kindergarten. After kiss and go, she returned to the house, always back in the kitchen by 9 a.m. For twenty-five minutes, the dwelling would be empty. Kevin visualised two or three ways of causing the havoc he wanted, but, in the end, he chose C4—easy enough to acquire through the al Qaeda website.

The Easter break gave him time to plan and, when the explosives arrived, he circled a date on his kitchen calendar. It would prove to be a beautiful day for a detonation, and he couldn't be more pleased with himself. With the wind blowing in a southerly direction, he knew the letterbox would remain intact and give up the message he had typed for the bungling urologist.

> "Your name is Lou and you're a louse.
> Say goodbye to your fancy house."

Wear one of those hi-viz jackets and everybody thinks you're a council employee or a utility person. Kevin pulled off the charade perfectly as he strolled from home to home checking the gas meters. At the Gutman residence, he boldly walked to the heating unit at the side of the house, wrapped the C4 around the compressor, inserted the blasting caps, and slowly returned to his car, parked around the corner in the next street. The scoundrel spent no more than four minutes on the property. The cool customer would then wait for the wife to return, and ignite the bomb just before she reached their drive. The heartless rogue would have preferred her husband to be the witness but you can't have everything.

The lady's car soon appeared at the end of the road and, when it passed his vehicle, the mad bomber detonated. It was the most explosive reaction seen since the release of Elton John's memoirs, and neighbours ran into the street, shocked and horrified. Parts of the house disintegrated, and pieces of furniture rained down on surrounding buildings and gardens. One poor joker was flattened by Gutman's refrigerator. They found the kitchen door in the next suburb.

Seeing the letterbox unscathed, the bomber drove away from the scene of the carnage. It would only be a matter of time before he would be matching wits with the world's most effective police force. At least, that's what their recruitment ad said.

Virginia!

It has to be said that radical medical procedures can distress more than one person. In this case, Virginia was so traumatised by the flow-on effect that she entered a convent, which didn't please her partner all that much. Her girlfriends, also shocked, would have nominated her as the last girl to become a Bride of Christ. Yes, they had all been taught by nuns, but only one student proved rebellious, irreverent and always late for mass.

Nevertheless, the rebel acquired excellent grades, which is why her parents were disappointed she chose to pursue a course in sports administration. The girl landed a job with a well-known men's basketball team and enjoyed the company of some very tall fellas. The guys also said she was a good sport.

Ginny met Kevin at a hen's night, but he should not have been there. Thinking he was going to Ken's night, a monthly booze-up organised by his pal Ken Craigie, he headed off to the ale house with anticipation and a thirst. On arrival, he was welcomed by the randy girls, expecting him to be the male stripper. Most of the ladies were well away on kick-ass cocktails, and it was left to the two sober folks in the room to connect.

In the ensuing weeks, they enjoyed tea for two, June in January, and some enchanted evenings. Following on from the hospital visit came the reality check, some tender aftercare, and, eventually, tea and sympathy. At this stage, post-traumatic stress had set in, and the angry ant insisted on adding large doses of rum into his infusion, which proved reason enough for his girl to seek refuge under another roof.

Getting into a convent is sometimes just as hard as getting out, as you have to get past an interview with the Reverend Mother. Virginia found the nun in a welcoming mood, unaware that she was on the sharp end of a recruiting drive.

"While you are here, child, you'll never walk alone if you walk with God. He'll help you wash that man right out of your hair."

I might mention that Mother Superior double-dipped as producer of the nunnery's musical comedy group. She had been a showgirl in a previous life.

The prioress handed the newbie some soap, shampoo, toothpaste, and other toiletries, and produced a black habit to replace the psychedelic blouse the fashion slave was wearing. As parting advice, the older woman canvassed some of the issues Ginny would confront.

"There will be many temptations while you are here, and you will realise that an insulated community does not enjoy many of the pleasures of the outside world or want to. However, the hardest thing for my girls to give up is the telephone and for that reason I'll ask you to insert your smartphone into the mobile crusher by my door. Good day, my dear."

That phone drop ranked as the most difficult thing the chatter queen had ever had to do. Friends and relatives could visit once a week for an hour, but it wasn't the same, was it? Of course, things could have been worse. The Carmelites are known for their monastic lifestyle and run silent convents in some countries.

The law!

Walter Wyatt made inspector three days before his fortieth birthday, an average promotion rate. Hardly overworked in the arson division, he took comfort from the fact that he was employed by the most effective police force in the world. It is amazing how many people believe their advertising.

A mid-afternoon explosion in a leafy suburban street didn't happen very often, but the on-duty detective arrived at the scene after receiving a call from the local precinct. There was nothing left of the house except the letterbox. Somebody collected the mail but didn't know who to give it to, so Wally put the three envelopes in his pocket. Neighbours had to be interviewed, and forensics would do their stuff. He touched base with the owner's wife, being consoled by a rubberneck from down the street. Hysteria reigned. The husband, a surgeon at Dumore General, was in theatre and yet to be informed.

Even before the investigation got under way, the word was out that explosives might be involved, but these rumour-mongers could not have been Mensa graduates. Wyatt's naïve offsider Shirley Sidebottom often provided the first analysis, and she rarely disappointed.

"Well, what we have here is a malicious act. What do you think?"

"You could be right, Shirl. They are talking C4, which rules out a gas leak, doesn't it? Can you get me a coffee? I think I saw a café down the way a bit."

Shirley was a nice kid but having her around slowed the boss up, and he needed thinking time. Fingering the envelopes in his pocket, he decided to give the letters the once- over. One of them, devoid of stamps and an address, had been hand-delivered. Surely Dr. Gutman would not object if the detective opened the slim envelope addressed to the surgeon? He did so with the utmost of care, aware that damning fingerprints might be found on the shiny white surface.

So, someone thinks Lou is a louse, thought the contemplative lawman. *Now, there's a motive.*

With little else to be done at the crime scene, the two investigators returned to headquarters and assembled the troops in the squad room.

"This is an act of arson without a witness," said Wal Wyatt. "We have one piece of paper on the whiteboard—a threat with no fingerprints to make it easy for us. This may be a lead to motive and we need to know what the victim did to deserve such a devastating attack on his reputation and property."

Obviously, the doctor needed to be interviewed, but he remained in surgery with patients lined-up, unaware of the destruction of his home. Settling for second best, gofer Shirley booked an appointment with the hospital administrator, who would guardedly comment on the surgeon's status, being aware that a malpractice suit might be involved.

In the meantime, the police station gossip machine cranked-up, and those on the front desk heard about the poetic threat. They then remembered the nurse who received a similar warning which they had ignored. Oh dear!

The senior sergeant and constable on duty at that time were called to the canteen, where Walter Wyatt offered them coffee in exchange for information. The constable's recollections were vague. His superior recalled practically everything.

"Her name is Felicity. I never forget a pretty face. And the message said something about heaven."

"She worked at Dumore General," declared the young man, delighted that he now remembered something.

A two-person deputation arrived at the hospital entrance and immediately parted. The lead detective headed for the third floor and the administrator's office, while Sergeant Sidebottom bailed up the senior sister for Ward 2C, hoping some connection would be made between Felicity and Dr. Lou. Upstairs, it proved hard going for the visitor, as the administrator would not release any personal details, still aware of the potential for a malpractice suit.

"I'm afraid that information is privileged, although it is true there have been some unfortunate incidents in the past twelve months. Every medical institution has them."

"Can I enquire what kind of incidents we are talking about?" said the interrogator, now becoming very interested in this line on enquiry. "Amputating the wrong limb? Removing a healthy organ? Leaving your instruments inside patients?"

"All of that," replied the smug supervisor, shuffling his papers in a manner that indicated the interview was over. The frustrated copper produced one last chestnut for the fire.

"Could Dr. Gutman have been involved in any of those? And what about nurse Felicity? I could return with a search warrant."

"Until then, Inspector, I wish you good day."

When the hardnosed cop caught-up with his sidekick in the car park, he didn't expect his mood to lighten, but it did. She had uncovered everything, and all down to a cooperative pal of Felicity's in Ward 2C, who related the whole story— the dropped charts, the botched op, plus the nurse's surname, her picture, address, and present whereabouts. Only minutes earlier she had signed off and headed for Paddy O'Reilly's to meet four of her girlfriends. Sidebottom didn't stop there. She wanted to be the font of all wisdom.

"I think O'Reilly's is an Irish pub, boss."

"You know, you may be right. Well done."

Where the beer is made from the tears of angels!

The five nurses squashed into a booth near the bar, an area designated as Shamrock City. They were loud, animated and the centre of attention, being the only women in the joint. Four of the girls didn't exhibit a worry in the world, but Felicity seemed apprehensive. It didn't take her long to explain the reason for her demeanour. She was scared.

The infamous poem was passed around the group and everyone agreed that she wasn't being stalked by Keats or Tennyson. This light moment eased the tension and the moments became even lighter as the pots of Guinness went down at a great rate. Eventually, Felicity excused herself and proceeded to the ladies room. She entered the middle cubicle, closed the door and did her business.

Was that the sound of the door opening again? Probably not, as none of her friends were in a state to open doors in a stealthy manner. Anyway, she heard the four-voice female chorus in the background, singing "Danny Boy."

Felicity's short walk to the wash basin ended abruptly. She became rooted to the spot, as a cold wave of dread engulfed her body. In front of her beside the hot water tap she spied a stack of "Sweet Chloe" knickers—French lace underwear for women with small bottoms. She never wore anything else. In fact, these were her undergarments, and she identified the six folded jocks in white, red, and black. One pair of skin-coloured panties languished in her laundry basket, and she was wearing the other pair. The frightened, freaked-out female, grabbed her undies and fled the bathroom, heading for the hotel entrance.

Wyatt and Shirley, just about to enter the premises, were bowled over, as the terrified lass bolted. The officers dusted themselves off, and then restrained the girl. Sergeant Sidebottom recognised her.

"Take it easy, young lady. We're the law. What has happened here?"

With explanations provided, they made the scared girl comfortable in the back seat of the pursuit vehicle. She was overwrought.

"He's been to my apartment. He may still be in the pub. Can you check? No, please don't leave me."

At this point, the calming influence of an older man took over, and the rear of the squad car became the centre of solace and comfort for the frightened girl. Inspector Wyatt soon had the sweet thing composed and cooperative.

"I think he's long gone, but there will be video footage to look at. In the meantime, can we retire to your apartment and check for a break-in.

On the way over, you can tell us what you know about your former patient Kevin. He's become our prime suspect."

All the methodical procedures were followed. Shirley stayed with the girl in the car, while her boss squared away the situation with her friends and asked the barman to put aside that day's security tape. When they arrived at Felicity's apartment, they found no sign of forced entry, but her smalls were missing from her drawer, now sitting comfortably in Wyatt's evidence bag. The investigator reassured the nurse that he was on top of the situation.

"When we pick up this slimebag, he'll be fighting a lot of forensics. I can assure you that every fingerprint on your panties will be assessed and used as evidence. It will be an open and shut case."

Wally Wyatt was totally unprepared for the blush that appeared on the girl's face and seemed confused by her next comment.

"Er, ah, is it really necessary to go that far? Perhaps if the results remained confidential."

The fellow still didn't understand her problem. Then it came out.

"I wouldn't want my boyfriend to see who had been handling my briefs."

Holy hell, thought the street-wise cop. *How many hands are we talking about? Will I need to double the forensic staff?*

His more immediate task was to solve the mystery of the break-in and he concluded that there must be a spare key. Affirmative that. The property manager lived on the ground floor and possessed keys to every apartment. They would pay him a visit on the way out, after reassuring the maid that a police van would be patrolling the neighbourhood right through the night.

The man-hunt!

Mr. Manager didn't answer the doorbell, and there were no lights shining from within. The other three occupants of the ground floor all agreed that the ageing bachelor rarely left the premises, so something must be wrong. The lead detective kicked the door down and, with his faithful deputy behind him, stepped into the hallway and searched for a light switch.

The only item of furniture in the hall was a large mahogany sideboard, dressed with a long cotton cloth and a framed photograph of Doris Day in a cowboy outfit. On the upper structure were eight key hooks. There was no key for apartment 7.

The manager's den offered more, with a small television set in the corner, and a wet bar by the window. It seemed that rum was the guy's favourite tipple, and the cop wondered if he might have been a sailor in a former life. Actually, his former life may have come to an end as early as that morning. The property manager was lying on the floor with a large dagger protruding from his chest. Once again, Sergeant Sidebottom came to the party.

"It looks like a kitchen knife, boss. I can see a block on a shelf with one blade missing."

The cool copper confined his interest to the murder location and spied a piece of paper by the corpse. As he picked it up, he imparted instructions to his offsider.

"Call headquarters and get Cody James over here. This is no longer an arson investigation, and it will be handy to have the force's best homicide man on the case. I also think we'll need to find alternative accommodation for her ladyship, upstairs. She's going to freak out when she hears about this."

"What about her boyfriend or any number of boyfriends for that matter?" suggested Shirley. "Or I could put her up at my place. I have a spare room."

"Done," replied her boss. "Let's keep her as close as possible until we find this creep. Go upstairs and get the girl and I'll write a note for Cody. It's not every day you receive the perp's name and address before you see the body."

"Alleged perp," suggested the princess of pedantic.

"Alleged perp," confirmed her superior, with a grim smile.

The ride to Shirley's place seemed uncomfortably long because of the total silence inside the car. The detective didn't want to comment on the case because the gal in the back seat was in a state of panic. However, he played over in his mind what had happened, and he knew the next stop for him would be Kevin's flat.

Then there was that note which he had left behind for the homicide people: page three of the poetry chronicles.

"My friend Virginia, that's her name.
Soon to be no more; another dead dame."

Who the hell was Virginia and what had she done to deserve this? Wyatt guessed that, having warned his first two targets in order to increase their level of apprehensiveness, the villain would now be looking for a fatal conclusion, with another poor soul on the hit list. *The guy had definitely lost his marbles. After all, who kills someone for a door key, except for Alfred Hitchcock* (Dial M for Murder)*?*

The policeman dropped off the girls, and then headed for Kevin's apartment, which wouldn't be appearing in "House and Garden" anytime soon. Picture one of those boring two-storey clinker brick catastrophes with no style or imagination, although a design highlight might be the double-sized, triple-glazed feature window. One of the residents had added a multicoloured sun blind which looked quite exotic—Caribbean Corner. The inquisitive detective knocked on the door of this unit, as Kevin failed to respond to the chimes activated by his doorbell.

It is hard to resist the authoritative knock of a policeman who has done this kind of thing before. In this instance, the pretty young thing who presented proved to be most cooperative, although the visitor found it difficult to concentrate with that ring protruding from her belly button. She wore slacks but the waist came up a lot shorter than expected. The other rings through her nose and eyebrow exemplified the contemporary choices of the younger generation, but he had seen it all before. With short-cropped purple hair, it hardly surprised that her name was Violet.

"Yeah, I know Virginia—Kevin's bit of crumpet. Nice chick but kind of uppity. Shame they split, I suppose."

"You don't know what soured their relationship? Another bloke? Another chick, perhaps?"

"Naw, nothin' like that. The guy is real straight, but they did participate in some decent bing pows towards the end. Lots of screamin' and shouting. She went off and joined a convent."

"You can't be serious," said the surprised policeman. He didn't think convents existed any more.

"I am serious. You know the old Gothic building behind the Church of Sad Souls in Blessington Street? The place with the high walls!"

As the officer from the arson squad sat in his car and contemplated his next move, he realised that waiting for the prime suspect to come home was not an option. He decided a visit to see the Reverend Mother at said convent would be opportune.

Kevin was already there.

In a lane abutting the dark side of the building, he parked his car right up against the high brick wall. After checking that his recently acquired stiletto remained firmly tucked into his belt, he clambered onto the roof of his Volvo and then scaled the remaining distance to the crest of the suburban fortification. With no chicken wire or broken glass in play, it proved to be quite straightforward. After all, who would want to break into a convent? Climbing down also presented no problem as a well-established vine gave him plenty of grip. He landed in the middle of a fresh produce garden, thus destroying tomorrow's salad. Freshly ripened tomatoes squashed under his size tens, and he deliberately lashed out at the butterhead lettuce, naked and exposed without its dressing.

The distance across the lawn to the cloisters measured about 100 metres, and the fading light would be his friend. Through a window he saw tables set for dinner, and at the other end of the outdoor corridor he made out the chapel, with the congregation at prayer. Suddenly, the organ started up and the familiar lyrics of "How great thou art" seeped out into the cold night air, playing with his mind. This was not about him. The family memories that came rushing back to him were not joyful ones: severe beatings, long sojourns in the naughty corner, and a definite lack of affection. No wonder he had turned into a homicidal maniac.

When the doors of the chapel opened, the nuns spewed out into the quadrangle and then assembled in groups, before starting their journey to the refectory for their usual modest meal. Kevin was hiding in the shadows as the sisters filed past him, two abreast with head bowed. Ginny brought up the rear with a tiny young thing beside her, whispering and giggling, possibly in contravention of house rules. When he stepped in front of them,

HORROR

he expected some sort of reactionary gasp, but none came. Virginia, as cool as you like, welcomed him to her world.

"Hello Kevin. Fancy seeing you here."

In fact, it was he who experienced the shock reaction, and this gave his former lover time to introduce the novitiate.

"I'd like you to meet Sister Samantha. Sam used to be a prostitute before she decided to take holy orders, and now she does it for Jesus. Why don't you run ahead, sweetie, and tell Mother Superior there will be a guest for dinner? You will eat with us, won't you, dear?"

With the hooker from heaven gone, the intruder saw his opportunity and grabbed Virginia roughly, at the same time tightening his grip on the knife under his coat. Her free arm found its way under the folds of her habit, looking for her spray can of mace, part of the welcome pack that all newcomers receive, because all nuns fear rape, especially on holy days of obligation.

Once again, the diabolical desperado deliberated. The offer of dinner sounded good as he hadn't eaten all day, apart from a nibble in the kitchen of the murder scene. Yes, the dirty deed could be done after chow. Why not?

This is when all plans went awry. Mother Superior arrived from nowhere with company: a middle-aged dude with glasses, wearing casual gear and a knee-length jacket he must have borrowed from his teenage son. He had to be a cop. The fiend decided to revert to his original plan and went for his knife, just as Sister Virginia reached for her mace. She beat him to the draw, and he staggered back onto the lawn in pain, clutching at his burning eyes. Nevertheless, he reacted more quickly than Wyatt and bolted for the safety of his perimeter entry point. With one large stride, he demolished another tomato vine and leapt for the creeper, which he knew would give him traction to the top of the wall. The inspector, arriving at the vegetable patch, saw the villain about to clear the last hurdle with what looked like a "Fosbury flop" action.

Kevin had been an elite athlete at school, and this technique propelled him to many high jump victories over his contemporaries. Going over the bar backwards allows you to bend around the marker and reach greater heights. What he didn't know was that Walter Wyatt had also been extremely competent in track and field events. He reached down and uprooted one of the stakes holding the tomato plant together. After a slight pause, he threw it.

The malicious murderer was only seconds from freedom when the garden javelin hit him squarely between the legs. Ouch! He felt his body shake in shock, and he could no longer propel himself over the wall. He dropped with a thud onto the veggie patch and offered no resistance as the spear-thrower shackled him and read out his rights.

Kevin's prosecution needed to be delayed due to his medical condition. His wound had not healed and he developed septicaemia. The amputation of his genitals took place at Dumore General Hospital, and Lou Gutman performed the procedure free of charge.

When the court finally convened, the verdict came as no surprise, but the sentence had everyone thinking. To be served concurrently, he received fifteen years for the arson, twenty-five years for murder, and thirty-five years for sexual harassment. That's the way it is these days.

How Do You Wear Your Genes?

William Burton came into this world at 1.15 a.m. on a Wednesday morning. His sister Jill arrived twelve minutes later. For the rest of her days, she would take a back seat, because of the rules relating to seniority.

"Age before beauty, little sister. I'll let you know my recommendations relating to everyone and everything."

Unsubstantiated records on file indicate that doctors at the Wagga Wagga Base Hospital delivered more twins than any medical facility in the country. Former test cricketer Michael Slater was born in Wagga. What a shame there weren't two of him.

The first inkling of any trouble associated with the Burton genes arose not long after the doting mother brought the babies home. With considerable foresight, the prudent provider purchased two divine-looking playsuits for the children, one pink, and the other blue. In a fit of pique, young Billy rejected the blue suit and reached out for the pink—a decision that would illuminate the path of his life, henceforth.

During their kindergarten years, the twins were very competitive, but the lass proved to be the most athletic. She always won the egg and spoon race, while he dropped the googy, as often as not. Some years on, the family moved to Yark in Victoria, which is well known to skiers, being located on the back road to Mt. Bulla. Their property was part of a burgeoning estate called New Yark, and William became the sole cab driver for the area. He was surly, rude, totally disagreeable, and a boorish know-all. I wonder where he got that from.

The girl blossomed in the rural atmosphere, but young Bill retreated into his shell. His innovative mind regressed, with few opportunities for artistic pursuits beyond mud wrestling and the tractor pull.

Perhaps this is why he turned nasty. As an uncontrollable teenager, the lad offended most people. He even scattered cement all over his teacher's vegetable garden. On the other hand, Jill presented as a joy to behold: sweet, smart, sporty, and going places. When they both came to town, she enlisted in the police force, and he became an organiser for the Pride March.

Some unkind souls said the only reason Jilly applied for the Mounties is because she looked good in jodhpurs. In truth, she looked good in anything.

Unlike the Canadians, the Victorian Mounties never get their man. Their bent is crowd control, sports events and public relations, and they never like to dismount from their horse. Jill was on duty when her brother made a spectacle of himself at the march he helped organise.

Entertainment icon Dame Edna Everage (also born in Wagga Wagga) led the parade, and Bill appeared on the second float, tied to a makeshift funeral pyre. Joan of Arc never looked so bad, and whatever message he wished to communicate was lost in translation —a barrage of eggs and rotten tomatoes came sailing his way. The amused sibling, by trotting her horse to one side of the exhibit, restricted the assault.

"Hello Billy, how's it going? I was going to suggest we get together for a late breakfast, but it looks like you're already done."

By the time they did catch up, her brother had cleaned himself up. Jill paid for the coffee and did most of the talking, while he withdrew into his inner self.

"I don't know why you're so controversial. Why not something cute and colourful like the dykes and their tulip float?"

She accepted his grumble as an answer, and that's how it often was. For this reason, their catch-ups became once in a while rather than now and then. Two years went by, which saw the horse heroine transferred to the homicide squad, as a junior sergeant. Meanwhile, Bill succeeded in offending other members of his leadership team and found himself demoted to Media Manager. After a few months in this job, he turned into a psychopath. It is not acknowledged that workplace issues exacerbated this condition.

Those who often read my commentary may come to the conclusion that a lot of psychopaths live in Victoria. Quite frankly, I think it is the government and the libertarians. The Liberals let us off the leash, and then welcome to hard Labor for the duration. Bill's first victim turned out to be a politician.

Andrew Pocock's brother played rugby for Australia, and he was popular. Andrew less so. The polly might have been lucky to be selected by his branch but, once nominated, he stood in a Liberal blue ribbon seat where defeat was unthinkable. They gave him a cabinet post and an important portfolio. What could go wrong?

Our previous rulers boasted Chinese friends and were regarded as red. The next administration would be green for sure. This left Bill and his lobby group looking at a fancy fellow with a blue carnation in his lapel. How he hated blue (although he later wore a blue uniform).

The bow tie which matched the politician's lapel flower didn't help either, but all would be forgiven if the man acceded to the wishes of the deputation from the militant organisation "Gay Day." All they wanted was a commonwealth grant to build a Statue of Liberation in the middle of Port Phillip Bay, at least thirty storeys high, with a lighthouse built into the statue's eye sockets. Due to the fact that limited numbers of LGBTQ people lived in his electorate, Pocock dismissed the submission out of hand.

That night, they found his body in the Yarra River, and the Prime Minister cut up rough.

"Bloody hell—another by-election!"

Jill Burton arrived at the scene as the men with long poles dragged the body out of the dirty depths. Her first question concerned the crime location by the city's iconic gambling venue, which might not have been as coincidental as first thought. Pocock actually approved the casino's first licence, amidst stern opposition. He also owed someone in the high roller's room 200,000 big ones. This information surfaced at a later date.

In death, he looked surprised—hardly an astounding reaction when somebody shoves a shiv into your solar plexus without warning. The medical examiner came up with his usual crap: Champagne and oysters for dinner, and no recent sexual activity—although that flagpole sticking out of his bum made one wonder.

"It's a gay rights flag, sir," said Jill, reverently. She would not become too friendly with her superior until peer acceptance designated her as one of the boys.

"They are made primarily for the annual parade."

"I think you have been with us long enough to call me Ken," suggested the chief inspector, as they walked across Flinders Street to meet the person who raised the alarm.

"Call me madam," said the middle-aged painted lady who answered the door at number 69, wearing a red dress that was all flounce and bounce. With all that make-up she wore, you could be excused for thinking it was Pancake Tuesday.

"Yes, Inspector, I reported the offense. I heard a splash and observed three men running from the river to a panel van. They drove off quickly."

In situations like this, the junior officer always asks the questions, so her superior can evaluate her skills. This junior officer was quick off the mark.

"What time are we talking about? And did you take down the number plate of the vehicle?"

"Well, I guess midnight, give or take a few minutes. I didn't see the plates, but the auto was black."

"Midnight, and the van was black," repeated the interrogator. "Do you realise, ma'am, all vans look black at midnight?"

It was apparent that the woman didn't like being interviewed by a junior and took umbrage at this perceived rebuff.

"O.K. It might have been red or blue or green, but it did have a Pride March sticker on the side window; and don't call me ma'am. I'm a madam."

Who knows whether comrade Bill plunged the dagger into Andrew Pocock? All three of them were probably involved, as they represented the hard core of "Gay Day." These sweet boys all worked part-time jobs, including Buck Roger, chairperson of Anarchy Australia No Liability. Considering his background and reputation, you would reckon him to be the one with the knife, while the others may have combined to insert the flagpole up Andrew's arse.

The politicians acted swiftly in the aftermath of the tragedy, and the nation's leader announced the ministerial replacement for Mr. Pocock. The liberation push would take heart from this appointment, as the new man was a real whacko. The fellow blamed the coronavirus on aliens infiltrating our beer. Building a statue in everybody's favourite water feature would be no problem.

In the meantime, the investigation continued, chasing after vans promoting the Pride March. The fuzz soon found themselves in the converted factory used as the administration headquarters for the shindig. Bill wasn't there and neither was Jill, who conveniently produced an excuse to be somewhere else.

What was there was a dark blue panel van, registered in 2012, with a familiar sticker on the window. Jay, the only person on the premises, would deny them nothing.

"You're looking at our community vehicle. We collect and deliver materials for the march and, as long as you sign in and out, it is available to everyone."

The transport logbook gave up one, Buck Roger, as the signature for the night of the murder, and Jay gave them his address. The gullible youth possibly suspected a logistics problem with the council authorities. Buck suspected nothing when he opened his door, and the lads swarmed in with a search warrant. What a bonanza!

Newspaper cuttings in every room paid homage to someone in the anarchy business, and the resident's overseas counterparts featured prominently. They found pictures of possible targets, and the occasional manifesto, which the Supreme Court would find interesting. Best of all, the searchers discovered a switchblade knife on the kitchen bench, next to Buck's mobile phone and money clip.

You would expect his prints to be on his own dagger, and they were. "But wait, there's more," said the medical examiner. Andrew Pocock had been eating a rare variety of Sydney rock oysters that night, and the remains of one of them had been pieced with the thrust of the blade. The residue remained attached to the weapon, and this proved enough to send Mr. Roger to the big house. A couple of days before the trial, his two accomplices quietly left town. They were never charged.

Did Jilly know of her brother's role in this tragic homicide? She may have guessed. There is little twins don't know about each other. She was not party to his relocation but became aware of it, and then helped him resettle when he returned to the city, many months later. This involved complete separation from his homosexual friends, and time spent in a sanatorium. Let's face it. The psychopath needed time to readjust.

You're not going to believe what came next. Little sister suggested he take the police entry exam. Sure, he was psycho and gay, but so was J. Edgar Hoover. How could they refuse him?

Constable Bill graduated a bit older than the average recruit, but he soon progressed to sergeant, and then became the backbone of the mobile traffic branch: motorcycle division. The chap loved his BMW work bike, and saved up to buy a Harley for himself. Whenever Jill came around, he would kid her about the under-powered divvy van she frequently used.

Then there were the days he didn't take his meds.

Some motorists choose to argue when they are pulled over by a motorcycle cop. What they don't know is that this department is one of the few sections of the force that doesn't always work in pairs. That other person is called a witness and can often be a deterrent for those contemplating a rash act.

The seemingly innocent driver slowed down and stopped when he glimpsed the flashing light in his rear vision mirror, but when the cop arrived, his natural persona took over. Sometimes, you can be too brash and overconfident. In fact, the kid was a dipstick, and the wheels were stolen. He also displayed a raunchy tattoo of Lady Gaga on his biceps. Taking one look at the tat, the officer told the driver to get out of the car, and produce his licence.

"Are you kidding me? It's pitch black out there. I have rights, you know."

The next sound he heard was the click of a Smith and Wesson semi-automatic. He felt the hard, cold steel up against his temple, and his confident composure diminished instantaneously. The Saturday spiv even regretted stealing the swish sedan.

"Is this your car, young man? You don't look like the type of person able to afford a top of the range Mercedes. How does it go?"

"Vvvvvveeeery well, but I think I prefer a Maserati. You know, more grunt, more girls."

Even though the lad prepared to exit the vehicle, he made no attempt to produce his papers. It was a shame only two people appeared on this deserted road at 2 a.m., because a third person would have advised him not to do what he did. The idiot made a run for it.

Sergeant Burton acted with considerable restraint and lack of panic, as he slowly raised his gun, aimed, and then let go three shots, which all found their mark. They would find the body in the bushes in the morning. Meanwhile, the cool cop closed the door of the Mercedes, mounted his BMW and roared off.

Those in the homicide squad are usually on call twenty-four hours of the day, which is why Jill's breakfast was interrupted. She slipped behind the wheel of her car, with mobile phone in one hand and marmalade toast in the other. Her junior at the crime scene was ready with his rundown.

"The deceased is Lenny "Light Fingers" LaRue. Twenty-five years of age, with a sheet as long as your arm—mainly "Grand Theft Auto.""

"It looks like he stole the wrong car," said the alert investigator, switching her attention to the three bullet holes in the victim's back.

"Did you find the shell casings? And the owner of the Mercedes?"

All this was in hand. With little else for the predictable policewoman to do, she checked with the medical examiner as to time of death, made a cursory walk around the abandoned vehicle, and then headed back to the office. Her boss would be waiting for a heads-up.

"Someone has taken road rage too far. Forensics will give me a report on the bullets tomorrow. I'm hoping we're not dealing with a thrill-kill. Some people watch too many movies."

Ken Ferguson relied heavily on the only woman of rank in his squad, and he wanted to mould her in his own image. This would be difficult because two impediments restricted promotion in their workplace, being female and being homosexual.

Bill Burton failed to incur much hostility because he wasn't effeminate, and yet to be promoted. This would come later. The psychopath was cool under pressure and rarely stressed out; blame it on his lack of guilt. Although rather withdrawn, he did possess some charm and made friends easily. Becoming an enemy, however, might be fraught with danger.

On the morning after the Mercedes incident, the off-duty policeman relaxed in a state of excitement, by watching a replay of the Sydney Gay Mardi Gras. On the urging of his sister, he had forsaken all his former associates, but he still enjoyed the glitz and glamour of Australia's best street pageant. You could bet his thoughts occasionally wandered. It was inconceivable that the motorcycle cop had banished from his mind all memories of the night before. He must have realised those bullets would be traced and identified as police issue.

"I've got some bad news for you, Detective Burton. Those three shell casings we recovered came from a Smith and Wesson semi-automatic. Has anyone stolen your gun?"

One can always rely on the forensics people to come up with something controversial. Jill couldn't believe what she heard. Ken Ferguson couldn't believe what he was told.

"Are you serious? The shooter is a cop?"

"Not necessarily," said his nervous underling, in a less than confident manner. "But we predominately use that particular firearm, as you well know. I suppose there might be black market circulation in the underworld."

"Sure," agreed the chief. "And Al Capone sold furniture."

When the finger of suspicion points inwards, divisional heads are always reticent to bring in the ethical standards people, whose code of conduct demands the highest level of integrity. These unfriendly snoops are never popular with the rank and file, and often receive minimal cooperation from the troops.

In this instance, it was difficult to find anyone who didn't think Lenny LaRue got what he deserved. Eliminating one more criminal from the planet didn't seem so bad. For some reason, the investigation didn't start where it should have: the mobile traffic branch, where one of their rough riders continued to be lax with his medication schedule.

Burton's propensity to associate himself with agitators who pushed minority causes led him to befriend a number of surly characters who, among other things, owned up to being vegetarians. They were lean, mean, and green. So, the budding agitator joined the climate change debate. This meant frequent protests, which involved the production of defamatory literature and signage for their various marches. Given his occupation, Bill needed to tread carefully and protect his identity at all costs

HORROR

One of the targets of this group, the minister for the environment, always pulled a protest crowd whenever he appeared in public. His forthcoming trip to Melbourne was eagerly awaited.

In normal circumstances, his trip from the air terminal to the city would attract a heavy protective presence, but the blue boys were busy elsewhere, with a "bikie" convention south of the CBD. So, the motorcade consisted of one black stretch limousine, with Bill Burton and his BMW out front. Bill advised the driver of the limo of possible protest trouble over the river, and to go where he went and to go fast.

What a mess in the western suburbs over the last few years! First, the widening of the airport link road, and then the under-river freeway. Also, an extension of Metro Rail, and the bridge over the Maribyrnong River, now 90% completed. The public expected it to open any day. Some folks thought it was already operating, but surprise, surprise, a union strike—just the usual ambit claim. Once they worked this problem out, that little gap over the water would be closed and the arteries would flow.

At Tullamarine Airport, the minister dashed for his ride, pleased he made it with only two direct hits from the rotten tomato brigade. The motorcyclist kick-started his bike and led the ministerial vehicle away from the curb and down the ramp to the freeway. Once on the open road, car and motorcycle established a steady pace within the speed limit, with both driver and rider relaxing somewhat. By the time the minister's car approached the river, the passenger in the back seat was dictating random thoughts into his machine. If the chauffeur hadn't been listening intently, he may have reconsidered his decision to follow the motorbike, which increased its speed as it came to the diversion that was the new river crossing. Well, 90% of the new crossing.

In retrospect, you have to think the guy standing beside the detour sign was one of those lean, mean vegetarians. Once he saw the limo veer towards the new bitumen, he removed the traffic instruction and scampered.

Evel Knievel always came over as an optimist, and you have to be such a person to do what he did. Billy displayed more bravado than optimism, when he propelled his BMW from one side of the bridge to the other. The elevation was just right for a motorcycle, and he made the crossing with ease. Sadly, the heavy limousine did not fly, but just flipped over the edge and plunged into the abyss below. A subsequent investigation determined that brakes were applied but not soon enough.

This investigation also exonerated Bill Burton. Because of the union strike, no witnesses stepped forward, and he couldn't explain why the driver of the government car didn't follow him along the usual route. Perhaps he thought the bridge was open? Did the minister urge him to get to town more quickly? In Canberra, the news hit home hard. The PM was angry.

"Another bloody by-election! We'll be out of office by Christmas."

The only survivor of this tragedy claimed to be traumatised by the incident, and the medics recommended the approval of his transfer request. They even promoted him. How nice, and what a coincidence that this happened just as the ethical standards people started to probe the mobile branch in relation to the roadside shooting.

Jill was delighted her brother had been promoted and rewarded him with a slap-up dinner. She did seem rather mystified that everything he ordered was green, not that the curry didn't taste red-hot.

"So, how are you coping with being a desk jockey? Do you no longer crave the feel of wind through your hair?"

"Sure I do," replied the reserved road warrior. "But we all wear helmets, so I feel nothing. What about you and the thrill when you arrest the lowlife you're after? What are you working on right now?"

Jill updated him on the Lenny LaRue killing, but neglected to mention the Smith and Wesson connection. Her dinner companion tried to be nonchalant and showed only perfunctory interest in her comments. After all, twins share this uncanny knack of knowing what the other is thinking. One suggests it would be embarrassing to be arrested by your sister.

November saw a new regime in Canberra, a new winner of the Melbourne Cup, and a new deputy commissioner of police in Melbourne—Ken Ferguson. With his promotion came the restructure of the homicide squad under Chief Inspector Burton. What a meteoric rise for the young woman. "All go," said bro, who was so excited for her. As a mark of respect, he decided to stop killing people, at least, for now.

The sadistic sibling had little to worry about, as the bridge enquiry had closed down. The scrutiny of the ethical standard dunderheads died in the water, and it was declared a cold case. Well, it did happen in winter.

HORROR

The new government, green and mean, made important decisions that alleviated the need to protest, and Billy's rage could hardly be directed at his fellow officers. He now worked for their union.

Two things grew and festered in his messed-up brain, which eventually might require action. He hated tattoos and graffiti, especially blue graffiti.

The artists would be an easier target than the inksters, many of whom were Comanchero, Bandido or Hells Angels. Heaven help him if he came up against that lot. Relinquishing his BMW and getting that promotion gave Bill the incentive to purchase the Harley-Davidson he always wanted. He rode it on most weekends, and also patrolled the dark streets at night, looking for action This is when the scribblers and squigglers unleashed their creative spirit.

Definitive Denis, the current star among the street art crowd, served his apprenticeship under the revered Banksy, the Bristol phenomenon who put global issues on every wall. Denis Kellogg left the Old Dart in a hurry, and Melbourne became his new home, as his relatives lived here, some of them in a penal abode. This didn't deter him. In fact, prison walls are the ideal canvas for his trade craft.

Local authorities periodically denounced graffiti, but they found it difficult to differentiate between creativity and vandalism. Their gaudy CBD lanes actually attracted tourists, and this encouraged those who aspired to become definitive. No such discrimination emanated from Bill Burton, who hated them all.

The day DD accepted a commission to portray the local Johnnies in a pig pen, he pretty well closed the door on any superannuation expectations. If Billy didn't get him, someone else would. Initially, the bugger was lucky because he could hear the purr of the hog as it rolled around the streets. The defiler always wore dark clothes and brought along lookouts, who warned him of any approaching danger. Sometimes, he chose to work on high, which gave him an escape route over the rooftops. To say the splatter and splay sketcher lived dangerously was an understatement.

Then, one morning, an early riser found Definitive Denis impaled to the door of a kebab café. A paint can had been rammed over his head, and the leaking red dye mixed with the blood to provide a gory denouement. The spear, also called a dory, had been part of the Spartan statue situated outside the adjoining restaurant, one which shared the footpath with local

Greeks for some fifteen years. Any number of spray cans lay abandoned beneath the victim's feet, and the killer used one of them to write his message on the café window—Daub and Die.

As a mark of respect, the owner of the shop closed down for two hours. He spent most of that time talking to the chief investigator. Jill Burton didn't need to be there, but the discovery of a body in the morning at Richmond couldn't be ignored, as she passed that way every day.

"So, Mr. Tabak, you say you knew the victim."

"Sure I did—Denis, a customer. The man liked our Shish Kebabs. Allah, Allah, now look at him. He's ended up like one."

"Quite so, and can I ask if you were aware of Mr. Kellogg's profession?"

"Well yeah, I suppose. You know, he was one of those street artists. To each his own, eh Inspector?"

Jill saw that the shop owner was nervous, and she knew why, having arrived with some information concerning the premises and the owner's record with the liquor licensing board. It is always best to do a probity check before you start asking questions.

"I don't suppose you ever commissioned the dead man to violate a wall on your behalf? I'm suggesting that now famous piece of artistic licence, depicting law enforcement officers in a pig pen."

Erdal Tabak was no longer nervous. That train had long gone. Now, dripping in sweat and visibly shaking, he knew the pigs would be out for revenge. He was sure of it. Nevertheless, the king of the kebab would hold out for as long as he could.

"Now, why would I do something like that?"

His interrogator smiled benignly, as she produced her phone, and started reading out the myriad of citations which the fellow had amassed over time.

"Eight convictions for illegal sale of liquor, four for gambling on the premises, and five for prostitution, also on said premises. Need I continue Mr. Tabak?"

"Gee, I only try to give my customers a good time."

The man obviously hated the Jacks, but this didn't make him a murderer. Might he be a potential victim? The impaler apparently knew the café owner to be implicated in the pig pen commission, which is why he chose to make his statement at Kebab Central. Hopefully, he would not take his grievance any further.

The testy Turk was pleased to see the departure of the nosy policewoman, but he did stretch the relationship a bit by offering her a pork shashlik to go.

He enthusiastically welcomed the media when they arrived in time for lunch, and he did a roaring trade. The body had been removed but not the catch phrase on the café window, which featured on the front page of all the dailies, with blood-curdling headlines such as "SPEAR FEAR" and "CEREAL KILLER." Of course, Mr. Kellogg was in no way related to the founders of the breakfast food company, but why let that fact interfere with a good headline?

Chief of Detectives Burton finished her quick read of the morning tabloid, as her staff filed into the incident room to be briefed on the case. The whiteboard, heavy with photos from the crime scene, only featured two individuals: dead Denis and Erdal Tabak. The investigation had a long way to go.

"Listen up, everybody. We have a murder with no witnesses, but there must be someone who can background us. Kellogg didn't work alone. Get out there and find his associates. Particularly anyone connected with the pig pen visual. We could be looking at one of our own. Don't let this cloud your judgement. In the meantime, I want to introduce you to Kirstie Shilton. Kirstie is a profiler with serial killer experience, having previously provided valuable intel in the capture of mass murderer Weet Bixby."

"Thanks Jill. Now, first of all, we are jumping at straws by labelling this a serial killing. Having said that, I do see worrying trigger points. The perpetrator has made quite a production of the slaying and gone out of his way to demonstrate his wrath. He wants us to sit up and take notice and is comfortable in the limelight. The saturation exposure by the media will only encourage him.

He might be deranged, but he's not stupid. The guy is also well-read. How many crazies put a punctuation point in their demented scribble? Talk to the street artists and advise them to keep a low profile. One of them may be next."

The voice that came from behind one of the filing cabinets was the youngest member of the squad, Julie McHarg.

"Why do you say male? Is it possible the perp is a woman?"

Kirstie was ready for this question, a perennial query.

"Physically, it would be difficult. Spearing the chap and then lifting him onto the door would take some strength. I wouldn't discount a number of people being capable. Perhaps some art lovers from the Richmond precinct?"

This joke didn't go over too well, as the prospect of a police perp was real, and most of the people in that room didn't know how they would react if this situation became reality. Kirstie gave everyone a quick smile and sought the security of the side door.

If he had been aware that such a person existed, Bill Burton would have enjoyed the cut and thrust between himself and Ms. Shilton, the profiler. As it was, he was pleased he had outwitted his latest protagonist, the hapless artist, Denis, the menace, Kellogg. Once the vindictive vigilante discovered that the so-called creative genius always consumed a lamb shashlik before each of his sessions, tracking him down proved no problem.

Definitive Denis had been interviewed in one of the Sunday mags, in which he declared his love for Turkish food. The stalker patrolled a few selected restaurants, and it was only a matter of time before the fellow turned up at one of them with some of his followers. The rest proved easy. But, what of those who would take him down? He would relish the opportunity to lock horns with his sister, and he knew she would be gobsmacked if she discovered the truth. Not that she ever would.

The first break in the case was down to the youngster, Julie, who tracked down Kellogg's two compatriots. They opened up as to what happened on that fateful morning when their friend had been done in. Jill and her comrades in the squad room listened, transfixed, as the young detective repeated what she had been told.

"The artist and his friends were aware of the anti-graffiti crusader patrolling the streets at night. They would pick up on the muffled sound of the world's largest vibrator, and hide wherever they could. The look outs often spotted him, and the best description available is medium height and wearing black leather. Not unusual for a bikie. The classic machine was also black.

At around 3 a.m. on the morning of the crime, the soon-to-be victim told his pals to go home. He would finish the paint job and then kip at

HORROR

the granny flat behind the Turkish café. The owner had given him the key, to use whenever he wished. Evidently, since he was busted on those prostitution charges, Mr. Tabak no longer rented out the two-room bedsit."

"Thanks, Julie," said her beaming boss, chuffed that the minute miss had gazumped the males in her department. Nevertheless, they were a team with a lot of work to do.

"So, we now have a description to go on, no matter how vague. Perhaps the night rider isn't our perp, but he or she needs to be brought in for questioning. I'm going to set up a roster for a twenty-four-hour watch on that particular part of town. Sorry, folks! All leave is cancelled until we get a result."

"Why Richmond?" asked Ken Ferguson, as he poured his homicide boss a stiff drink, to celebrate the end of a long day.

"There is plenty of industry in a concentrated area, so that means many walls. The graffiti artists love it. Also, the factories all close down at night, reducing the risk of interference, until recently. The lone bikie has been known to try to run them down, but, up until now, there has been no real physical violence."

Ferguson was happy to see something positive happening, because he dearly wanted an early success for his upgraded department. He put his reputation on the line for his protégé and, as there had been some opposition to his task force recommendations, the knives were out.

Later that evening, the knives were still out. The Burtons had chosen the Ming Palace for their periodical catch-up, both being proficient with chopsticks. The young one waited until they finished their dumplings, before breaching the subject uppermost on her mind.

"Billy, we've had a break in the spear murder case."

"Ahhhh, the cereal killer! Very clever, those media chaps with their headlines. Does this mean you're going to arrest Uncle Toby Oates?"

"Come on. You know you can't say that. Uncle Toby is a valued member of our indigenous community. The man is going to provide the "Welcome to Country" for the forthcoming Commonwealth Games."

"Of course he is," said the man who loved to goad his sister on her politically correct views, although he suspected they were moulded by prissy policy from Spring Street. "So, what is the break in the case?"

"Well, we have eyewitnesses who can identify a lone rider, who patrols the area at night. He rides a Harley."

"I ride a Harley. It could be me."

"I don't think so, brother. The witnesses say he is a cross between Chris Hemsworth and David Beckham, with a fierce temper. You're such a sweetie."

Jill had no idea why she decided to embellish the truth. It was probably an automatic response. Her training supervisor repeatedly advised her to always keep something back to confuse the felons. Not that she would categorise her bro in this way.

"I would value your opinion, given that you still mix with the tearaways on two wheels. Can you ask around the leather-clad community? The person we're after could be one of our own. It's a sensitive issue at HQ."

This last statement hung in the air, as the siblings nibbled away on their food, but the question needed to be asked. Who was more sensitive than the psychotic predator with the Sichuan King Prawn between his chopsticks? Bill Burton, in the last twelve months, had supported Afghans, Argentinians, Africans and the American Indians. The activist even signed a petition to replace the Mount Rushmore presidents with Cochise, Crazy Horse, Geronimo, and Sitting Bull. There are four bastions of bestiality for you and the ingredients for a classic movie to surpass Marvel's Avengers.

When Bill arrived home, he may have tried to tabulate how many killings he needed before they made a movie of his exploits. Kirstie the shrink included "Delusions of Grandeur" as part of her grab bag of analytical symptoms. Half the division heads at HQ would fit that category. The man with a spear had now become the man without fear. Fortified by his fame, he wanted more. Bring on the next degenerate.

A creative person seldom revisits their past successes, which is why Jill's Johnnies had no luck with their Richmond patrols. The local precinct captain, Dusty Barton, bemoaned the fact that his overtime costs soared with no result to show for it. With all the publicity, the super-spreaders with the spray cans had gone to ground, and one wondered whether the lack of a target would satisfy the night rider's appetite for blood, now quite overwhelming. This is when the tattoo generation displayed their ink.

Not the Comancheros or the badass Hells Angels. It was the girls in the ladies' football competition. You would have thought a former executive of "Gay Day" might have given them some slack, the participants being mostly feminists in the LGBTQ community. No sir. Nobody hated tattoos like he did.

Was he up to slugging it out with footballers? Good question because some of these dames were big units. Thankfully, he didn't need to. A far more expedient means of validating his vengeance presented itself.

The Tits and Tatts Society was a social group that met once a month at the Freezer Room in the Vodka Commissar, a large drinking establishment at the heresy end of Chapel Street. The secretary of said society accepted Bill's membership application as Billie B, Qantas flight attendant. Should the truth be known, he enjoyed coming out in drag and was sure he would fit in admirably at the forthcoming mid-year social. Naturally, the peripatetic policeman did a reccy on the premises and discovered the place to be a firetrap—absolutely perfect for what he had in mind.

First-timers arriving at Vodka Commissar would soon realise all the ice wasn't delivered to the Freezer Room. The hotel was a pleasure palace, and many of the customers appeared stoned, although well cordoned off by the armed security guards, a hedge against any visit from the law. The Freezer Room advertised itself as cold and carefree, and something like 300 revellers regularly designated it as the coolest spot in town, if they could get in. Getting out was also a problem. How much did the owners slip the building inspector? The space only incorporated one entrance/exit, and bouncing Billy padlocked the door before moving on to the boiler room, where management manipulated the temperature of all areas of the hotel. The maniac intended to freeze everyone to death.

The intruder was challenged by security staff just as he opened the boiler room door, giving him no other option but to go for the colt revolver in his purse. Yes, the nearest guard saw it emerge but too late. He took two slugs in the stomach. Somebody screamed, and another guard fired back. All of a sudden, a surge of customers spewed out into the street, and a shooting match started outside the boiler room. At least a dozen patrons' dialled emergency as Billie B locked himself in with all the plant equipment and turned the aircon temperature in the Freezer Room to twenty below.

Some fifty metres down the road, the fiend's sister was breaking bread with her co-worker Julie McHarg. They liked the energy and vitality of Chapel Street and felt relaxed in their downtime, being out of their work clothes. Their phones both went off, seconds after the commotion intensified at the Vodka Commissar.

The detectives rushed into the hotel with their guns drawn and were confronted by two door bitches, who didn't know who they were. One of them reached for the stiletto in her stocking and plunged the dagger into Jill's abdomen.

Her gun clattered to the ground, and she gagged, as blood spurted out and gushed over her Burberry cashmere poncho. Seeing her partner slowly drop to the floor, Julie reacted automatically. She shot the blonde with the knife and, for good measure, the other bitch. This was no time to ask questions.

Was there chaos all around her? You bet your sweet bippy there was. The ice maidens, who were still cool but no longer carefree, kept hammering on the door, as the temperature dropped alarmingly. The guards feverishly attacked the boiler room door with an axe, and God help the person inside, currently attending to his make-up. Bill knew the brutes on the other side of the door all carried guns and would use them. He wanted to look his best. As a final act of defiance, he turned the temperature down from twenty below to thirty below.

The drama played out as you might expect. Once the locks were broken, the door caved in and four security guards pumped a total of twenty-five bullets into the helpless queen, slumped over the air conditioning unit. There was an attempt at a royal wave, but it didn't come to much.

Bill Burton died at 1.15 a.m. and his twin sister twelve minutes after that. They both lived on this planet for exactly the same amount of time, which didn't surprise those people who swim in gene pools. All the partygoers survived, but, once they thawed out, most of them failed to renew their membership to TATS. Julie McHarg found herself on the end of a sermon from Ken Ferguson, devastated that he had lost his favourite detective. In the space of a month, the young woman had investigated two cold cases, but it would be just the start of a brilliant career.

The lady's ascent up the greasy pole proved to be spectacular, considering her sex. It was never easy being female in the organisation she worked for, but because she contributed to so many successful prosecutions, there was no alternative but to promote her. The former homicide elf ended up as deputy commissioner, and only retired because of her age. Even today, some of her accomplishments are still talked about, colloquially called Jules' Rules.

Harmony and synchronisation are everything in this world we live in, and don't let anyone tell you anything different. Not a day goes by when we don't read the news and wonder. Even the participants involved in this traumatic event had to share the headlines with a sporting announcement—the Australian cricket side being declared the best dressed team in the world. Their captain, Mark Taylor from Wagga Wagga, would accept the trophy.

HOLLYWOOD

The Investigation

In an effort to restrict the fabrication of fantasy to acceptable levels, covert scrutineers throughout the land monitor those who would challenge the parameters of poetic licence. Few people would know this, I'm sure of it. Hollywood's studios with their superheroes and imaginative scribes are always under the microscope.

It is rare for a greenhorn journalist from the Midwest of America to walk into a high-profile job with a big city media outlet, but Clark Kent managed same on the basis of one interview with the editor, Perry White. Need I say the other two applicants were black?

Two weeks into Kent's tenure and the editor discussed the new appointment with his gun reporter Lois Lane. The new age woman, in no way critical of the new man, seemed mystified by some of his habits.

"He's got a perfectly functional telephone on his desk, but I keep seeing him in that call box down by the deli."

"You think that's strange," said the man who employed him. "He's thirty-one years of age and not married. Was he alone in the box?"

Lois could have taken umbrage at such a remark, also being thirty-one and unmarried. For a woman, this was the stuff of rumour and insinuation. Kent's asexual demeanour would become a matter of curiosity at a later date, but, in the meantime, the two observers would withhold their judgement until the man had a chance to prove himself. It is a hard road to success in the newspaper business, but with Ms. Lane as his mentor, the fellow would be given every opportunity.

By coincidence, that telephone facility by the deli had sparked interest down at police headquarters. Officers on the beat had reported coming across homeless people wearing ties and classic business suits with designer labels. They all claimed they had found the clothing on the floor of a phone booth.

The first report of a person flying across the sky in his underwear came the morning after Independence Day celebrations, so authorities dismissed it as a hangover hallucination. Then there was the lass tied to the railway tracks in Kansas. Was it the Atchison, Topeka, or Santa Fe locomotive which Superman stopped with his bare hands? Once again, officialdom, not wanting to encourage speculation, denounced the incident as an office Christmas party gone wrong.

Talk of a superman was nothing new. In the early days of Metropolis, Mayor Jimmy Talker told everyone he could do just about anything and people believed him. However, he couldn't fly, and this guy in his underpants broke the sound barrier regularly. Of course, the inability of friends and acquaintances to see past his thin disguise proved a damning denunciation, according to those conducting the investigation. Perry White, Lois Lane, and Jimmy Olsen must have all been idiots, because Clark Kent removed his glasses for cleaning on numerous occasions. How could they not recognise the Man of Steel?

The criticism didn't stop with the good guys. Investigators found that the importation of kryptonite into the country was a blatant breach of government protocol, with no attempt made to acquire an import licence. The studio blamed one of the executive producers, who thought his position to be a tax-sensitive one. He didn't think he had to actually do anything.

The officials involved in this type of public hearing are usually sticklers for authenticity and this enquiry proved no different. The representative from DC Comics looked decidedly uncomfortable as he was grilled from pillar to post by Chairman Elliott Bentwood.

"We notice with some gratification that your protagonist presents each morning, fresh and well-scrubbed. Nevertheless, after having made submissions to the Real Estate Commission and the Fair Rents Board, we came to the conclusion that the gentleman has no fixed abode. Can you explain this, sir?"

"Well, er, ahhhh ... there is the place in the North Pole," stammered the flummoxed minion, fielding the kind of bombastic barrage which should have been taken on by somebody beyond his pay grade. Stoically, he stood firm, aground in a sea of anguish, sweating profusely. You might say he was taking on water at an alarming rate.

"Did you say the North Pole?" asked the man spearheading the interrogation.

"Well, yes, I did. Only a small cave, but Superman uses it as a sort of weekend retreat. I don't think he takes women there or anything like that. The fellow is a very moral person."

"I'm sure he is," commented Elliott Bentwood, who was not really sure at all. "You're not telling me the chap commutes to the Daily Planet every day from the North Pole, are you? Absolutely preposterous! What is the flying time for a trip like that?"

The street-fighter in the hot seat was saved by a lunch break. One thing patently obvious in this morning session of investigation was the bent of the committee to find fault with this long-running favourite character, beloved by youngsters the world over. For some time, rumours circulated that snotty-nosed officials were contemptuous of the abundance of too many superheroes and were advocating a good solid pruning. But at what cost? Why try to sanitise the brand by getting rid of the pioneers, if this was their intention?

Observers with much to lose included stakeholder Georgia Parkway, a granddaughter of Lois Lane. She took lunch with her friend Della Street III, nervous because of her commitment to various Perry Mason productions—another long-standing franchise in the cross-hairs.

"These people are out to get us," said Georgia, as she stabbed at a piece of sushi with her chopstick. "Sure, Superman hasn't changed his underwear for eighty years, but that doesn't mean he's not pleasant to be around. Modern day deodorants are first class. Am I right?"

Della agreed with her pal, which she often did, but she did see problems arising in the afternoon session.

"The committee is bound to want to discuss paternity matters. I'm quite sure Supergirl and Superboy are illegitimate, and that supposed wedding between your man and Wonder Woman was surely a sham."

"Are you sure you don't mean 'Shazam?' He used to be Captain Marvel and look what happened to him—another golden oldie rebadged for the benefit of the current generation. Where will it end?"

The end would be that very afternoon in one of the courtrooms built by Universal Studios, which is where the interrogators conducted proceedings. Della worried about her friend and her royalties, should they rescind current arrangements. She had knowledge of the trials and tribulations of the cast of Perry Mason, when they closed down their television series. Public prosecutor Hamilton Burger ended up as a branch manager for McDonalds, and Paul Drake could only find work on a poultry farm north of L.A. There is nothing wrong with these jobs, but it's not show business is it?

Surprisingly, those at the high table wanted to talk about income streams. George Reeves and Christopher Reeve had gone to God, but their residuals were collected by a medium, Madam Olga. Olga claimed to be in touch with both gentlemen on the other side, and submitted that they appeared happy for her to manage their money. She arrived at the courtroom in a Ferrari.

Also in the Lord's garden were the writer/artist team who started it all: Jerry Siegel and Joe Shuster. Sadly, they sold their rights to DC Comics for next to nothing at a time when most people had nothing. Because of a public backlash, the creators were provided with a minor royalty provision, but this didn't preclude them from criticism; the moral majority were incensed with the possibility and probability of Superman's X-ray vision being used for lewd behaviour. The colour of Lois Lane's undies was her concern and only shared with the producer and close friends. In recent times, behavioural issues plagued movie sets on many levels, and the judgement panel on this witch hunt included some ferocious females.

Georgia wasn't fussed about Jane Honda, because her intimate gear was see-through, anyway. Holly Golly and Prudence Gosh, on the other hand, were professional virgins with no known experience involving a six-foot-two hulk of any description. Secretly they might well enjoy being ravaged by such a man, but publicly they gave their all for the sisterhood. Prudish Pru cast the first stone.

"Does anyone in this chamber recall any sexual advances being perpetuated by the Last Son of Krypton, be they male or female?"

A hand popped up at the back of the room, and the chair recognised a little old lady called Modesty, who definitely looked on the wrong side of sixty.

"Superman had his way with me every night for a number of weeks. I remember it well."

"Can you tell us all, madam, where this took place?"

"Certainly I can. In my apartment, in my bed."

"My God," exclaimed the prickly princess, as she searched the faces of her fellow committee members for traces of like-minded outrage. Totally enthralled with the lady's story, they all hoped the finale would be worth waiting for.

"We don't wish to prolong what must be a distressing situation for you, but can you tell me how long this vile molestation lasted?"

Although most of the folks in the room were breathing hard, or whispering among themselves, they all heard the reply, delivered resolutely in her phlegmatic manner.

"It always finished when I woke up."

Bob Hope would have paid big money for the laughter that erupted on the back of this comment. Chairman Bentwood doubled over with his mirth spasms, and Della Street clapped enthusiastically. It meant the end for Prudence Gosh and all the harassment innuendo she may have stored up. In fact, it was pretty much the end of the hearing. One last submission came from a ten-year-old boy. He waxed lyrical about his favourite superhero, who could fly faster than a speeding bullet and jump tall buildings in a single bound. That bit about truth, justice, and the American way could have been the clincher. Even though the speech had probably been written by the boy's father, those at the table of arbitration crossed their hearts and signed off on the licence renewal.

Somebody noticed Jane Honda shed a tear; or was she acting?

Hands Across The Water

He came from the Land of Oz and ingratiated himself with the U.S. president. Determined gumshoe Paddy Pest thwarted three assassination attempts on Gus Snoodle's life and, in so doing, acquired an enviable reputation in Washington. He secured a Green Card and the eternal gratitude of the Republican Party. Back home, the local authorities celebrated because the more time he spent out of their country, the better they liked it. Patrick Pesticide could screw up big time and often did.

His relationship with intelligence agent Stormy Weathers was also cause for concern. ASIO didn't employ a lot of exceptional spies but this one excelled on many fronts. To keep her happy, the spymasters farmed out a few jobs to the little man with the giant ego.

The couple travelled to Los Angeles for the annual CIA awards night. The Criminal Investigators Award recognised those unsung heroes whose investigative work transcended all others. Stormy was up for "Spy of the Year," and her associate rated neck and neck with Maxwell Smart for "Most Inept Secret Agent on the Planet."

It would only be a matter of time before these two acclaimed protagonists came face to face. The chick magnet known as Eighty-Six introduced his fiancée to the Aussie pair.

"Paddy, Stormy, I'd like you to meet Ninety-Nine. We're getting married in the fall."

"How nice," replied Paddy, who often changed the subject when marriage came into the conversation. In contrast, his lady friend tended to gush over the smallest details.

"Will it be a church wedding? I love church weddings."

Smart and Pest looked at each other in frustration, and immediately retired to the bar. Fifteen minutes later they were firm friends, and this is when Max made his surprising offer, an offer he was not authorized to make.

"My controller has asked me to put together a team for a super-secret investigation. He's also in town, and we're being briefed tomorrow. I would love you and Stormy to join the unit and give us an overseas perspective."

The main man expected his underling to recruit a squad from existing Control employees, but, as the Aussie mingled with Washington heavyweights, he welcomed him to Spy City. Nobody anticipated the crime to be so heinous.

"Somebody has kidnapped Homer Simpson. And it's not Frank Grimes."

Who represents the typical American psyche more than Homer Simpson? He is insensitive, intolerant, insulting, and in denial. Should he disappear from the menu of daily discussion, life may cease to exist as we know it. For this reason, all possible resources would be made available to those brave men and women who would be resolute in the pursuit of these fiendish transgressors. A small core of Control agents, aided and abetted by their courageous cousins from the colonies, would endeavour to return the American way of life back to normality.

This was the mission statement emanating from Control headquarters. Inside the chief's office, they were getting straight down to business.

"This sounds like a KAOS plot to me," said Smart, but pretty much everything sounded like a KAOS plot to Max. To say he was fixated on this international organisation of evil is an understatement. Jealousy may have been the reason, as his counterpart and arch-enemy Siegfried often boasted about his superior pay packet and benefits, which were substantial for a director of personnel.

Deputy Chief Max enjoyed senior status, and would likely maintain this position, irrespective of how many screw-ups he participated in. The alternative was Agent Larabee and nobody wanted that.

"I don't know, Maxwell." This comment came from Ms. Weathers, who surprised all by venturing into the discussion so soon after her introduction. Did the alert observer detect raised eyebrows from the other woman in the room? One could almost feel the tension. Not Stormy, of course. She just prattled on, regardless.

"If your KAOS friend wanted to kidnap a significant person, he would settle on Lisa. She's far more intelligent and might be able to help KAOS with their decision-making."

"Or Marge," suggested Ninety-Nine, who didn't want to be left out of any brain-storming moments. "She would be comfortable with any hair-raising scheme that Count Siegfried conjured up."

The chief noticed Paddy shaking his head. Such confidence! He needed to know more.

"You obviously don't agree, Mr. Pest. What is your view? We'd all like to hear it."

The wonder from Down Under smiled, as he often did. Here he was in the engine room of America's most clandestine intelligence organisation, and they were turning to him for an educated opinion. Not that he should make much of it. Next in line came Fang, the dog. The K9 division boasted more successful operations than anyone.

"KAOS are looking to improve their operating task force, and they can extract a substantial ransom from the Duff Brewery for Homer. These people can't afford their favourite spruiker to be out of the bar for too long. Otherwise, their sales will plummet. Am I the only person thinking this way?"

All this made sense to the chief and that's all that mattered. He let them all loose and headed for his prayer mat. In the spirit of global brotherhood, Max offered his new-found friends succour and accommodation at his lodgings, but it took a while for the newcomers to become acquainted with the various gadgets in the L.A. safe house. Paddy was particularly taken with the fellow's shoe phone. He just had to acquire one of those.

Dangerous, dicey, dodgy, death defying

Catching a cab in the City of Angels is all of that, but the crime-fighters needed to cross town before the television people came online with their afternoon entertainment options. If word got out that Homer Simpson would not be appearing, Little America would be revolting. They were bad enough already.

"Paaadeeeee!" screamed Stormy, as one underage urchin ran past her with intent. "Did you see that? The little shit put his hand up my dress."

Patrick Pesticide had contemplated this kind of obscene act when he was a tyke, but he never possessed the nerve. Now he decided to wallow in his "holier than thou" attitude.

"I did suggest that a chastity belt would be a wise investment. I'm sure the agency would have paid for it," murmured the possessive companion. Recently, the durable duo participated in a Commonwealth operation with James Bond, and there might have been some hanky-panky. Stormy denied it.

On arrival at the Fox studios, Max and Ninety-Nine began to interview the performers, while the Aussie pair sought out the producer of the hit series—not a happy man.

"Where is our goddamn star? We've exhausted all our back episodes, and we need him back on the box. So does his wife."

"Does she fear for his life?" asked Stormy, once again being prepared to share the pain with her female compatriots, even though she had never met Marg Simpson.

"Not at all. The residuals dried up, and she wants to put Lisa through a double degree at Berkeley. She also needs some readies to release Bart from reform school."

While this conversation was taking place, Max discovered that filming had stopped due to a union demarcation dispute. Some clown wanted all the funny lines and, yes, his name was Krusty. These kinds of clashes are grist to the mill for the seasoned performer, but cartoon actors never know when to stop. Krusty could well have been the one to abduct Homer. He came across as a devious kind of character.

When the deputy chief of Control introduced himself, the jester viewed him with disdain. However, his eyes lit up when Ninety-Nine arrived on the scene. Who could resist a skirt of that calibre?

"Hi there, sweet chops. Are you with this dude? I can't believe he's a secret agent; he looks more like a greeting card salesman to me."

As this was actually Max's official cover, you had to hand it to the comedian to get it right. If only Agent 86 could get it right. He felt comfortable with Germans, Chinese felons like "The Claw" and other despicable human beings, but cartoon characters had him bemused and bewildered. Nevertheless, he probed deeply and directly, as he always did.

"We're investigating the disappearance of Homer Simpson," said Max, as he looked the overconfident comic squarely in the face. "We've heard about your differences. Artistic differences, perhaps?"

"Sure, I admit it," replied the joker with the bad haircut, now less animated. "But I wouldn't hurt the fellow, yet someone did. I saw the broken door to his dressing room and the guard in agony."

"He was man-handled and spirited away from his quarters?" exclaimed Ninety-Nine, hoping to obtain an accurate account from an eyewitness.

"You can't say that, miss. I believe person-handled is the correct expression."

Allowing for this inexcusable lapse of political correctness, the truth had surfaced and the Springfield breadwinner really had been kidnapped. Now Max knew exactly where to go with his inquiries.

"Tell me, did you see the abductors, and were they wearing ABC or NBC overalls? Some people will do anything for ratings."

The helping hand

Publicising a kidnap is never a smart idea. It encourages any number of demands from any number of crazy people. The first one came through to the production company within 12 hours of the snatch.

"We've got Homer Simpson, and if you want him back it will cost you 5 million large—cash money, no bitcoins."

Sitting behind a recording device in the boardroom was the hope of a nation. Unknown to Max and Ninety-Nine, the production company hired legendary Hawaiian investigator Harry Hoo to look into Homer's disappearance. The islander was on friendly terms with the agents of Control, but Fox didn't want them to join forces in case Smart's ineptitude ran off on their man.

However, his mate from the sunshine state, always keen to touch base with old pals, caught up with the couple and their two friends in the studio canteen.

HOLLYWOOD

"Moment please. Am I meeting illustrious investigator Maxwell Smart and his beautiful partner Ninety-Nine?"

"Get out of here," screamed Max, "Look honey, it's Harry Hoo. Can you believe it?"

After introductions, the inscrutable Chinaman joined the happy group, at least, happy for now. They were not aware they would all be working the same case.

"What are you doing in LA?" asked Control's man on a mission. "No, don't tell me. There are two possibilities. Well, er, ah...perhaps you'd better tell me."

"Pleased to do so, my friend. I investigate whereabouts of international icon, beloved by many—philosopher, gourmand, beverage tester and family man."

Paddy Pest came to the conclusion that if he wasn't talking about Jimmy Hoffa, it had to be Homer Simpson, and the production company was being devious. All the sleuths in the canteen now knew where they stood, with no hard feelings. They would go their own way and report to the Control boffins later in the week. The Fox people had become resigned to the fact that Harry from Hawaii was now under government influence.

Over the following few days, the usual suspects were interviewed including Mr. Burns, Principal Skinner, Moe Szyslak and Rabbi Hyman Krustofsky. The chief welcomed all the investigators to his office to submit their reports. He provided orange juice for every-one.

"Listen-up people. The president is concerned there hasn't been a development in this case. If his grandchildren discover that Homer is missing, all hell will break loose. I'm recording each of your submissions, so who's on first?"

"Sorry about that, Chief," said Max, "but I'm on first. Hoo's on second and Paddy will finish, as he isn't used to the Cone of Silence."

"Oh no, not the Cone of Silence." This response emanated from everybody.

Agent Smart's dedication to security was, for the most part, applauded and encouraged by all staff members, but whoever came up with this useless echo bubble should be certified. Notwithstanding this, they all huddled under the bulletproof glass overcoat and made their submissions, although Stormy announced that she would sit this one out. She knew Paddy often broke wind in a confined space.

Max would be the first to submit his findings, but the chief, being a stickler for protocol, needed to dispense with convention, before continuing.

"What about the family and close relatives? Do they understand the circumstances of the situation?"

This was one for Agent Larabee, and he reported that he had ticked all the boxes.

"Sure thing, Chief. The immediate family are concerned, while Jessica and O J couldn't care less."

As Larabee didn't appear as if he would be extending his testimony, Max sipped on his juice, before providing a breakthrough with his opening remarks.

"At approximately two fifteen in the afternoon, the daytime guard outside Homer's dressing room was assaulted from behind. He saw no-one. A loud noise, attributed to the destruction of the door, was heard in the make-up room, some fifty yards away.

Two minutes later in an alley by the stage door, a rather stout person with a white beard was seen carrying a protesting individual under his arm. They boarded a conveyance that could only be described as a sleigh. A bystander testified that the abduction was carried out by Santa Claus."

"Oh Max," interrupted his fiancée. "What a marvellous breakthrough. How old was the bystander?"

"The witness claimed to be seven years of age, Ninety-Nine."

"You are aware, Max," said the chief, "that it hasn't snowed in Los Angeles in 200 years. And a Christmas conveyance in June?"

Wanting to relieve his friend of the embarrassment suffered by being chastised by the boss, Harry Hoo interrupted with his assessment and provided his pal with a modicum of support, no matter how ludicrous.

"There are two possibilities. Vehicle is rickshaw from Chinatown; similar to sleigh. Kidnapper is Mandarin madman with young chil-ren. Second possibility...No kidnap. Mr. Simpson run off with cartoon lady with big bazookas."

Given the fact that Homer proclaimed to be a family man, this latter judgment seemed highly unlikely and, therefore, the resources of the intelligence community had come up with very little. Somewhat embarrassing, one would have thought.

Although his head ached from the echo bombs under the Cone of Silence, Paddy Pest became the pragmatic voice of reason in a room overwhelmingly infected by fantasy and imagination. All this without any help from his offsider, currently attending to her nails.

"I think Homer has gone swimming with concrete boots."

This was a comment that no-one wanted to hear, so they lifted the Cone of Silence. Stormy Weathers looked up from her nail polish.

"You don't mean the Mafia?"

"I do," uttered Paddy in his most serious voice. The discount detective had locked horns with these Italian thugs on numerous occasions, on several continents.

The "Cosa Nostra" didn't handle criticism well, and the Simpson scriptwriters often resorted to ugly satire in order to make their point. According to Pest, Al Mascarpone, the big cheese in this town, should have been in the frame for the abduction.

At the mention of his name, Fang from K9 division growled aggressively. No love lost there, and they had history. In assessing the dog's reaction, Paddy was glad the mutt with menace was on their side. He seemed to be a formidable pooch.

Many people believe the U.S. Mafia only operates out of New York, Chicago or Las Vegas. Nothing could be further from the truth. There are many Italians living in the greater Los Angeles area, but most of them have changed their names in the hope of a Hollywood contract. Some are heavily involved in production. One of the biggest animation studios around is ScreamWorks, where intimidation and coercion go hand in hand with their job overtures. Is it possible Homer was made an offer he couldn't refuse?

Two days after the meeting at the Control office, Lisa Simpson fronted the media and denounced the kidnappers for their actions, at the same time pleading for the safe return of her beloved father. Her pain and anguish was obvious to all who watched the prime-time address, and brought an instant worldwide response from sympathetic parents, including the presidents of China and Russia. Both of these countries retained a much-feared "Black

Ops" team, either of which could be responsible for the felony. Of the two possibilities, Harry Hoo was rooting for the Soviet Union.

"Mr. Simpson have noticeable five p.m. shadow. Vould make good Vladimir for chil-ren's program."

Given that the investigators had little else to go on, they probed the possibility of a soviet spy with big knockers, which would integrate both of Harry Hoo's think-tank scenarios. Such a woman worked at the Russian Embassy and Maxwell Smart was granted an interview. Katerina Lubyanka, a KGB cypher clerk, primed her nipple camera, and prepared for the meeting. She was surprised at the naïve nature of Max's first question.

"I seem to detect a foreign accent. Our records have you down as an UCLA graduate."

"I am from Ukraine, Mr. Smart. You have been to Kiev, yes?"

"Well, not really, although I do like their chicken. Is this the region where you come from?"

The control agent's cover as a newspaper reporter had not deceived the embassy people, but they always wanted to assess the quality of the opposition, so their best female spy was more than happy to trade barbs with the famous Maxwell Smart.

"I think you confuse me with Chicken Man. I am red sparrow from whore school in Putingrad. As part of tuition, we are entitled to breast implants. Vould you like some Vodka and Borsht? If you stay for dinner, we 'ave Poison du Jour."

Max didn't stay for dinner because he knew he wouldn't be getting fish of the day. Neither did he think this Kat with claws was involved in the kidnap of Homer. The fellow might be well-read in Athens but surely not well-red in Moscow? Russia didn't approve of all homo-sapiens.

The conspiracy theories!

The first sighting of the missing man occurred at a McDonald's outlet in Glendale, which is where ScreamWorks had their studios. Certainly, a major cause of conjecture. Another conspiracy theory concerned a North Pole vendetta against Disney, which owns 20th Century Fox Television.

In their 1994 movie, "The Santa Claus," Disney may not have disbursed royalties to the old guy with the white beard. Let's face it. The reindeer need to be fed with more than snow and ice.

Every kidnapping has its red herrings, including the previously mentioned ransom demand, instigated by an opportunist. In this instance, the fool used his own phone, and the police quickly apprehended him. The judge decreed that he be incarcerated in the "Dumb & Dumber" section at San Quentin Prison.

With not a lot happening, the L.A. Police Commissioner offered to bring in Detective Axel Foley from Detroit, but it would not have looked good if their screw-up made Control's screw-ups look bad. That's when the package arrived at the safe house on Hollywood and Vine. The parcel contained Homer Simpson's wedding ring, which, it turned out, was radioactive. They even put Fang in a HazMat suit.

The ring was significant, as kidnappers usually send a finger rather than a wedding band. Did this mean someone wished to identify love and marriage as the key indicator of this abduction, if, in fact, it was an abduction? Could an emotionally unhinged Homer be part of the plot? Did he feel mistrusted, marginalized, manipulated, and emasculated? Was he mentally moribund? Maxwell Smart had his suspicions.

"I think he's in this with Santa Claus. What do you think Ninety-Nine?"

"Well, it could be a cry from the heart. Or sexual harassment! You don't have to be Weinstein to consider that."

Agent 13, a qualified marriage guidance councillor, emerged as the go-to man in this situation, but he was presently holed-up in a rubbish bin at LAX. Most people would presume he leads a lonely life, working in washing machines, sewers, fire hydrants and cigarette dispensers, but the chap is happily married with five kids and is the obvious choice for marital advice.

At the nearby Hollywood Burbank airfield, a World War II bi-plane was spotted on the tarmac, fuelling speculation that an attack on Disneyland might be imminent. In fact, it had been hired by Paddy and Stormy to search for the missing man. And they got lucky.

Having asked the pilot to perform a low sweep over Amalfi Drive, they discovered a portly fellow, looking decidedly yellow, and sunbaking by a large swimming pool. Could you believe it? The home was owned by Weaven Kneelberg, a major shareholder in ScreamWorks Animation.

On the second sweep, Paddy focused his binoculars on two things: the bar fridge full of Duff beer and the unsigned contract on the table next to Homer's sun lounge.

Although Weaven Kneelberg liked to stay out of the limelight, he was very much the money and muscle behind ScreamWorks, and the power behind the phone. His employment proposal, on the back of the kidnap, may just have been a promise made to a man easily swayed by envy, lust, and greed.

Once Paddy had pinpointed the superstar's whereabouts, the law and the lawyers took over. They arrived at the Amalfi Drive property before the man could sign the contract and discovered a prop from *Star Wars* in the garage, which looked like a sleigh. Ninety-Nine then appeared and escorted the recalcitrant home to his loving wife and family.

Gracie Films proved to be extremely grateful, and provided Paddy, Stormy and Harry Hoo with a generous stipend. Unfortunately, Max and Ninety-Nine were on government wages and unable to participate in gratuitous rewards. This situation was not improved when the boasting call from Siegfried came through. All KAOS agents now received a productivity bonus and paid maternity leave. Could you believe it?

Nevertheless, Maxwell Smart is and would be a Control agent for life, and loving it.

Maxwell Smart and Paddy Pest

Sam Spade Down Under

It was a few minutes after the Cinderella hour on a black evening in May, and downtown Caulfield seemed the wrong place to be. Out of the night, the muted sound of a magic flute cut into the foreboding silence like a fart at a chamber music recital. Immediately, I got the vibe and shifted my ride into overdrive. With dexterous skill, I wheeled the throbbing beast over the tram tracks and headed for the source of the syncopation.

The neon winked at me like a working girl on wages, and I could tell the place had style. I was drawn to it like a Kiwi to a dole queue.

"Good evening, sir. Welcome to Rix Bar. Tonight, we're featuring Tinsley Waterhouse Lounge Lizard."

For any self-respecting lush, the bar was a joy to behold. The establishment offered seven different varieties of whisky, and the barman was called George. It was probably his name. He picked me for a bourbon boy and, before I knew it, a double nip of Wild Turkey cradled in my vice-like grip. The guy on my left was drinking Champagne alone, and nobody cared. It was like the Red Eagle pub without any advertising people. I then observed that Mr. Moët was wearing odd socks.

I accept that I'm not the fashion police, but French bubbly and feuding footwear seemed a bit out of step. I decided to attempt knowledge gratification by a circuitous route. I introduced myself.

He claimed to be the resident piano player, and, surprisingly, he did look a bit like Liberace. When Tinsley finished his set, Oswald would step up and tickle the ivories for fifteen minutes. The chap wore odd socks to project his personality. The house supplied the Champagne.

My interest in the Rachmaninoff riff he was playing was hijacked by the familiar fragrance of a long-forgotten lavender bouquet, and the apparition that arrived brought with her the scent of a woman in control.

The sheer silk party dress she was almost wearing had to have cost twice my weekly earnings. Having spent the day at the races, last week's salary was now a distant memory.

Before I could explain about Flemington and the wet track, she was fathoms into a Fluffy Duck, at my expense. As my pinkies embarked on a voyage of discovery towards the intimate recesses of her inner thigh, I touched on the subject of the gigantic quadrella dividend and how I only picked three legs. As her thrusting kneecap buried itself into my unprotected groin with pinpoint accuracy, I realised I wouldn't be getting the fourth leg that night. Oswald, when he returned from his keyboard, noticed me doubled over and in pain—the smile on his face totally unwarranted.

"So, you met Testicular Tess. She never misses, does she? Can I interest you in an Alabama Slammer, or another Wild Turkey?"

At that moment, Ozzie and I became firm friends, and Rix Bar would be a place I frequented, as time went by. This had been my first solo Saturday night since my long-term relationship floundered amidst a flurry of emasculating denunciations. It's hard to bounce back from that kind of thing. Dames! Who needs 'em?

Fond memories can sometimes be forgotten if they are replaced with other fond memories, such as the celebration of Oz's birth.

The birthday boy received lots of socks and jocks, and we all gathered around the Werner upright to sing a few songs, after the other patrons had been pushed out the door at 3 a.m. The wallopers arrived at 4 a.m.

Could you believe it? A brothel complaining about the noise? One supposes the girls were jealous because we enjoyed ourselves more than they did. In those days, you could make a donation to the Police Benevolent Fund, and all your troubles would disappear. In fact, the boys in blue would sometimes stay for one or two.

A lot of people used Rix as a base for their business dealings. O.K., we're talking funny business, but as long as there is a cut for management, nobody's nose knows nothing. However, keeping schtum about the shenanigans associated with the bird—that was another matter.

"You're talking about the Lebanese Magpie."

"I am, indeed," I said to the stalwart on the stool by the window. This regular never said much, but he would listen to anything, even one of my stories.

Noel Faro, the Portuguese antique dealer, arrived one night, all dishevelled and flustered. The plump profiteer threw down three slammers before you could say Humphrey Bogart, and, as I recall, ordered three more. Figuring he might be buying, I gave the bar a fly. I was being optimistic. The man had arms like a crocodile.

"What's the matter, my friend? You look like you've seen a ghost. Did you drop one of your Fabergé eggs? Or is someone after your bacon?"

Counterfeit art is not uncommon business in this city, and selling forged masterpieces can sometimes lead to retribution and restitution. Most people counted their fingers after they shook hands with Noel. I didn't offer to help, but he understood I would be available if he managed to stump up a retainer. His return remarks did leave the door open to such a possibility but only in a vague kind of way.

"One understands your concern, Mr. Wade, and I will consider your services should matters deteriorate. Perhaps, for the moment, you could escort me to my car, on my departure. I am concerned for my safety."

"Hey, what's this Mr. Wade business? We've been friendly long enough for you to call me Ham. I'll be more than happy to walk you to the car park."

Yep, you heard it right. My name is Ham, short for Hamilton, my birthplace in Victoria, not New Zealand. A few years ago, I toyed with the idea of becoming an actor, but how would that ever work? Now, I'm a private eye, part-time of course, also pulling wages from a security firm, who benefit from my previous capability as a cop.

The walk to Faro's car proved tense, as we were spotted by two goons in unfashionable overcoats, possibly packing, and probably pissed off. The hard rain would not have improved their mood, as both of them tried to nestle beneath the same umbrella. After loading and despatching the antiquated gnome as quickly as possible, I headed in their direction. They turned on their heels and walked away, which surprised me. Did I look that tough?

Back among friends, I rearranged my damp clothing under the eye of Odd Socks Oswald. Having finished his set, he was about to be effusive.

HOLLYWOOD

"I'll bet the fat man told you about the wings of wealth? That's why he's been sweating like a wet potato. Didn't you notice?"

Ham Wade doesn't dig potatoes. If the man had been sweating like a pig, I would have picked up on it. Why folks like to pour their heart out to the piano player, I'll never understand, but this guy claimed to be an authority on everything from cotton buds to cannon balls. Mr. Flexible Fingers didn't wait to find out whether I would be happy to be part of the conversation. He told the story as if he had written it.

"About thirty years ago, this dude in Beirut stole a very expensive bejewelled effigy from their main museum, a Sardinian warbler. By the time the thief and his feathered friend arrived in Melbourne, it was a magpie, courtesy of a talented taxidermist. The immigrant, having been welcomed to this country on the back of the government's multicultural policy, settled in Collingwood.

Some folks recognise the Collingwood Magpies as the greatest Australian Rules football team ever, but our friend didn't comprehend this, favouring soccer, the world game."

I hated to interrupt a good yarn, but was this guy for real? In the time I had known Ozzie, he never once revealed himself as a storyteller. The fellow assured me this was a true tale and accepted my offer of another Champagne cocktail. I reminded the bartender of the house's commitment to cover the muso's costs. By now, half the room had become captivated by his story.

"Evidently, the jewels and precious stones attached to the Sardinian warbler were priceless, but Mr. Malouf didn't need the money. He wanted the fortune to be ready and waiting for his children when they grew up, so he hid their legacy in plain sight—mounting the Lebanese Magpie on a marble column in his front yard. All the people who passed his house thought him to be an avid football fan. In fact, once he learnt the fundamentals of the game, he became one, and polished the dust off the monument every Saturday before an important match."

How I regretted my part in the fat man's escape. I should have let the two hoods shoot him. Notwithstanding those ungracious thoughts, I needed enlightenment as to how he fitted into the fairy tale. Portugal is some distance from Lebanon, especially if you're winging it. Once again, I tuned-in to Ozzie's story.

"It didn't take long for the press to hear about this Saturday morning ritual, and once they discovered that polishing became a portent for winning, they screamed it from every masthead. On the eve of the 1960 Grand Final, the statue was stolen and Collingwood lost the match. This club appeared in eight more grand finals in the next thirty years and didn't win one. Malouf then died of food poisoning and the Lebanese Magpie faded into obscurity."

Was it the lateness of the hour, or the story without a punchline? The joint emptied like a Mexican bedpan, except for Ozzie, me, and George, the bored barman. How could I see it through? Why didn't I go home with Testicular Tess?

"The missing magpie resurfaced ten years later, when the water authority dredged the Yarra River. It was wrapped in a footballer's jock strap, and the taxidermy had withered in the water. Some sapphires and emeralds had become visible, and the dredging company onsold the prize to a local trader. That's when the murders started."

Oh, God! It's the start not the end. Oz looked at me as if he couldn't understand why I wasn't enthralled. The only person on overtime produced another round, and we rejoined the tiresome train ride to tedium. I wanted to kill myself. Was that unreasonable?

"It had taken a lot of years, but bad people in Beirut finally pinned the robbery on Malouf. They traced his movements to Melbourne, where they discovered a large Lebanese community, many of them prepared to do brutal things. To date, seven bullion and precious metal dealers have been murdered, and the rumour around town is that Noel Faro is the man currently in possession of the fabulous feathers. This is why he is very nervous right now."

In the end, I'm glad I stayed the journey, because I reckoned my chubby pal might want to put me on a retainer, in which case those two guys in the carpark would now earn my respect. They might be able to shoot straighter than I thought.

Bed became a welcome relief, and I slept with a heater under the pillow. It pays to be careful. Before I nodded off, I wondered about Faro and his precautions. Whoever tried to sell the precious artefact would become a merchant of menace and the target of many. The portly prince from Portugal lived and worked in his high-rise penthouse, which provided some security. Who would have thought they would use a dame to get at him?

The antique dealer was one of a kind, operating from his ninth floor Toorak apartment. His living quarters backed on to his showroom, conveniently situated beside the elevator. You needed an appointment to view the goodies, and that involved a rigorous vetting procedure before he opened the door.

His female visitor used her charm to get past security, all hard-hitters from the local mosque. She came across as dark and desirable and comfortable in her high-fashion hijab. Later, he maintained that such visitations were not unexpected for a man whose reputation in Oriental and Middle Eastern art defied scrutiny. What was unexpected was the Irish brogue that came out of her mouth.

"Good afternoon, Mr. Faro. My name is Bridget O'Shaughnessy. I've come here for the bird."

The pistol produced looked like a peashooter, but the fat man was close enough for it to do some damage. She was close enough to recoil from the mace spray, activated from the artificial carnation in his lapel. The squirt found its mark, and the clandestine colleen dropped her gun, as he stepped forward and engulfed the beauty in a beastly bear hug that knocked the stuffing out of her. Yes, she fought back. They lurched around the room, as she endeavoured to escape from his gripping embrace, and he tried to avoid all the irreplaceable works of art in harm's way. Was this the reason they crashed through the glass patio doors and ended up on the balcony? Maybe! Having been summoned, with the promise of a retainer, I had just arrived in the street beside the building, when the girl went over the railing, screaming in Gaelic? I had never realised it was such a demonstrative language.

Yours truly reached Faro's door ten minutes before the police. The art dealer was pleased to see me.

"Thank God you're here. A mad Irishwoman just attempted to rob me. Can you believe it?"

At this stage, I assumed I was on consult, and attempted to calm the fellow down. Being cool is part of my image. It doesn't always work.

"Yeah, I see the recently departed took the shortcut to ground level. Was she after the sky rat?"

The man looked at me incredulously, obviously in awe of my investigative capabilities.

"You know about the bird?"

"I do, but my guess is you don't want the Johnny Hoppers in on the secret."

This confirmation came with his acceptance of my service quotation, which included daily fees plus expenses. There would be no time to find out what he wanted me to do, because the law came a knocking. Unlatching the inner door, I came face to face with an old pal. Tim Tambling had been a sergeant when I wore blue. He was still a sergeant.

"Get out of here. Hamilton Wade, if I leave and breathe. Whaddya doing here, Ham? There must be a broad involved."

Sure, there was a broad involved, but how would I explain that I was the meat in the sandwich? Tim's partner didn't look like a fun guy, and he started asking the hard questions.

"There's a dead woman, laying on her back in the garden, downstairs—a dead woman last seen on your balcony. When I say "your balcony," can I ask who actually lives here?"

This is when I handballed all enquires to the fat man, and he fielded them for about forty minutes. The presence of the women's derringer helped with Faro's self-defence claim, and they eventually let him be. With the forensic people swarming all over his apartment, I suggested we retire to Rix.

Tinsley Waterhouse Lounge Lizard was jamming hard, with Ozzie alone at the bar, looking desolate. With no-one to chat to, our arrival must have seemed like a mirage at the end of the information highway. He greeted us like family.

"Hey guys. Great to see you. What's new?"

Talk about a leading question! I brought him up-to-date, while Faro bought the beverages. The musician's cynical query was ill-timed, with the man of the moment about to rejoin the conversation.

"So, who tossed her over the balcony rail? Surely not Roly-Poly?"

There are cold stares and cold stares. Oswald got eyeball Antarctica, and melted into the background as our fulsome friend provided his rational summation of the tragic event.

HOLLYWOOD

"Anyone would consider the lady's death to be an unfortunate accident, and I am remorseful and full of sympathy for her next of kin. However, she pulled a gun on me. Now, gentlemen, if we could change the subject to something less distressing."

I thought this would be a good time to bring up the matter of my employment, as I still didn't know what he wanted of me. Naturally, the meter was already running. I'm sure he understood that.

"Be my bodyguard for the next few days, Ham, and stake out my apartment block. There are people who want to kill me."

"And steal the wings of wealth," I added.

"Exactly! Have I told you about my other visitor, today?"

This didn't sound like it would be a long story, in comparison to Ozzie's epic narrative, but, in any case, my ears were financially bound to the stout gentleman standing beside me, so I listened to what my employer had to say.

"He introduced himself as a Lebanese businessman but looked more like a heavy from Hezbollah. The distasteful character was forthright in his demands, and do you know what he said?"

Odd Socks Oswald had been quite quiet since being put in his place earlier, but gossip mongers find it difficult to moderate their excitement, with natter and chatter in the air.

"Gee, Noel, you know you can tell us and it won't go any further."

"My friends, I don't think I ever saw such a vile-looking rogue in all my life. He demanded that I give him the bird, or else he would kill me."

In reality, the fat man's assessment was not wrong. Salman Ella was a sick man, and it wasn't just because he was a Muslim terrorist. As a child, he used to torture worms and other innocent creatures, so being a Hezbollah heavy was a perfect fit for the fellow; and Mr. Faro had recognised his capability. The piano player couldn't wait for the outcome of the story and pressed his pal for further details.

"Holy shit, he said he would kill you. What did you do?"

"What could I do? I gave him the bird."

This outcome proved to be an anticlimax for Ozzie, because he just sat still with his mouth open. It was left to me to interpret the vernacular expression used by the big fellow. Considering his Portuguese heritage, one had to congratulate him on his knowledge of local slang and idiosyncratic idioms.

"I believe Oz that our friend gave him the two-fingered bird, which is a time-honoured response, guaranteed to enrage and infuriate. One assumes there was a steel security door between both parties to this conversation."

I'm sure Faro was glad he employed someone who was on the ball. He confirmed as much, but I harboured self-doubts. I couldn't see how Bridget O'Shaughnessy fitted into the picture. He could.

"Later that night, the fellow's wife or partner turned up: the Irish Muslim."

"Wow," said Oswald, now fully appreciating the round one's predicament. "Let's hope there is no son on the payroll. Can you imagine the breeding—a Hezbollah father from an IRA mother?"

The style leader with the odd socks went off to fulfil his musical obligations, and I decided to put some hard questions to my buddy Noel, relating to two matters I had been sweating on for quite some time. Surprisingly, he answered them.

"O.K., Mr. Boss Man. I now appreciate how dangerous my job is, but I want answers before I commit. Where is our feathered friend, and how much is it worth?"

He ordered another two slammers and waited for the bartender to deliver the cocktails, before looking me straight in the eye, and providing the climax to this tale, which will satisfy no-one.

"The bird is where it should be, Mr. Wade, in the prop room of Warner Bros. Studios, on the Gold Coast. We're going to make a movie of *The Lebanese Magpie*. It's worth a lot of money—to me."

About The Author

Gerry Burke was born in Healesville, Victoria, home to one of Australia's quirkiest animals, the platypus. He was educated at Xavier College, before taking-on an accountancy course while employed by an international mining company. This was a commitment that lasted for twelve years, partly spent in New Guinea. Dramatically, the author then switched careers and joined an advertising agency in Melbourne, as a copywriter.

Gerry's advertising career took him to Britain, America, Hong Kong, Singapore and a number of Australian cities. He was employed by some of the world's largest ad agencies, before branching out and starting his own company on his own terms. GerryCo provided advertising, marketing, film and video production to local and overseas clients.

In parallel with these activities, Gerry maintained an ongoing interest in the thoroughbred horse racing industry, as an owner and breeder, having raced more than twenty thoroughbreds.

The author's humorous stories and commentary were first made available for general consumption in 2009, with the release of his first book, *From Beer to Paternity*. A number of short story collections followed, in which the ubiquitous discount detective Paddy Pest was introduced to the unsuspecting public. *The Hero of Hucklebuck Drive* was the author's first novel in 2015, and *The Europeans* was his fifth. He has reverted back to the short story format for this collection, volume number twelve. To date, eight of his books have received nine international awards in the categories of General Fiction, Humour and Science Fiction.

Gerry is single and lives in Melbourne, Australia, with a number of possums and two doves, Lindsay and Anne. Rex, the dog, ran-off with a bitch from a leafier suburb.

www.gerryburke.net

Is that it?
Is that all there is?

Author's Previous Works

AMERICAN BOOK FEST BEST BOOK AWARDS — FINALIST
My Book of Revelations — Stories that burst the bubble of believability

AMERICAN FICTION AWARDS — FINALIST
The Europeans — a saga of settlement Down Under

BOOK EXCELLENCE AWARDS — FINALIST
The Europeans — a saga of settlement Down Under
The Snoodle Contract — a provocative power play of political perfidy
The Replicants — they come in peace or so they say
Be Dead and Be Damned — murder with malice in Melbourne

U.S.A. BEST BOOK AWARDS — FINALIST
Pest Takes a Chance — humorous stories from the Paddy Pest Chronicles
Pest on the Run — more humorous short stories from the Paddy Pest Chronicles
The Hero of Hucklebuck Drive — another Paddy Pest mystery

INDEPENDENT PUBLISHER — BRONZE MEDAL
Paddy's People — tales of life, love, laughter, and smelly horses

COMMUTERS' COMPANION
The Lady on the Train — humorous Paddy Pest yarns for children over thirty

SHORT STORIES & OPINION PIECES
From Beer to Paternity — one man's journey through life as we know it
Down Under Shorts — stories to read while they're fumigating your pants